MEMORY OF A MURDER

Library of Congress Cataloging-in-Publication Data

Staggs, Earl.
　Memory of a murder / Earl Staggs.
　　p. cm.
　ISBN 978-0-87033-604-1
　1. Psychics–Fiction. 2. Serial murderers–Fiction. I. Title.
　PS3619.T344M46 2008
　813'.6–dc22
　　　　　　　　　　　　　　　　　　2007047558

Manufactured in the United States.

For Carol,
who suffers my shenanigans more than a
saint should have to.

CHAPTER

1

"Adam Kingston! Get your skinny butt out of that bed."

Her voice cut through his sleep and made him cringe. He pulled his face out of his pillow, forced one eye open, and turned his head far enough for a squinting glance around. Yes. He was in his own bedroom.

He opened the other eye and focused on the figure standing at the foot of his bed. Slim, well-dressed, skin the color of cocoa, arms folded across her chest, dark eyes boring into him. He plunged his face back into his pillow and mumbled, "Dammit, Ellie."

"Get up."

"What time is it?"

"After eight."

"How much after?"

"A minute or two. Get up."

"I can't get up. I'm dead."

"You can die later."

Adam pulled the sheet over his head only to have it jerked off him. He groped for it with no success. He rolled onto his back and checked to see if his skivvies were covering what they were supposed to cover, then looked up at Ellie.

"Where's Phil?"

"Home in bed."

"How come Phil gets to sleep and I have to get up?"

"Today's his day off."

Adam groaned. "It's my day off, too, dammit. Come on, Ellie…" He interrupted himself with a yawn that shivered all the way down to his toes. "I just got back from a trip and didn't get to bed 'till after three. What the hell are you doing in my bedroom at this ungodly hour?"

"Junior's in trouble and I need you to do your thing."

That did it. Adam sat up and swung his legs over the side of the bed, his feet landing on the rumpled slacks he'd peeled off only a few hours ago. Junior. Phil Russell Junior, his godson. Bright, responsible, levelheaded, top of his class in college, never been in trouble in his life. Adam glanced at Ellie as he pulled up his pants.

"What kind of trouble?"

"He hasn't called me for two days."

Adam shot her a hard look. "That's it? He hasn't called?" He plopped onto the bed. "Jesus, Ellie. He's nineteen years old and he's in Daytona having a good time. He's fine."

"He always calls me every day, and he hasn't called for two days. Something's happened to him, and I want you to do that thing of yours and tell me what's going on."

"Ellie…"

She spun on her heels and marched toward the door. "Coffee's on," she tossed back over her shoulder. "Get dressed and get out here."

Adam shook his head and watched the woman he'd known for more than twenty years leave the room. He and Phil Russell became best friends in high school in spite of their obvious differences. Adam, the tall, gangly white boy and Phil, the shorter, well-built black kid. Ellie was a nurse at the same hospital in Philadelphia where Phil did his residency. Adam and Caroline stood for them at their wedding, and the four of them had been like family through both the lean and good years.

Ellie was forty-three years old, a year younger than him and Phil, and the biggest worrier in the world when it came to the people she loved. She was also the most stubborn and hardheaded woman he had ever met. If she was concerned enough to come to his apartment, use her key to get in, and roust him out of bed to do his thing, he knew damn well he had no choice.

His *thing* was psychic ability. The experts had other names for it, but were never able to explain it. They didn't understand it themselves. They couldn't even tell him why it started twelve years ago after the accident that nearly took his life. At first it terrified him. After two years of their testing and probing, he overcame his fear of it, stopped trying to understand it, and told them to leave him alone. Since then he'd worked as a consultant to the FBI and other law enforcement agencies, occasionally taking on private clients. It helped that he had been an FBI agent himself before the accident.

He looked for the shirt he took off and tossed before tossing himself in bed, found it, and headed for the bathroom.

Adam entered his kitchen a few minutes later to find his coffee poured and Ellie sitting at the dinette table, rubbing her temples over a cup of her own.

She looked up at him. "Sorry for dragging you out of bed, but you know how I am."

He leaned across the table and kissed her cheek. "Yeah, I know. I'm sure Junior is okay." He sat down and took a cautious sip from his steaming cup. Too hot. "I can't promise you anything. You know it doesn't always work."

"But you'll try?"

"I'll try." He rubbed his weary eyes and tried his coffee again. Still too hot. "What do you have?"

Ellie reached down to her lap. "Here's the most recent picture of him." She handed a snapshot across the table.

Adam remembered the picture. He'd taken it himself at Junior's nineteenth birthday party a month ago. The handsome young man stood by himself, proudly showing the new wristwatch Adam had given him.

He laid the picture on the table and sighed to himself. Ellie didn't fully understand what she was asking him to do. Remote viewing. The experts especially couldn't explain that part of it. It meant sending his mind somewhere distant, not just having images flash across his mind when he touched an object or visited a crime scene.

Years ago, he'd spent a few weeks at a government facility where he and a group of others with psychic abilities were trained in remote viewing. They telepathically visited sites all over the world, looking for missile installations, hidden caches of arms, MIAs, any number of things. Long-distance spying. He hadn't stayed with them long, and since then had avoided using it except when absolutely necessary. It wasn't easy, often gave him a headache, and the voyeuristic aspects of it made him feel creepy.

And, as often as not, it didn't work. The recent picture of Junior, his own connection to the watch, and his personal attachment to his godson might be enough to make it happen.

Adam raised his cup, blew into it, and took a swallow. Still hot, but drinkable. He looked across the table into Ellie's face, saw her impatience growing, and put his cup down.

With his fingertips lightly touching the snapshot, Adam closed his eyes and relaxed his mind and body. After a few moments, the sensations began.

The feeling of being in a dark elevator, rapidly accelerating upward, then traveling at incredible speed through a spiraling tunnel. Gradually the speed decreased and colors drifted into his subconscious. Green. Brown. Gold. Slowing even more. Stopping. A strange room.

Bright light from the left. Sunlight through a window. Clothes and shoes scattered on the floor...a bed, sheets hanging over the sides...two figures sprawled on the bed...Junior and a girl, both nude, sleeping peacefully...a sudden burst of blinding light...the feeling of movement again...stopping...somewhere else now...outside, in bright sunlight...a man walking toward him...scruffy clothes, long hair, thick beard...feelings of desperation, exhaustion...

The images faded, and Adam felt himself returning at rapid speed through the bright tunnel, then descending into darkness and slowing. The familiar dizziness that always followed a remote journey washed over him.

He kept his eyes closed and thought about what he had seen. The scene of Junior and the girl had been one of contentment, two people sleeping, no danger or alarm. The images that followed were totally different and had no connection to Junior and the girl. A man he could not identify coming toward him. He had gotten a completely different feeling from those images. A dark feeling that sent a chill down his spine.

It had happened before. At crime scenes or when he touched objects, he often received confusing images unrelated to the case he was working at the time. Maverick images, he called them. Sometimes they became clear to him days or weeks afterward. Sometimes never.

Ellie's voice brought him all the way back. "Well?"

Adam looked across the table. Ellie's eyes searched his face.

"Ellie, you have nothing to worry about. Your little boy is fine. He's done some partying and is sleeping it off peacefully. Relax. He'll call." He saw no reason to mention the maverick image.

Her eyebrows raised. "Partying? What kind of partying?"

Adam grinned. "The kind of partying college students on a break are supposed to do. It's a law." He raised his own eyebrows and leaned toward her. "Surely you remember those days."

She studied him for a moment, then her features softened. "Oh, I remember very well. Too well. Are you sure he's all right?"

"I'm positive." He also saw no reason to mention the girl. He knew Phil Senior would be pleased about that part though. "By the way, do you know all the kids Junior went to Daytona with?"

"Yes, of course I do. Why?"

"Was one of them older than the others, long hair, full beard, kind of scraggly looking?"

She shook her head. "No. Why? Is something wrong?"

He reached across the table and patted her hand. "No, nothing's wrong. Junior's fine, I'm fine, you're fine, the whole world's fine. Now go home and get that lazy husband of yours out of bed."

Ellie took a small sip of her coffee, then stood. "You men! All you ever want to do is sleep."

Adam followed her out of the kitchen into the large area that served as a living room at one end, a dining area at the other. He and Caroline strained their budget years ago for a sixth floor condo in the Colonial Towers on the Boardwalk at Thirty-fourth Street. They loved the panoramic view of the Atlantic Ocean and Ocean City's endless white sand beach. Before her death they had lived in Baltimore and had come here to the Maryland seashore for vacations and weekends. Now that he lived alone, it was his permanent home.

Ellie stopped in the living room. "When are you going to do something with this place?"

"What's that supposed to mean?" Adam felt a lecture coming on, hoping nothing was out of place. He kept his clutter in the extra bedroom he had made into a den. His bookshelves were in there, his desk, a computer he never used, a TV he seldom used, and the treadmill he had bought two years ago on express orders from Phil, the health-fanatic doctor.

"Don't start on me," he said. "There's nothing wrong with this place."

"Nothing a little redecorating wouldn't cure."

Ellie walked to a picture-covered living room wall. Adam had hung the pictures himself, in every conceivable size and color of frame, the entire wall, floor to ceiling. He and Caroline in the early years of dating, their wedding, and nearly every event remotely worthy of capturing on film during their time together. While the arrangement pleased him, he knew a decorator would run from the room in tears.

"It looks like a museum," Ellie said with a broad wave of her arm. "Take down those pictures, get some new furniture, something modern, get some bright colors on the walls."

Adam rolled his eyes. They had had this conversation before. He and Caroline picked out the furniture and decorated the apartment together, and he didn't want to change anything. He still felt her presence here. It was home, and he liked it just the way it was.

He threw up his arms and let them slap against his thighs. "That's it, lady. You're outta here. First you drag me out of bed and then you criticize my home. Go home and nag your husband."

Ellie wagged her head in exaggerated disgust. "You're hopeless. At least put some life in here. Get yourself a pet." She walked toward the door.

Adam followed. "Yeah, right. A dog, maybe, to chew up the furniture and crap all over the floor. Or a cat to leave hair all over everything. And who'd clean up after them when I go away for weeks at a time? You?"

"Not on your life, bud. So get some goldfish or birds or something. Anything to liven the place up some."

"The place is just fine, thank you very much. Now get out of here before my neighbors start gossiping about me having an affair with my best friend's wife."

Ellie snorted. "You should be so lucky."

At the door, she turned and gave him a hug. "Thanks for checking up on Junior."

He kissed her on the forehead. "Anytime."

Ellie opened the door and stepped out. As she walked down the corridor toward the elevator, she called back, "By the way, your underwear's worn thin. I'm going shopping today. I'll pick some up for you."

Adam closed the door, leaned back against it, and let another yawn work its way over him. The remote viewing trip had produced only a mild headache, and it was nearly gone. He thought about going back to bed, but knew he wouldn't be able to sleep now. He gave another passing thought to the strange man he'd seen after spying on Junior, then pushed it aside. If it meant anything, he'd know soon enough. If it was only another meaningless glitch, nothing would come of it. He headed for his den.

The treadmill seemed to smile as soon as he entered the room, as if to say, "Come on, old man, get your punishment." Adam groaned, pulled a sweat suit from a hook on the back of the door, changed into it, and mounted the monster.

And quickly stepped off again. He was too tired, he hadn't had enough sleep, and he needed more coffee. He went into the kitchen, poured a fresh cup, carried it into the dining room, opened a sliding glass door, and stepped out onto his patio.

The green-carpeted patio ran the width of the apartment and extended out twenty feet. Adam stood at the concrete retaining wall and looked toward the Atlantic Ocean. From the horizon to the surf, the morning sun spread its glaring reflection in a jagged golden path across gently tumbling waves. On the wide beach between the surf and the Boardwalk, seagulls and sandpipers scurried over freshly combed sand, searching for crumbs of food missed by giant cleaning machines.

As far as he could see in either direction, hundreds of sea birds floated above the surf, diving and snatching when they spotted a morsel behind a receding wave. Their frenzied squeals punctuated the constant rush and slide of water against sand to complete the familiar symphony of a seashore morning.

On the Boardwalk, six floors straight down, he watched a pair of cyclers in matching yellow outfits weave gracefully and silently through a quartet of joggers. Soon the Boardwalk and beach would fill with vacationing families. His thoughts drifted back to days when he swam in the surf while Caroline sat on the beach reading a book, looking up to see him get bowled over by a wave and come up laughing, laying her book aside, running to join him.

A long, deep breath filled his lungs with salty air. It also brought a strong reminder that he needed a shower. Badly. He raised his cup, drained it in a gulp, and went inside. He would shower and dress and head out to the library. With all his recent traveling, he had missed a few best sellers this year and wanted to catch up. His calendar was empty, and he could afford to relax for awhile. The Bureau paid handsomely for his services, but he hoped they wouldn't call on him again for at least a couple of weeks. He needed a rest.

After a long, lazy shower, Adam turned off the water in time to hear the buzz of his intercom. He sloshed to the foyer on wet feet, wrapping a towel around him as he went. He recognized the voice of the dayshift doorman from the lobby.

"Mr. Kingston?"

"Hey, Henry. Good morning to you. Need a cup of coffee?"

"No, sir, not today. Thanks, but there's a, uh, man down here. Says he wants to see you. You expecting anyone?"

Adam smiled. A retired postal worker, Henry's purpose in life now was to protect residents of the condo building by screening all nonresidents who entered. He took great pride in his vigilance.

"No, I'm not expecting anyone. Who is it?"

Adam waited through a moment of muffled voices before Henry spoke again.

"He says his name is Weathers. Says it's important, and he wants to talk to you. Mr. Kingston, I, uh, I..."

"What is it?"

Henry's voice dropped to a whisper. "I think I should send him away. I mean, he's not wearing a suit or anything like those FBI guys. He's, well, more like one of those street people. You know, the kind that hits on you for a handout? Maybe I should get rid of him."

Adam's curiosity kept him from telling Henry to send the man on his way. He could go to the lobby and meet him, but he had things to do first. Like drying off, getting dressed, having breakfast.

"Tell you what. Ask him to come back in an hour. Tell him I'm in the shower."

"In the shower. Right, Mr. Kingston. Will do."

Adam thanked Henry and headed for the bedroom, toweling as he walked. He had one leg in a pair of slacks when he heard the intercom buzzer again. He jabbed the other leg in and hurried to the foyer.

"What is it, Henry?"

"Mr. Kingston? He, uh, says he'll wait for you, if you can come down after your shower."

"Well then, if he insists on waiting, tell him I'll be down in half an hour." The man could wait until he finished dressing and had a bite to eat.

"But, uh, Mr. Kingston?"

"Yes."

"I don't know, I mean, him hanging around the lobby, looking like he does. I don't know about that."

Something clicked in Adam's mind. "Does this man have long hair and a beard, dressed kind of scruffy?"

"Yes, sir. That's why I don't think he should—"

"Henry."

"Yes, sir?"

"Send him up."

CHAPTER

Brenda McCort merged into early morning traffic heading for Baltimore. It was her day off, but after a phone call from Captain Jackson, she left her apartment in Glen Burnie halfway through its overdue cleaning. The cleaning could wait. She was thirty-eight years old, divorced, and living alone. What difference did it make?

Another unidentified body. This time a man shot, wrapped in black plastic trash bags, and left in the trunk of a car. Three days ago, the skeleton of a young woman was found buried in the basement of a house on Century Street.

She had worked ten John or Jane Doe cases since making detective five years ago and solved eight of them. Maybe that's why she pulled almost every one that came along now. Someone dying alone and unknown bothered her more than a normal homicide, but none bothered her more than the young woman found on Century Street.

"Don't let it get to you, McCort," Captain Leo Jackson had lectured in that fatherly way of his. "It's just another case."

"Bull," she had said. "No one kills another human being and sticks them in the ground like that and gets away with it. Especially a young woman just beginning her life."

As she drove, Brenda decided to ask the newspaper to run the picture of the woman's clothing again. Somebody must know something, and that might stir some memories.

Twenty minutes later, she made a left off Russell Street onto Lombard, then in the middle of the block, another left into the West Side Parking Garage. When she came off the winding ramp on the fourth level, she saw everyone there. Scene techs, Medical Examiner, four patrol cars, and Kaminski.

As she approached Detective Timmy Kaminski, he gave her his silly grin.

"Enjoying your day off?" he asked.

She replied by sticking her tongue out and punching him in the ribs. He was five years younger, an inch or two taller, and a little paunchy. Officially they were partners, but one person could do much of the work involved in investigations, so they worked apart as much as together. It was the best way to keep up with their heavy caseload. She was also godmother to his twin daughters.

"So what have I missed?" she asked.

"Not much. They're still dusting. Take a look."

As they threaded their way through the gathering, Brenda exchanged greetings in response to a "Hi, Bren," and a teasing, "About time, McCort." She ignored the "Who's the looker?" from a young patrolman who must have thought he was out of range. She didn't mind getting one of those once in a while. She'd always been grateful to her mother for passing along a decent face and figure, but would have rejected her father's mouse-brown, flyaway hair if she'd had a choice. She owed him, though, for the hazel eyes most people seemed to like and for some of his height, five-eight of his six-three.

Still, the young patrolman's remark gave her a twinge of self-consciousness. She had dressed in a hurry, grabbing a yellow skirt she now remembered was a tad tighter and a few inches shorter than she normally wore to work. Too late to worry about it now.

Inconspicuously, she hoped, she pushed down on the skirt with both palms and centered her attention on the car.

The dark green Buick Skylark was five or six years old and had a mangled rear bumper. The trunk lid was crunched and sticking straight up.

Just above the bumper, bent almost in half but still readable, hung a Pennsylvania license plate reading *SUE M.*

The new Assistant Medical Examiner, short and blond, knelt a few feet behind the car examining the nude victim. He lay on a bed made from the black plastic bags in which he'd been wrapped. Strips of duct tape protruded from beneath him. The man appeared to be in his fifties, and Brenda saw a bullet hole in his left temple.

"How's it going, Shirley?" Brenda knelt beside her.

"Nearly finished, McCort," she said without looking up.

The new ones are so professional and meticulous, Brenda thought, and take twice as long. "Captain Jackson said he was a John Doe. Still no ID?"

"Nothing. No clothes, no jewelry, not even a ring. Suntan marks on the wrist indicate he wore a watch. Tattoo on the left shoulder. That's it so far. I'll have the full report for you tomorrow."

"Thanks," Brenda said. "Can I see the tattoo?"

Shirley frowned at Brenda, then smiled. "Sure." Her demeanor said she didn't appreciate the interruption. She moved her bag of tools aside so the man's left shoulder was visible.

"It's an old one," she said, "and not a professional job."

Brenda agreed. The poorly drawn eagle looked like one of those tattoos prison inmates inflict on each other. Beneath the eagle were some numbers. She pulled a notepad from her jacket pocket and copied them.

"Thanks," she said.

Shirley returned to her work without replying.

"So, Kaminski," Brenda said as she walked to the side of the Buick Skylark with him one step behind. "What happened?"

"Well, it seems the Skylark came in shortly after eight this morning. The man in the booth remembered because he came on at eight and it was the first one in. At approximately 8:45, a valet brought up that blue BMW over there. He went to back it in next to the Skylark, misjudged or something, and rammed the Skylark. The trunk lid flew open. When he looked to see how much damage he'd done, he saw the package in the trunk."

"Where's the valet?"

"There." Kaminski jerked his head to the right.

Brenda saw a thin, dark-haired young man leaning against a wall with his arms folded and his chin on his chest. He appeared no more than seventeen.

"He had to be going pretty fast to do this much damage," she said to Kaminski. "He was backing up, you said?"

"Ever see these valets in action? You'd think they were in training for the Indy 500."

"Too bad. He'll probably lose his job."

Kaminski snorted. "Wait'll the beamer's owner gets here. Losing his job could be the high point of his day."

Brenda looked at the BMW sitting a short distance away with rear-end damage worse than the Skylark's. Kaminski was probably right about the kid's day. Her own didn't seem such a tragedy anymore.

CHAPTER
3

Adam waited in his foyer a long two minutes before he heard a soft rapping on his door. He opened it to see a man in a frayed, dingy, tan windbreaker, a dingier gray T-shirt, and shapeless, belt-less, blue trousers. The man's bush of dark brown hair fell to his shoulders like tangled brown twine. His thick mustache and beard obscured his face except for gaunt cheekbones and shadowed pits under bushy eyebrows. He did not seem hostile or dangerous. He appeared weak, barely able to stand.

Adam tried to sound congenial. "Can I help you?"

"You're Adam Kingston?" The voice was raspy.

"Yes, but…do I know you?"

"No. I read about you. What you do. I'd like to talk to you. If I can." He spoke in short, clipped bursts, as though it were an effort.

"What did you want to talk to me about, Mr…. . What was it?"

"Weathers. Chip Weathers." He stared at Adam's outstretched hand before wiping his own across his chest and accepting the handshake. "Something happened. A long time ago. I need your help."

Adam's curiosity compelled him to listen to what the man had to say. "Come in, Mr. Weathers."

He stepped aside to let his visitor enter, then led the way into the living room. He motioned toward a beige sofa against the wall on the left. "Please have a seat, Mr. Weathers."

Weathers sat on the end of the sofa nearest the front door. He eased himself down and perched on the lip of the cushion. Adam wondered how long it had been since the apparently homeless man had been invited to sit on a sofa in someone's living room.

"Would you like something to drink? Coffee? Water? I may have some soda if you like."

Weathers hesitated, then said, "No. Thanks."

Adam flashed a polite smile. "If you change your mind, let me know." He thought a drink of water would do his visitor a lot of good, but didn't push it. He sat in the armchair that matched the sofa. A narrow rattan coffee table separated them.

Adam's wall of pictures seemed to have captured the attention of the man on the sofa. "A lot of pictures," he said. "Nice."

"Thanks. I've got more, but I ran out of wall." Adam appreciated the compliment, but was anxious to know why he'd gotten this strange visitor. "Now," he said, flashing the polite smile once more, "I believe you said you wanted to talk to me about something."

The man appeared as if he wanted to speak, but instead reached into a pocket of his windbreaker and brought out a folded, wrinkled handkerchief. He laid it across his lap and carefully unfolded it. Adam saw it had been wrapped around a piece of newspaper folded into a square. He also saw a small piece of white cloth. The man unfolded the paper as deliberately as the handkerchief, then handed it across the coffee table.

"I guess the best way to start," he said, "is let you read this."

It was half a page with the logo of *The Sun*, Baltimore's daily newspaper, at the top and dated August 13, three days ago. The headline read: "Body Discovered in Basement on Century Street."

Beneath the headline were two pictures. One showed a narrow basement room with concrete block walls and a pull-string light-bulb fixture dangling from exposed rafters. A wood staircase clung

to the wall on the left. Under the steps, the concrete floor had been
torn up and a hole dug in the dirt.

The other picture showed rumpled, dirt-stained clothing
arranged on a table. A pair of white women's slacks. A sandal, the
kind with thin straps. A woman's blouse, white with thin dark stripes.

Adam read the article beneath the pictures.

*Workmen repairing a sewer line discovered the skeletal remains of a woman
beneath a basement floor at 834 Century Street in East Baltimore. According
to a police spokesperson, the age and identity of the woman and how long she
had been buried are unknown. The Police Department provided the above
photograph of clothing removed from the body in the hope that someone might
recognize it. Anyone with information is asked to call their local police station.*

"Is this what you wanted to talk to me about?" Adam asked.

The man nodded.

Adam felt a chill like an ice cube sliding down his back. He
peered at the paper again. "Do you...know something about this?"

Weathers wiped a hand across his mouth. He coughed, then
cleared his throat. "Mr. Kingston, I think... ." He paused, took a
deep breath, and exhaled loudly. "I think I killed that woman."

Adam stared at him, wondering if he'd heard correctly. "You
think you killed her? What do you mean you *think* you killed her?"

"Look at the picture of the clothes."

Adam scanned the picture again. "What am I supposed to see?"

"The blouse. Where the pocket should be."

Adam looked again. The blouse in the picture had thin dark
stripes running from top to bottom. Where a pocket would normally
be, over the heart of the wearer, there was nothing. "Okay," he said,
not clear what it meant, "there's no pocket."

Weathers picked up the small piece of cloth from the handkerchief and handed it across the table.

Adam took it, examined it, then compared it to the newspaper photograph. The cloth he held in his hand was the right size, had the identical pattern of stripes—faded, but probably dark blue at one time—and there were thread holes on both sides and across the bottom. The fabric he held in his hand seemed to be the pocket missing from the blouse in the picture.

"How…where did you get this?" Adam knew it was a dumb question. The sensation of ice on his back felt like a glacier now.

His visitor lowered his head and stared at the floor. He spoke in the quivering voice of someone close to tears.

"Mr. Kingston, I…I was there. I know I was there. I must've killed that woman and put her…buried her…in that basement. That's why I'm here, why I need your help. I have to find out who she was…what I did…why I… ."

Weathers slowly raised his head, and Adam saw his dark brown eyes clearly for the first time. He'd always been able to read people through their eyes—their *windows*. He'd seen remorse in the eyes of people who killed in a fit of passion, unbridled grief in those who lost loved ones, and guilt in the eyes of suspects. Through the moist glaze of this man's eyes, he saw emptiness. Deep brown wells drained dry. Yet, they were the eyes of a man who said he thought he killed a woman and buried her beneath a basement floor.

Adam stood. "Mr. Weathers, I need a cup of coffee." He felt a sudden need to swallow something hot and bitter. He also felt a need to stand and move, get into another room, get his thoughts together. As he walked into the kitchen, he said, "I'll get something for both of us, then you can tell me the rest. Coffee all right for you?"

He didn't hear an answer, only noises. A muffled groan, a loud crashing sound, a thump. He ran back into the living room to see his visitor lying on the floor between the overturned coffee table and the sofa.

CHAPTER

Brenda McCort examined the inside of the Buick Skylark and talked to the scene techs. So far they had found no fingerprints. It'd been wiped. The glove compartment had been emptied of everything, including the registration card.

After making a few notes, she walked away from the Skylark to the chest-high wall of the parking garage. Across Lombard Street, ancient blacktop roofs with tacked-on air conditioning units and fire escapes extended for several blocks like an old rug littered with erector set pieces. If they couldn't ID this guy, she'd start by showing his morgue picture at all the hotels in the area. That was always fun. She saw five from where she stood.

Brenda watched traffic moving by on the street below. People on their way to work, going shopping, leaving for vacation, worrying about all they had to do, how they'd be able to pay their bills, and complaining about the heat. Another day in their lives. The man lying on the concrete floor behind her had seen the last day of his.

She turned to watch when she heard the Medical Examiner's van leaving. John Doe was on his way to the morgue. When it disappeared onto the ramp, she turned back to the wall.

*   *   *

After his breakfast, he walked across Shoney's parking lot to his rented car, thinking about the young waitress. Seventeen, maybe eighteen. Thin legs, but fat lips. He felt the beginning of an erection as he thought about what those lips could do. Maybe he'd come back to see her when he finished his business in Ocean City.

He climbed into the big car as quickly as he could and flicked on the air conditioning. A large man who perspired easily, he hated it when sweat trickled from his bald scalp into the hair around the sides. He wrestled out of his suit coat and tossed it into the back seat, then unzipped the large nylon travel bag on the passenger seat. After rummaging inside, he found a clean handkerchief and swabbed his face with it.

While he waited for the car to cool, he ran his fingers over the luxurious soft leather of the seat. He had rented a Mercury Grand Marquis with all the options, the most expensive car the rental company had. Money was no object. He used Albert's credit card.

After a few minutes, he felt comfortable and steered onto Lombard Street. He turned his wrist and read Albert's watch. Five after nine. He could make it to Ocean City by early afternoon and, with a little luck, might get it done today. Then he could hit a nightclub and score some flesh for tonight.

As he drove, he pulled a business card from his pocket and memorized the address scribbled on the back.

Colonial Towers. Boardwalk and Thirty-fourth Street

He tore the card into small pieces and tossed them out the window. Then he settled back and enjoyed the air-conditioned comfort of the Grand Marquis.

Cross the Bay Bridge, stay on Route 50 all the way to Ocean City. Sure be nice to get it done today, get laid tonight.

A few blocks down Lombard Street, cars ahead of him slowed. Just before he got to the Westside Garage, everything stopped.

He saw why. A cop was holding up traffic to let a black van out of the garage.

Shit. The meat wagon. They found Albert already. Shit.

He thought back. He'd wiped the car clean. Everything he'd touched. Steering wheel, shift lever, door, glove compartment, trunk. Everything. They wouldn't even find prints on the bags and the tape. He'd worn gloves. Nothing to worry about.

He relaxed and called to the black van as it drove away, "Have a nice trip, Albert."

When traffic moved again, and he came abreast of the garage, he couldn't resist. He had to see the show.

He pulled off the ramp at the fourth level and saw cops everywhere. Uniforms and plainclothes. Even a television crew.

"Hey, Albert, you little prick," he whispered through a wide grin. "I made you famous. TV and all. How about that?"

He inched ahead, pretending to look for a place to park. When he saw the BMW's smashed rear end and then the Skylark, he realized how they found Albert so fast. He gave a respectful nod to the young uniform who directed him around the area cordoned off with yellow tape.

*   *   *

Timmy Kaminski joined Brenda at the garage wall. "Great. No ID, no prints, no nothing. How come you get all the easy ones, Bren?"

"Luck of the Irish, I guess."

"Wanna be Polish? Beth and I'll adopt you."

She grimaced. "No thanks. Can't take the food."

He faked a laugh. "Very funny. Anything new on the Century Street case?"

"Not much."

"No leads from the clothes?"

"Blood traces. Hair samples. Blonde and dark brown. Much more of the blonde."

"So she was probably the blonde."

Brenda nodded. "The shirt and pants were good quality polyester, but six major stores in the area carried the line a few years ago. The one sandal buried with her came from a trendy shop on Charles Street that went out of business eight years ago. We know she wasn't a bargain basement shopper, for all the good it does."

"Good thing it was polyester," Kaminski said. "Anything else would've been worm food by now. Doesn't that give you some idea of a time frame, though? When did people stop wearing that stuff? Twenty years ago?"

"Ten, fifteen, maybe. But it lasts forever. Some of us senior citizens might still have a piece or two hanging around."

"Yeah, I've noticed," he said, checking her up and down and taking an elbow in the ribs for his trouble. "Ouch. I'm gonna start wearing pads around you, McCort." He rubbed his side. "How about the bone pickers? They come up with anything?"

"Only that she was petite and in her early to mid-twenties. Cause of death, multiple fractures to the skull. I gave her approximate age to the media, but I'm holding the cause of death and hair color."

"How's your house-to-house going? Anybody remember her?"

"Not yet. But I've only talked to about half the people in the neighborhood so far."

"Don't tell me the great McCort is slowing down."

"Not on your life, kiddo. I'll finish it Saturday."

"Why Saturday?"

"Better get your notebook out. Here's something else they didn't teach you at the Academy. Century Street's a working class neighborhood. The natives work hard on weekdays and are not too friendly after sundown. Saturdays, they sit on their stoops, drink their brewskies, and will talk to anyone. Even cops."

"I knew that." After another minute, he said, "Let me know if there's anything you want me to do on this one."

She leaned toward him and touched her shoulder to his. "Thanks, pal."

"So where you going now?"

She frowned. "Home. I left my vacuum cleaner running."

"Might as well," he said. "This one'll have to hang till Shirley Stick-Up-Her-Butt finishes her report. Or we get a make on the plate. Even that might be a bust. Probably a hot car. Prints'll take a couple of days, if they find any."

"Weren't you in the service, Kaminski?"

"Yeah, Navy. What's that got to do with anything?"

"You remember your serial number?"

"Sure. Same as my Social Security number. Why?"

"In the old days, they used a different numbering system. I had an uncle who was so proud of being a Marine he had his serial number tattooed on his arm, something like this."

She tore the page from her notepad on which she'd copied the numbers tattooed on the victim's shoulder and handed it to him. He examined them with raised eyebrows.

"Hmmm. Worth a try. I'm going to the pit from here. I'll throw it in the system and see what comes back. You know," he said as he stuck the piece of paper in his pocket, "it's no wonder you're my idol. When I grow up, I want to be as smart as you."

"Don't ever grow up, Timmy. You're too cute. Besides, you won't like it."

He shrugged. "Okay, I won't."

She shook her head and gave him a weary sigh. "You're a real piece of work, Kaminski, and I'm outta here. See you in the morning, and it's your turn to bring donuts. Don't forget."

Timmy Kaminski gave her his silly grin again. "Have a nice day."

She gave him the tongue again and walked away. A few feet from her car, she stopped. A big sedan was driving by. She waved it on.

Rubbernecker. A crowd of cops always brought them out.

*　　*　　*

He smiled politely and took a good look at the bitch cop in the tight yellow skirt as she waved him by. Her eyes caught his attention. *Brown. No, hazel. Sexy. Great body.*

Instead of continuing past her, he stopped and rolled down his window. He was close enough to read the ID card hanging beneath her badge.

Brenda McCort. Detective. Homicide.

"Excuse me, officer," he said with a broad smile. "What happened here?"

She glanced at him, then looked over the hood of his car in the direction of the mangled Skylark. "Just an accident, sir. Better move along."

"Was anyone hurt?"

"Move along, sir." Without looking at him again, she waved a hand, ordering him to drive away, like he was nothing, an irritation.

"Sure thing, officer. Have a nice day." He smiled again and rolled up his window as he drove away.

"Screw you very much, Detective Brenda-Tightass-McCort," he said to her image in his rearview mirror. "Maybe we'll meet again someday."

She was a little older than he liked, mid-thirties he guessed, but he liked her eyes and the way she filled out that yellow skirt. He'd never balled a cop before. Someday he'd give one a try.

Shit. Bitch cops want it as much as any other bitch.

Once on the ramp and out of sight, he couldn't hold it any longer. He laughed all the way to the street. It didn't bother him to pay two dollars for the few minutes he was in the garage. The show was worth it. Besides, it was Albert's money, and he sure as hell wouldn't need it. He made a right onto Lombard and settled in for the three-hour drive to Ocean City.

CHAPTER

5

Adam sat at his kitchen dinette table drinking coffee. After lifting the unconscious man onto the sofa, he called Phil Russell. Their conversation had been brief.

"Dammit, Adam. This is my day off. I'm going shopping with Ellie. Call 9-1-1."

"I don't want 9-1-1, Phil. I don't want the police involved in this. Not yet. Besides, you hate shopping."

"I promised Ellie I'd take her, and I'm going."

"Tell her you'll be home in an hour. Tell Ellie it's for me. Tell her I love her."

"Everybody loves Ellie."

"Okay. Tell her I'll eat her meatloaf without any wisecracks."

"You must be desperate."

"I am."

At that point, Phil sighed and said, "I'm on my way." Now he was in the next room examining Chip Weathers.

Adam finished his third cup before Phil charged into the kitchen.

Phil Russell never walked, even from one room to another. He charged. Adam said Phil's tendency to attack any destination in front of him was responsible for his setting a high school record for most touchdowns in a single season. One of his favorite arguments with Phil had to do with who really deserved the credit for those touchdowns. Was it Phil "the Rabbit" Russell, or the quarter-back who threw him all those passes, Adam "the Sling" Kingston?

Phil kept in great shape. Except for a touch of gray at the temples, he looked like he could still slip into the Rabbit's uniform and crunch out a few yards.

"Adam, there's not a whole lot I can do here," Phil said as soon as he entered the kitchen, "but as far as I can see, there's nothing wrong with him that a few days sleep and a few good meals won't cure."

"Did he say anything?"

"Not much. He asked where he was. When I told him, he wanted to know where you were. How well do you know this man?"

"I don't know him at all. He showed up at the door, said he wanted to talk to me about something, and that was it. He fainted, collapsed, or whatever it was, on the floor."

Adam had decided not to tell Phil everything he knew about his visitor. Phil would give him hell for not bringing in the police. Besides, he didn't know the whole story yet.

Phil leaned against the counter by the sink. "Collapsed is probably the best way to describe it. Not surprising, a man in his condition."

"What do you mean, his condition?"

Phil helped himself to a glass of water from the faucet and took a fast swallow. "I don't see any signs of alcohol or drug abuse, but he's on his way to exhaustion, dehydration, malnutrition, the usual. I see it all the time at the clinic. They sleep in alleys, eat whatever they can scrounge, and the only time they see a doctor is when somebody scrapes them off a sidewalk. You want my professional opinion?"

"Are you charging me for this visit?"

"You bet your ass."

"Then I want my money's worth."

"Okay. All I can do here is rule out the major things. Heart attack. Stroke. He needs to get to the hospital for a complete checkup."

A voice surprised both of them. "No hospitals."

Adam and Phil turned to see him standing in the kitchen doorway. He'd removed his grimy windbreaker, but the gray T-shirt he wore was worse.

"Thanks, anyway," he said, "but no hospitals. I had enough of that a long time ago." He did his best to smile, but what could be seen of his pale face behind his bushy mustache and beard didn't seem to have the strength to pull it off.

Phil said, "It wouldn't hurt to get checked out. And if you're worried about the cost, don't. I can arrange it."

"I appreciate that, but I've been enough of a bother already. I want to talk to Mr. Kingston, then I'll be on my way."

"How do you feel?" Adam asked.

"I'm okay," he said with a shrug. "Sorry for conking out like that."

"Don't worry about that," Adam said. "I'm glad you're all right. How about a cup of coffee?" He didn't wait for an answer. He got up to pour the coffee at the counter and nodded toward the dinette table. "Sit down, please. I can't offer you real cream and sugar, only the no-fat stuff." With a jerk of his head toward Phil, he added, "Doctor's orders."

"Don't blame me," Phil shot back. "You're the one who binges on chocolate donuts. Forget the coffee. I know you poison your own guts with a couple gallons a day, but he needs something else. Any juice in here?" He opened the refrigerator.

"Should be some orange juice," Adam replied, feeling dumb with a half-filled cup of coffee in his hand. He emptied it in the sink. "Look behind the donuts."

Phil shook his head and muttered, "Should've known." He pulled out the pitcher of juice. "How about a clean glass?"

"Try the dishwasher."

Phil glared at him. "Should've known that, too."

Adam winked at Weathers. "See what I have to put up with?"

Phil Russell reached the glass of juice across the table. Adam watched his visitor hold it in both hands and take several large gulps. He could see that cold orange juice was a rare treat.

Phil checked his watch. "I'd better go. Ellie's waiting."

With a devilish grin, Adam said, "With a long shopping list in hand, I'm sure. I hope you have a fun day. I really envy you."

"Shove it, Kingston. She'll probably stretch it out twice as long because of you."

"Thanks for coming. I owe you one."

"Oh, you'll pay, my friend, trust me." To Weathers, Phil said, "I wish you'd reconsider that checkup."

The smile was stronger this time. "Thanks. I'm fine."

"The offer's open. Later, Adam." Phil caught Adam's attention and jerked his head in the direction of the front door.

Adam followed Phil to the foyer. They stood with the door partly open and whispered with their heads close together.

"Adam, what the hell have you gotten yourself into this time?"

"I don't know yet, but he came all this way to talk to me. The least I can do is listen."

"Are you sure it's safe?"

"Reasonably sure."

"Be careful."

"Like always."

Phil shot him a stern look. "That's what worries me. I gotta go."

"There's just one more thing, Phil."

"Now what?"

"About the meatloaf? I lied."

Phil's face went from stern to a wide grin. "Dammit, Adam, someday that woman's going to divorce us both because of you." He was shaking his head as he closed the door behind himself.

Adam stared at the door. Maybe Phil was right, and he shouldn't get involved. Maybe he should tell Chip Weathers to go straight to the police with his story. But he was intrigued by what he'd heard so far. The least he could do is listen to the rest of it. What was it Caroline used to say?

Why do you let yourself get dragged into these things?

Okay. He would listen. But that's all.

CHAPTER

6

Adam returned to the kitchen and saw his guest's empty glass. He refilled it with juice. "I was about to have breakfast when you came," he said. "Mind if I go ahead and whip up something while we talk?"

He left it at that. He would fix enough for two, but he didn't know the proper etiquette when offering a meal to a starving man. He decided on a cheese omelet and toast.

"Sure. Sorry I messed up your day, Mr. Kingston."

"No problem," Adam said as casually as he could. He pulled his large skillet from the oven, set it on the stove, and adjusted the dial to medium. "Tell you what, though," he said as he selected ingredients from the refrigerator, "why don't you call me Adam, and you're...was it Chip?"

"Charles. Chip'll do."

"Okay, Chip, you're about to watch a master chef at work."

Adam broke five eggs into a mixing bowl, added shredded cheddar cheese, and his estimate of half a cup of milk. He decided against adding diced onions and peppers, thinking a more bland meal would be better for his guest. He would still add Bacon Bits at the end though. He stirred the mixture with a fork and poured it into the hot skillet. Next, he put bread in the toaster, then set plates and silverware on the table. When that was done, he decided he had stalled long enough. He had a lot of questions.

"The woman, Chip. Who was she?"

"I don't know."

Adam pretended to watch the skillet. "But if you were there when it happened…"

"That's all I know. How could I have the pocket from her blouse if I hadn't been there? We must have struggled—pulling, grabbing, whatever—and it ripped off in my hand."

"Are you saying you don't remember?" Adam kept his attention on his cooking, but heard his visitor shift in his chair and clear his throat. Like someone trying to think of the right words to say something.

Chip asked, "How much do you know about amnesia, Mr. Kingston?"

"Not much, I'm afraid," Adam said as bubbles appeared on the surface of the omelet. Soon he'd have to flip it over.

"Total amnesia. That's what they told me anyway. My whole life before that day was wiped out like it never happened."

The toast popped up. Adam stuck in two more slices. "When was that?"

"Sixteen years ago."

"Who said it was amnesia?"

"Doctors, shrinks. University Hospital. You familiar with it?"

Adam nodded. He knew it all too well. A helicopter took him there twelve years ago—after the accident. It was three months before he left. He rolled the omelet and sprinkled Bacon Bits on the surface.

"Why were you there?"

"All I know is what they told me. They found me in the street, covered with blood, a big gash on my head."

He paused. When he continued, his voice was soft and wistful, more like he was thinking out loud.

"You know how some people remember things all the way back to when they were babies? Me? As far back as I can go is the day I woke up in that hospital room. I was twenty years old, I was strapped to a bed, and the room was full of people in white coats and blue uniforms."

Adam glanced at Chip who stared through the window at the end of the kitchen. "Blue uniforms. Cops?"

Adam stood by the table now, skillet in one hand, spatula in the other. "What happened? How did you get hurt?"

He shoveled the omelet onto their plates.

"No one knows. At first they thought I'd been mugged, but I had my wallet. That's how they knew who I was. There was money, I had a watch on my arm, a ring. They scratched the mugging idea."

Adam put a plate of toast on the table and sat. "You said they had you strapped to the bed." He picked up his knife and fork and with a gesture, invited his guest to do the same. "You must have given them a rough time."

"The cops said I gave them a real battle. They were okay about it though. Took the straps off after a while, after I started talking to them, trying to answer their questions."

Adam watched Chip fork a piece of omelet and raise it to his mouth. Somehow he'd expected a starving man to attack his food like a savage, but Chip ate slowly, in small bites, chewing it well. A discipline learned from years of not eating regularly, Adam decided. Like a desert wanderer sipping water slowly. He tasted his own breakfast. It was good, but he missed the onions and peppers.

Chip Weathers took several more bites and a long drink of orange juice before he spoke again. "I couldn't tell them anything. That's when they came up with amnesia. They said not to worry about it. I had a bad concussion, and it was normal to have a memory gap at first. They said it would probably return after a few days. They were wrong."

"Your memory never returned? Nothing at all?"

"Nothing. They tried everything. Even hypnosis. They finally gave up and sent me home."

Adam finished spreading jelly on his toast and handed the jar across the table. "You said they found you in the street. Where was that?"

Chip took the open jar, stared into it, and then sat it on the table. He did not speak until Adam looked up and their eyes met.

"On Century Street. In front of the house where they found that woman's body three days ago."

Adam felt the need to stand and move again. He went to the counter to refill his coffee cup, taking his time. Everything in Chip's story seemed to fit. The injury, the house, the piece of cloth. But the amnesia? Was it permanent? How hard was it to fake?

Adam knew he would have to research amnesia if he got involved in this. But he probably wouldn't get involved. He was only listening. He returned to the table. His next question must have been written on his face.

"I thought about going to the police," Chip said, "if that's what you're wondering. Thought about it a lot. I figured they'd either laugh at me or lock me up and throw away the key. Either way, I'd never know what really happened in that house. That's why I came to see you. I read about you in that magazine. *Newsweek*, I think it was. It said you can look at things and touch things—like pictures—and figure out what happened. That psychic thing you do."

"How did you know I'd be here?"

"I didn't know."

"I travel a lot. Sometimes I'm gone for weeks at a time. What would you have done if I'd been on a trip?"

Chip shrugged. "Waited. No big deal."

Adam stopped eating and studied his visitor. It occurred to him that he'd never had a conversation with a homeless person. As an FBI agent, he questioned a few, but had never thought much about their way of life. *No big deal.* As if time meant nothing. Of course not. Time passed, days went by, one after the other without any significance beyond existing on the shadowy perimeter of society. Time was nothing more than a space between one place to sleep and another, one meal and the next.

Adam looked at his breakfast, half-eaten, and pushed it aside. His appetite was gone.

"I want to say something," Chip said, placing his fork beside his empty plate, "before we go any further." He wiped his mouth with the back of his hand and took a deep breath.

"If I killed that woman, I'll do what I have to do. I'll go to the police. I know you'd have to if I didn't. That part doesn't bother me. I don't care about that. They can do what they want with me. But—and I know this sounds crazy—but I have to know what happened that day." His voice grew louder. "I have to know who she was. Who I was. Why I did…whatever I did. I don't care what happens after that. It won't matter. I just have to *know.*" He raised his fist as though he were going to pound the table, caught himself, lowered his hand, and whispered, "Sorry."

Adam waved his hand. "Don't worry about it."

The truth was, he didn't know what to say. The only thing he was sure of was that breakfast was finished. He busied himself with clearing the table.

"Listen, Chip, I have a great view from the patio. Why don't we get some fresh air?"

Adam led the way from the kitchen, through the dining room, and was sliding the patio door open when Chip spoke, "That's a great picture."

Adam saw Chip had stopped by a posed portrait on the wall of him and Caroline.

"Your wife?" Chip said.

"Yes."

"She's very beautiful. Where is she?"

"I lost her. Twelve years ago." He stepped onto the patio. "Cancer."

CHAPTER

7

With the sun overhead, the patio was in full shade from the one above. Adam made his way between two lounge chairs and stood at the waist-high retaining wall. Chip followed, and the two men looked through bright sunlight into a soft blue sky laced with wispy cloud trails.

A large seagull floated into view ten feet from where they stood. It stopped, hovered for a second, then threw a high-pitched bark and dove straight down. Adam watched the bird plummet until it leveled off a few feet above the Boardwalk.

From six floors up, the Boardwalk at this time of day was a massive throng of heads and shoulders moving in all directions at once. If one small group stopped, a traffic jam resulted. Had it been that long since he and Caroline had been part of that crowd?

Chip said, "I'm sorry. I didn't mean to say the wrong thing. About your wife, I mean."

"It's okay. It was a long time ago."

He was lying. It was yesterday. And the day before yesterday. Every day for more than twelve years.

"Do you have a family, Chip?"

"A sister and her husband. My parents died in a car accident two years before all this happened. Some cousins somewhere. California, I think."

A moment passed before Chip asked, "Will you help me find out what happened that day? I know if I can remember that much, I can get the rest of my memory back, too. The shrinks said something about a traumatic shock blanking everything else out. Fill in the blank space, and it all might come back. No guarantee, but it's the only shot I've got."

"Why did you wait all this time?"

"I didn't. I tried for a long time, but it was hopeless. All I knew was where they found me, but it was only a street. I didn't know about that house or about…her…until I saw that picture in the paper three days ago."

Adam settled into the lounge chair behind him. "There's no guarantee I can help, Chip. It was a long time ago, and there's not much to go on. Then there's the police. It could be they've identified the body by now, somehow connected it with you. They could be looking for you."

"I know that."

"If you were involved in what happened to her, you could end up in jail for a very long time. Or worse."

"I know that, too." He stepped away from the wall and nodded at the other lounge chair. "Mind if I…"

"Not at all. Make yourself comfortable."

After adjusting his backrest halfway down to match Adam's, Chip spoke softly. "All the pictures on your walls inside of you and your wife. You must have a lot of memories wrapped up in those pictures. I'll bet you could look at them and tell a lot of stories."

Adam leaned his head back against the cushion of his chair. "Sure could."

"Mind if I ask you something? You don't have to answer if you don't want to."

"Sure." Adam rolled his head toward Chip, curious now.

Chip stared into the endless blue sky. His voice seemed to come from somewhere out there.

"How would it feel if you came home one day and didn't recognize any of those pictures? Say someone brought you here one day, told you this was your home, the woman in the pictures was your wife, but you didn't recognize her. You had no memories. No stories. How would that feel?"

Before Adam could think of an answer, Chip continued. "When the hospital cut me loose, Lisa and Eric, my sister and her husband, took me home. They had pictures, too. Of the guy I was supposed to be. Baby pictures, school pictures, Little League, vacation trips. A whole life. I must've worn those pictures thin going through them over and over again. All I saw was some stranger with my face."

Chip fell silent. A pigeon fluttered to a landing atop the patio wall, stared at him a moment, then flew away as if it had seen nothing of interest. From somewhere distant, the sound of a siren grew and faded.

"There were pictures of a man and a woman," Chip said. "I looked a lot like him. He was tall, powerful-looking, the kind of man a boy could look up to. She was beautiful. Small and on the frail side, classy, like a queen or something. My parents. And I didn't even know them.

"Lisa and Eric tried hard to help me remember. I tried, too. After a while, there was no use trying any more. I didn't belong there, so I left and never went back. Now, after all this time, somebody digs up a floor in an old house and..." His voice had faded to a bare whisper. "I want to go back, Adam, and this is the only chance I'll ever have."

Adam saw Chip's reddened, unblinking eyes fix on something in the far distance. In Chip's drawn, haggard face, he saw—almost felt—the emptiness carried as baggage for sixteen years.

Chip's question pulled at him. He tried to imagine it, how it would feel to not recognize loved ones. He closed his eyes, and his pictures came into focus in a parade celebrating the best part of his life. The old ones when there was a shortage of money, but not of things to do or places to go. Tent-camping weekends in the mountains, Caroline holding the first fish she ever caught, the two of them on a roller coaster at Hershey Park with eyes and mouths wide open. The one she took of him on their first trip to Ocean City. They spent the whole day on the beach, then slept in the car and drove home the next morning. Everything was an adventure in those days, and he could recall every one of them as if they happened yesterday. Memories captured and held in time, etched in solid gold.

Adam couldn't answer Chip's question. The words didn't exist. But he understood why Chip was willing to go to jail if that's what it came to, why he would gamble the life he had now on a chance to regain the one he'd lost. A trade off.

"I can't promise you anything, but I'll try."

Chip faced him, but didn't speak. He didn't have to. It was in his eyes.

Adam let his head sink deep into the soft padding behind it. Phil Russell popped into his mind with a question of his own. It was the one he asked earlier when he left.

Adam, what the hell have you gotten yourself into this time?

It's simple, Phil. I agreed to help him find out if he killed someone.

Why did you do a fool thing like that?

So the poor guy can spend the rest of his life behind bars.

What's wrong with that?

He could see the expression on Phil's face as clearly as if Phil were there.

Adam glanced at his new client. Chip lay motionless, his head rolled to one side, his eyes closed. There was no reason to call Phil this time. Chip was snoring softly with a smile on his lips.

Good. There was something he wanted to do. Something he should have done before he agreed to help Chip. He eased himself out of the chaise lounge and went inside.

CHAPTER

8

After parking the Mercury Grand Marquis two streets away, the man with Albert Cookson's credit card and driver's license in his pocket sat in the hot sun. His bench was bolted to planks on the Boardwalk and faced the Endicott House, a sand-colored, stucco hotel eight stories high.

Behind him, the beach was alive, packed all the way to the surf with shade umbrellas of all colors, blankets, and sun worshippers sitting, sleeping, and smearing suntan lotion. The shouting from a volleyball game, screaming kids running back and forth throwing buckets of water on each other, and dozens of portable radios playing different kinds of loud music irritated him.

Perspiration flooded his face. He pulled a drenched handkerchief from his pocket and swabbed his scalp again.

In front of him, a mass of sweating bodies with blank eyes filed by shoulder-to-shoulder in both directions like zombies. Some had ice cream melting down their arms. Most had yapping kids tugging at their baggy shorts. But they were dressed appropriately, and so was he. At a convenience store in Salisbury, he'd changed into white shorts, a loose-fitting flowered shirt, and sandals. He'd bought sunglasses and an Orioles baseball cap to keep him from getting a sunburn on his bald scalp. In this outfit, he felt inconspicuous. His weight didn't make him stand out. Half the passing people were fat.

He studied the Endicott House. It stood on the south corner
of the Boardwalk and Thirty-fourth Street and took up nearly half
the block going toward Thirty-third. On the north corner, across
Thirty-fourth, the Colonial Towers was smaller than the Endicott
but the same height. He had already checked the other side and rear
of the Colonial Towers. Except for a freight door in the back, the
only ways in or out were the front entrance from the Boardwalk and
a side door in the middle of the building on Thirty-fourth Street.

He looked from one building to the other. The Endicott House
rose from the edge of the Boardwalk. The Colonial Towers sat back
twenty feet. From a window in the front corner of the Endicott,
overlooking Thirty-fourth Street, he'd be able to see both entrances
of the Colonial Towers. Fourth floor would be perfect, fifth would
be okay. But would they have the right room available? If not, he
might have to use the roof. Only one way to find out. He reached
between his legs, picked up his heavy bag, and weaved his way
through the mass of zombies.

*   *   *

Adam found what he wanted on the coffee table in the living
room. He took Chip's handkerchief, the torn pocket, and the
newspaper article into the kitchen. With those items on the
dinette table, he relaxed, touched them lightly with his fingertips,
and hoped he could come up with something. The images came
almost immediately.

A room…faint light…bed, dresser…shadowy figures, pushing, fight-
ing, loud voices…two people?…three?…too dark to tell…something moving
among them, up, down, gray, flat, rectangular, rising, falling…a woman's
scream…the basement room now…someone under the steps, back turned…

bending, straightening, bending...a shovel, digging...a man running from the house...cars, horns, sirens...

The images stopped, and Adam leaned back and thought about what he'd seen. How many people were in that room? Was it only shadows, the movements of two people in a life or death struggle, that gave the illusion of more than two?

He hadn't learned a lot, but there were a few things. The struggle wasn't in the basement, but in a bedroom. Maybe the same house, maybe not. The basement floor was not concrete when the grave was dug.

Was Chip the man with the shovel? Maybe. The man running out of the house certainly was. Sixteen years younger and without the beard, but it was Chip.

The gray rectangular shape moving up and down could've been anything. Or nothing. It might have been another maverick image.

Adam searched the newspapers from the last few days and found two follow-up articles on the discovery of the body. The only new information was that she was between twenty and twenty-five when she died. No further description, and no mention of the cause of death. No mention of any suspects. And she was still referred to as *the unidentified young woman*. The police were hopeful someone would recognize the clothing in the photograph and come forward.

The phrases *withholding evidence* and *harboring a fugitive* crossed Adam's mind. He pushed them aside. Even when he was with the Bureau, he'd bent a rule here and there. Within reason, he told himself.

Did Chip Weathers kill her? Adam's gut instinct told him Chip wasn't the type who would take another's life, but he'd learned long ago how wrong a judgment like that could be. As a young, idealistic

FBI agent, he thought he could *tell* about people. Experience and more than a few mistakes forced him to exorcise that belief.

Under the right circumstances and with the right motivation, anyone can take actions that result in the death of another. He'd once heard murder described as *a tapestry woven from twin brittle threads; one the frailty of life and one the volatility of human emotion.*

Was Chip a man who, sixteen years ago, did something under circumstances of the moment that resulted in a young woman's death? And if he did kill her, was it something he did on purpose?

Gut instinct or not, it didn't matter. Chip wanted the truth either way.

Adam found himself thinking about the young woman who died. Who was she? Why did her life end so terribly?

He knew there could be parents somewhere, possibly a husband and children, who still suffered their loss. He knew what it was like to lose a loved one. It was hard enough under any circumstances, but not knowing what became of her would have to be unbearable.

*   *   *

He set his travel bag at his feet and explained what he wanted to the elderly woman with stiff, gray hair behind the counter.

After what seemed much too long, she responded, "I'm sorry, sir, but there's nothing available where you want it. The only single rooms left are on the south side of the building or toward the rear."

He gave her a sad smile. "Aw, that's too bad. I really had my heart set on staying at the Endicott, and I wanted a view of the ocean. Are you sure there's nothing at all? How about a double room or an efficiency?"

She looked at her chart again. "The only thing would be 406, but that's a three-bedroom suite."

He grinned. "Suite 406 will do fine."

"Will that be cash or charge?"

"Visa." He slid Albert Cookson's credit card and driver's license across the counter and waited with a pleasant look as she went through the authorization procedure.

After a quick glance at the picture on the driver's license and a quicker one at the man's face, the lady behind the counter returned her attention to her paperwork. Not a second's hesitation. The picture switch had only taken half an hour. Albert's signature was easy.

CHAPTER

While Chip Weathers slept on his patio, Adam vacuumed and straightened the apartment, cleaned the dishes from breakfast, and emptied the dishwasher. He also took a short catnap of his own. Afterward, he called Ellie. Phil Junior had indeed called her, suffered through her lecture, and renewed his promise to call every day.

"Oh," Ellie added, "he met a wonderful girl and is bringing her home to meet us."

"That's nice," Adam said.

At five after five, Adam stood in his kitchen wondering what to do next when Chip came in from the patio. "Well," he said, "I wasn't sure I'd see you until tomorrow."

Chip grinned. "I'm sorry about falling asleep like that."

"Don't worry about it. I did a little snoozing myself. How do you feel?"

"Much better."

He certainly looked better, Adam thought. He had some color in his face and looked closer to thirty-six than he had before. He calculated Chip's age from his being twenty when he was picked up on Century Street sixteen years ago. A few hours ago, he might have guessed fifty.

"Listen," Adam said, "if you'd like to freshen up, the bathroom's the first door on the right down the hall. Grab a shower if you want. There's a fresh toothbrush, and I laid out some clothes you can use. I'm a little taller than you, but they should fit all right. Then we can talk."

Adam busied himself pouring a glass of water and waited. Out of the corner of his eye, he watched Chip examine his hands and shabby clothes. Then, with a grimace and a shrug, Chip mumbled, "Maybe I'll just...wash up a little."

Adam listened. The toilet flushed. The sink ran for a moment. A long silence. Finally, he heard the shower running. He smiled.

Chip returned to the kitchen half an hour later in the blue cotton slacks and blue-and-white polo shirt Adam had selected. Not too fancy, washed a few times, loose-fitting on Chip's smaller frame, but a hell of an improvement. Adam wondered how his longhaired, bearded client would look after an hour or so in a barber's chair.

Adam had set the dinette table with a tray of cold cuts and cheese, lettuce, sliced tomatoes, mayonnaise, mustard, pickles, bread, and two large glasses of iced tea.

"You're just in time," he said. "Hope you're hungry."

Chip stared at the food with wide eyes. "Man. Two meals in one day. You're going to ruin my diet. By the way, I meant to give you this before." He pulled a folded piece of paper from his pocket and handed it to Adam as they sat.

Adam recognized it as a check, but he wasn't prepared for what he saw when he unfolded it—two thousand dollars made out to Adam Kingston. In the top left corner, it read "Charles P. Weathers Jr. Fund," with an address in Hunt Valley, Maryland. He was familiar with Hunt Valley, a sprawling complex of high-rise office buildings and rambling distribution and manufacturing facilities north of Baltimore.

The signature on the check was an illegible scrawl, but below the signature line were the printed words "E. M. Richards,

Administrator." Below that was "EMR Investments, Inc." The check was dated August 14, two days ago.

He stared at the check, then at Chip. "What's this?"

Chip, busy building a sandwich, replied, "That's a, uh, whatta-you-call-it? A retainer. I know you get paid for what you do. If that's not enough…"

"That's not the point."

Adam was confused, and he always became a bit irritated when that happened. He laid the check on the table and pointed at it.

"What is this fund, and who is E. M. Richards?"

"That's my brother-in-law, Eric."

"Okay, Eric Richards is your brother-in-law. Can I assume Charles P. Weathers Junior is you?"

Chip nodded.

"Now what about this fund in your name?"

Chip hesitated. "Adam, I…if you don't mind, I'd rather let Eric tell you about that."

Adam decided not to press it—for now. "All right. If that's the way you want it."

After taking a minute to reduce his irritation back to simple confusion, he watched Chip take a bite of his sandwich and decided to make one for himself. When he picked up the check to put it in his pocket, images formed.

A large room…windows, wide, high, an office…loud, angry, male voices… "something I have to do"…"crazy, throwing money away"…a desk, a man sitting, dark hair, suit, tie…Chip, standing, shouting…"have to do this"…the other man, sneering, "phony psychic"…"fortune teller"…"con man"…Chip, pleading…"help me"…"last chance"…

The images and voices faded.

Adam made his sandwich, troubled by what he had seen. Chip and Eric arguing about money. But Eric wrote the check anyway. Why? Whose money was it?

The two men ate in silence, but Adam couldn't help thinking about Eric's words.

Phony psychic. Con man. Fortune teller.

He couldn't wait to meet Eric Richards.

After they finished eating, Adam refilled their glasses. "Chip, we need to talk now. You're my starting point on this and I need to know everything you can tell me."

"I don't know much, but I'll tell you everything I can."

"Let's start with Eric. You saw him recently, the day you got the check. Do you see him often?"

"No. Hardly ever. That was the first time in, I guess, five years."

"How about your sister? Do you see her?"

Chip shook his head. "I haven't seen Lisa since I left their house sixteen years ago. I found out they split up after that, and she moved away. I don't even know where she is."

"She never tried to contact you?"

"Not that I know of. Lisa and I were never close. At least, that's the feeling I got when I stayed with them after the hospital. She was five years older, and I guess I was the bratty kid brother. She was nice to me, but kind of standoffish, if you know what I mean."

"What about Eric? Did he keep in contact?"

"Sort of. He hired a private detective to check on me. It took me a while to catch on, but every few weeks I'd see this same guy sitting in a car or standing on the street, watching."

"How do you know he worked for Eric?"

"I asked him. After I caught on that he was spying on me on a regular basis, I approached him and asked why. I don't know if I scared or shocked him, but he told me Eric hired him. Eric was worried about me and wanted to make sure I was all right. His hired watchdog and I came to an understanding. He'd keep on doing his job, reporting to Eric, and I'd ignore him. It's been that way for a long time now."

"It's nice to know Eric cares about you," Adam said. He was tempted to ask about the check again, but decided against it. Chip clearly didn't want to discuss it. He could push Chip to tell him, but first things first. He needed to know what was happening in Baltimore with the police investigation. If they knew about Chip's involvement and were looking for him, none of it would matter. Leo Jackson might help. He glanced at the clock. After six. Too late today. He'd call Leo first thing in the morning.

Adam busied himself with clearing the table and putting food away as questions filled his mind. Why did Chip live the way he did when he had access to money? Eric Richards was apparently a successful businessman who not only showed concern for Chip, but also had control of a trust fund in Chip's name. Why? And why had Chip's sister turned her back on him?

Chip interrupted his thoughts. "Adam, I want to help as much as I can, and I'm sorry I can't tell you more. What do we do now? What do you want me to do?"

"There's nothing we can do until tomorrow morning. Why don't we call it a day?"

"Whatever you say."

Adam felt awkward but the words came out anyway. "Do you, uh, have a place to stay?"

Chip shrugged. "Of course." A flicker of a smile played across his lips. "That's never a problem. There's a shelter not far from here. The food's not as good as yours, but it's...comfortable."

Adam wondered how long it had been since Chip had spent a night in a real home. He thought about offering money, but decided against it. He sensed he'd made Chip uncomfortable enough already.

"Okay," he said, "if you're sure."

"I am. Want me to come by tomorrow?"

"Why don't we meet next door? The Colonel's Kitchen. We'll have breakfast and talk some more. Nine o'clock all right?" At least he would make sure his client ate a decent breakfast.

"Fine by me."

"Good. I'll walk out with you. I need to stretch the old legs a little."

CHAPTER
10

With the sliding door open, he had a clear view of the Boardwalk and the front entrance of the Colonial Towers through the wrought-iron railing of the narrow balcony outside. And with his chair inside the darkened doorway, no one could see him. His rifle lay at his feet, assembled, loaded, and fitted with the silencer. The noise from outside would prevent anyone hearing the muffled shot. His handgun, a box of trash bags, a large roll of duct tape, and two containers of ammunition were in the travel bag on the floor beside the chair.

He leaned forward to get a better glimpse of the Boardwalk four stories below. Not as packed as before, but still a lot of people walking by.

He'd already decided he would visit a few lounges afterward. All the big hotels had lounges, and they attracted women. He'd bring her to the suite. Maybe he'd get lucky and find a good-looking one. One that took credit cards.

He checked Albert's watch. Six-fifteen. Another hour and a half of good daylight left. Nothing to do but wait.

He wanted a head shot. Head shots were best.

*   *   *

The clock above the front entrance read 6:40 p.m. when Adam led Chip through the lobby of the Colonial Towers. They passed the Petersons, an elderly couple from the eighth floor. He exchanged smiles and greetings with them. Nice people. Their curious glances at Chip were hardly noticeable.

The doorman, Henry, peered over his newspaper from his desk near the entrance. Probably wondering why Chip wore different clothes than when he came in, Adam thought. He gave Henry a friendly wave.

As soon as they stepped onto the Boardwalk, Chip said, "Hey, that looks like fun."

Four boys, all around ten years old, tossed breadcrumbs in the air. Above them, two dozen seagulls floated, flapped, squawked, and grabbed the treats in mid-air. Adam thought of the many times he and Caroline did the same thing. Chip was right. It was fun.

The boys stood at the edge of the Boardwalk, facing Thirty-fourth Street, halfway between the Colonial Towers and the Endicott House. Adam and Chip joined the small group of passersby who stopped to watch them.

*　　*　　*

He picked up his rifle as soon as he saw them come out. He'd been watching kids throw crumbs to the birds while keeping close watch on both exits of the Colonial Towers. The kids started with only a handful of birds, but there must be ten times as many now—squealing, squawking, bobbing up and down—some as high as his fourth-floor window.

Everything was going his way. With all the noise from the kids and the birds, no one would hear the shot.

When he saw the two men walking in his direction, then stop to watch the kids, he knew it was his lucky day. He took a breath, held it, aimed, and squeezed the trigger.

At the same instant, a large seagull fluttered directly across his sight.

"Damn bird!"

The distraction made him miss the shot he had wanted. He lowered the rifle and squinted. The crowd was in his way. No chance for a clear second shot. He dropped the rifle on the floor and walked to the open door. He saw no one pointing his way. They had no idea where the shot came from. He smiled, stepped inside, and searched through his nylon bag for his binoculars. Might as well have a closer look, he thought, as he returned to the patio.

*   *   *

Chip smiled as he watched the boys. "Adam, did you…"

He spun around, made a loud grunting sound, grabbed his stomach with both hands, doubled over, fell to his knees, and toppled face down on the Boardwalk.

Adam saw Chip spin and fall and tried to grab him, but missed. He knelt beside Chip's outstretched body and saw a hole in the back of Chip's shirt, just above the waist. A crimson splotch encircled the hole.

Chip groaned and tried to turn over. Adam helped him. Now lying on his back, Chip's hands clutched his stomach. Blood seeped through his fingers. His teeth were clenched and his face contorted in pain.

He muttered, "I think I've been shot. Jesus Christ, Adam, somebody shot me."

Adam looked up. People stared and closed in around them. "Stay back," he shouted. "Call an ambulance."

He saw a man unclip a cell phone, then concentrated his attention on Chip. A wet, dark circle spread outward beneath Chip's blood-soaked hands. Adam yanked his handkerchief from his pocket, raised Chip's hands enough to slide it under them, then replaced Chip's hand with his own to add pressure.

"Hold on, Chip. You're going to be all right. Just hold on."

Still on his knees, Adam raised himself as high as he could without taking his hands off Chip's wound and looked around in every direction.

Who? Where?

He hadn't heard a shot and realized no one else had either. If the people around him had heard it, they'd be running for cover instead of blocking his view as they moved in for a closer look.

The curious crowd was all around them now, murmuring, asking each other, "What happened?" An elderly woman in a floppy straw hat mouthed, "Oh my God."

Two small boys squeezed between the legs of adults and stared with saucer eyes and gaping mouths. A young mother held a toddler in her arms, one hand covering the child's eyes. Over her shoulder, a man on a patio with binoculars. The crowd grew and edged closer.

Adam yelled, "Move back! Please! Move back!"

Chip groaned and rolled his head from side to side. With his eyes squeezed shut, his mouth pulled into a tight grimace of pain, he sucked large breaths through his teeth. Adam kept assuring him he would be all right, to hang on. Chip lost consciousness seconds before the ambulance and police arrived. Adam rode with him to the hospital.

Chapter

11

Within seconds of their arrival at the emergency room, the stretcher carrying Chip was surrounded by men and women in white and green and wheeled inside a curtained cubicle. Adam was left standing in the middle of the congested emergency room. And in everyone's way it seemed. No matter where he stood, someone rushed in or out of Chip's cubicle forcing him to find a new spot.

A short, square-faced nurse with close-cropped blonde hair saved him. She approached him holding a clipboard.

"Are you a relative?" she asked.

Somewhere in her mid-forties, she stood barely to his shoulder and wore a look of relaxed acceptance that said the excitement of an emergency room had turned to routine long ago.

"No. A friend. How is he?"

"He lost a lot of blood, but that's under control. He'll go for X-rays in a few minutes, then we'll know more. There's a waiting room through those doors if…are you injured?" She stared at his blood-smeared hands.

Adam raised them to chest level. "No. I got this from putting pressure on the wound."

"Well then, how about we get you cleaned up?" She led him to a sink.

As Adam scrubbed, he noticed her looking at him, her head cocked to one side.

"You're Adam Kingston," she said.

"Yes, I am. I'm sorry, but I..."

She smiled and waved her hand. "I don't expect you to remember me. I met you briefly at the fundraiser for the clinic in April. You were with Phil and Ellie Russell. Then I read about you in *Newsweek*. It was like a miracle when you found that little boy."

"I'm afraid they gave me too much credit," he said. "There were a lot of people involved in the search. Besides, the picture they ran of me was so bad I was hoping no one would see it."

She laughed. "Not likely. Not around here anyway. Phil must've shown it to everyone in the hospital."

Adam grimaced. "Good old Phil. I'll get him for that."

She laughed again and handed him a paper towel. He dried his hands, tossed the towel into a wastebasket, and held both hands out for her inspection. When she nodded her approval, he said, "You mentioned a waiting room?"

She grinned up at him. It was one of those upside down, squinting grins where the mouth bends downward instead of up, and the eyes squeeze almost shut. "Okay, Mister Humble Hero," she said. "Follow me."

Dot Whiting, RN, according to her name badge, led him through double swinging doors to the waiting room. She said she would let him know as soon as there was any news about Chip's condition and, by the way, she didn't think his picture in *Newsweek* was that bad.

Windows along one sidewall of the waiting room looked out into a parking lot. Against the far wall, in one of the blue plastic chairs lining the room, an elderly man with a cast on one leg from his thigh to his foot looked very uncomfortable.

Across from the windows, a young woman in jeans and T-shirt cradled a tiny baby across her chest, rolling her arms back and forth in a slow rocking motion. In the seat next to her, a boy about five slept open-mouthed, his head snuggled against her shoulder. His head bobbed in rhythm with the movement of her arms.

Adam settled into a chair across from the young family and looked at the clock above their heads. Almost seven-thirty. Less than an hour ago, he and Chip left the Colonial Towers. It all happened so fast, he hadn't had time to think. Now he did.

Who fired the shot? Why? A random shot fired into a crowd? A stray bullet meant for someone else? A careless, accidental discharge?

He knew they were hopeless questions at this point. Most important was whether Chip would make it. He'd seen gut shots before, seen people die from internal bleeding and damage to vital organs. He hoped Chip had gotten here in time. He could only sit and hope for the best. He remembered talking to two policemen while the ambulance crew worked on Chip back on the Boardwalk. They asked him to meet them at the hospital. Maybe they would have some answers when they came.

He could do nothing but wait. He hated waiting. It made him irritable.

Across the room from him, the young mother raised her shirt and breastfed her baby. The little boy continued to sleep beside her.

After thirty minutes that seemed like a couple of hours, the little boy snored softly, and the old man with the cast on his leg limped away with Nurse Whiting's assistance. She gave Adam the upside-down grin as she passed.

Adam's rear end was numb from sitting in the hard chair, his patience hung on a frayed thread, and he wanted a cup of coffee. He decided to roam the halls to find one when a man came through the doors from the emergency room. He stopped, looked at Adam, then pulled a small notepad from his shirt pocket. He stood there, thumbing through pages.

Adam recognized him as one of the plainclothes police officers from the Boardwalk. He hadn't paid much attention then and
couldn't remember his name. When the young man looked up from
his notepad and walked toward him, it occurred to Adam that he
resembled a young Robert Redford. Blond, well-built, beach-boy
looks. He even dressed the part. Tan sport coat, gray slacks, cream
colored shirt, no tie.

Probably works out a lot, does martial arts. The new breed.

"Mr. Kingman?"

"Kingston."

He checked his notes again. "Yes, Kingston. I have a few questions. I hope you don't mind. Oh, I'm Detective Wilson. Stuart
Wilson. We met at the scene?" He flashed a wide movie star smile.

Perfect manners. Perfect teeth. Definitely new breed.

"I remember you," Adam said, trying to be cordial in spite of
the sour mood brought on by the waiting.

The detective selected the chair next to Adam's, moved it so
they would be facing one another, and sat. When he checked his
notepad again, Adam's last shred of patience slid away.

"Detective, did you find out who fired that shot?"

Wilson looked up from his notes. "No. Actually, we haven't been
able to do that yet." He tried the movie star smile again, but only
took it halfway. "You see, there seems to be some, well, confusion."

You seem a little confused yourself, kid.

"There were plenty of witnesses," Adam said. "Someone must
have seen what happened."

"The, uh, confusion seems to be about the direction your
friend was facing when he was struck. Naturally, that would have a
bearing on where the shot was fired from. In other words…"

Adam interrupted. "He was with me, right beside me."
Irritation filled the void left by his patience. "We were facing the
same way."

Detective Wilson went to his notepad once more. "But you,
uh, stated, Mr. Kingston, that you were facing south at the time
the shot was fired. Some of the other witnesses stated that your
friend…Weathers, was it?"

"Yes, Weathers."

"…that Mr. Weathers was facing the other way, north, when he
fell, which means the bullet would have come from that direction or
perhaps from the beach."

Adam glared at the young man. "Listen carefully, Detective
Wilson. We were standing together, side by side. Why in the hell
would we be facing opposite directions? He spun around after he
was shot."

Over the detective's shoulder, Adam saw that the tone and
volume of his voice had awakened the little boy across the room.
The youngster stared at him with wide eyes. His mother rocked her
baby faster. Adam smiled at them to apologize, then lowered his
voice to a controlled level, and found another apologetic smile for
the detective.

"I'm sorry. I'm a little on edge. It's been a hectic day."

"That's understandable, Mr. Kingston, and I'm sorry to take
your time like this. But, you see, in police work, we have to talk
to all available witnesses, and sometimes their stories don't coin-
cide. You see, when traumatic incidents occur, like what happened
tonight, eyewitnesses often give conflicting accounts. We have to
sift through the differing…"

"Please," Adam broke off the lecture as politely as his forced
restraint would allow, "if you have no further questions for me, I
have to go to the restroom."

Detective Wilson shifted his weight on the chair. "Oh...yes... of course. Well, actually, there are a couple more questions." He dug into the right-side pocket of his jacket, then the left, pulled out a ballpoint pen, and poised it over his notepad.

Adam fought the urge to shake him senseless.

"Let's see now," Wilson said, frowning at his notes. "Yes. Do you know, Mr. Kingston, if Mr. Weathers had any enemies? Anyone who would want to harm him."

"None that I know of."

"Did you happen to see anyone yourself who might have fired the shot?"

"No."

"Did Mr. Weathers say anything to you, either before or after the incident, that might help us determine what happened?"

Adam crossed his arms across his chest, pursed his lips, and put on a thoughtful expression. "Yes, as a matter of fact, he did say something right after the incident that might help you determine what happened."

"Good. What did he say?"

Adam leaned toward him and whispered. "He said, 'Somebody shot me.'"

Wilson stared at him and blinked several times.

Adam stood. "Detective, I would like to go to the restroom now."

Wilson deposited his pen in one pocket, his pad in another, crossed his legs, then uncrossed them. "Uh, okay. That'll be fine. Anyway, I have to see about confiscating the bullet as soon as they recover it from the...I mean from his...well, ballistics, you know."

CHAPTER
12

Adam didn't have to go to the bathroom, but he did anyway. It felt good to stretch his legs, and he needed to calm himself. He had worked with police officers all across the country, and not one of them had given him a lecture on the inherent problems of conflicting eyewitness accounts.

Who the hell did he think he was talking to?

But he had to admit Wilson had no way of knowing he was talking to a former FBI agent with twenty years of investigative experience. Perhaps, just perhaps, he'd been a trifle impatient with the young detective.

On his way back to the waiting room, he spotted an alcove with vending machines. Yes! A coffee machine. As he watched the cup fill, he remembered something. Chip was shot from the front, spun around, and fell face down with a bloody hole in his back. The bullet had gone all the way through. The detective had not seen it because Chip was lying on his back when the police arrived. If the bullet was to be found, it would be at the scene of the shooting. Wilson needed to know that.

Adam hurried to the waiting room, trying not to spill the hot coffee. He sat it on his chair and checked the emergency room. No one knew where the detective had gone. Adam went outside and checked the sidewalk and the parking lot. No sign of him. Oh, well. Wilson would get the word soon enough.

Adam returned to the waiting room and his coffee. The young mother and her sleepy children were gone. He took his first sip as Phil and Ellie Russell burst through the door at the other end of the room.

Phil wore a dark suit and tie, and Ellie was elegant in a red dress and pearls.

"Adam, what happened?" Phil had Ellie by the hand, pulling her along.

Adam stood to greet them. Before he could speak, Phil stopped a few feet away and scanned him. Ellie bumped into Phil's back.

Phil said, "They told me you'd been shot."

Ellie pushed around Phil. "Adam, are you all right?"

Adam held up his hands. "Whoa, guys. I'm fine. Who said I'd been shot?"

"An intern in ICU," Phil said. "I called to check on a patient, and he said you were here and had been shot. What the hell's going on?"

Adam groaned. Nurse Whiting. The news was probably all over the hospital by now and with the usual accuracy of word-of-mouth broadcasting.

Ellie touched Adam's arm. "Are you really all right?"

"I'm okay. Honest." He kissed her on the cheek. "Now, if you'll both relax, I'll tell you about it."

As he finished telling them about the shooting, Nurse Whiting came through the door behind them carrying X-rays. Phil stood and stepped in front of her. "Are those the gunshot films, Dottie?"

"Oh, hi, Phil. Yes, they are." She peeped around him and waved. "Hi, Ellie." Then her eyes rested on Adam, and she gave him that grin again.

Phil took the X-rays and held them to the light. "Who's on it?"

"Dr. Greenberg."

Phil looked at Adam. "I'll see what I can find out. Wait here."

"Like hell I will." Adam sprang from his chair and followed Phil and Nurse Whiting through the swinging doors. He'd had enough sitting and waiting.

Adam stood behind Doctors Phil Russell and Dick Greenberg while they studied, pointed at, and ran their fingers over Chip's X-rays.

Phil turned to him. "We're pretty sure the bullet passed through his midsection without any major damage. It missed his spine and aorta by a hair, and his spleen was undamaged."

"Then he'll be okay?"

"Looks like. So far, anyway."

"So far?"

Dr. Greenberg replied, "We're waiting for test results. We'll have to repair some internal damage, but it looks good."

"When will you know for sure?"

"Soon," said Phil. "Now get out of here. Go keep my wife company. I'll tell you as soon as we know more."

Adam pushed through the double doors into the waiting room. Ellie sat where he'd left her.

"Phil thinks there's a good chance he'll be all right."

He sat in the chair beside her and smiled.

She said, "I'm glad," but she didn't return the smile. She studied him with tight lips, narrowed eyes, and one arched eyebrow.

Since there was no way to avoid it, he threw himself on her altar by saying, "Ellie, you look absolutely ravishing tonight. Is that a new dress?"

Her other eyebrow shot up. She examined her lap and smoothed wrinkles that weren't there. Then she picked imaginary pieces of lint from her dress and dropped them at his feet. Finally, she looked at him with the worst imitation of benign calmness he had ever seen.

"Yes, as a matter of fact, it is," she cooed, in a voice dripping with honey. "How sweet of you to notice. You see, for the first time in weeks, Phil had a day off, and we had every intention of enjoying a relaxing evening at the Del-Mar Inn. But instead, we had to rush to the hospital because a certain pain in the ass had reportedly been shot."

"Now, Ellie, it's not my fault the story got twisted around. You can't blame…"

She raised her hand.

He shushed.

"Upon arriving at the hospital," Ellie continued, "we found that the pain in the ass had not been shot after all."

"Ellie, I'm sorry I ruined your evening. I…"

Her hand shushed him again.

"Ruin my evening? Oh, no. You don't have to apologize to me." The honey in her voice had turned to vinegar. "Oh, no. You don't owe me anything."

"Ellie."

"What?"

"I love you, and I'm sorry about your dinner."

"Don't you dare try to weasel out of it like that, Adam Kingston. I could boil you in oil right now. And you know damn well I'm not talking about a stupid dinner."

He nodded and hung his head. "I know."

"Then please tell me, if you'll be so kind, why you're running around and getting shot at again. You quit the cops and robbers business a long time ago. You think Phil and I don't have enough to worry about? We have to start worrying about you all over again?"

"No, Ellie. Nothing like that. It's just that I have this new client and, uh...it's kind of a long story."

"Well, it seems I have a bit of time on my hands right now—thanks to you—so let's have it."

He told her about his day, from Chip Weathers coming to his door to the shooting on the Boardwalk. He didn't mind. Ellie had always been a good sounding board.

When he finished, Ellie's mood had softened. "Do you think someone purposely tried to kill him?"

He shook his head. "It doesn't make any sense. People like him don't make enemies. No, I think the bullet was random or meant for someone else. Some psycho, maybe, wanting to make the front pages. Hell, it could have been an accident, a kid playing with daddy's gun, any number of things."

"Okay," Ellie said, "the next obvious question is was someone shooting at you instead of him? And don't tell me you never made any enemies when you were with the FBI."

Adam laughed and patted her hand. "Ellie, I've been out of all that for more than twelve years. Believe me, anyone with a grudge against me from those days is either dead or rotting away in jail somewhere."

"I hope you're right about that. You *will* check, won't you?"

The way she said *will* made it a command, not a question. "Yes, dear, I'll check out all my old enemies. First thing in the morning."

"Good. What are you going to do about your client's problem?"

"For one thing, I need to have a long talk with Eric Richards, his brother-in-law."

"What about his sister?"

"That's another curious wrinkle. His brother-in-law seems more concerned about him than the sister, even hired someone to check on him from time to time. His sister dropped out of his life completely. He doesn't even know where she is."

"Maybe she's embarrassed at the way he turned out."

"Maybe. I'm hoping Eric Richards can fill in a lot of gaps."

"When are you going to talk to him?"

"Right now, if I can come up with a phone number."

CHAPTER

13

Adam cursed himself for leaving his cell phone at home, but he hadn't planned on going any further than the Boardwalk. He remembered seeing a change machine in the vending room he'd visited earlier and a pay phone in the hallway. Armed with a handful of coins, he called Directory Assistance. There was no listing for Eric M. Richards. He did get a number, however, for EMR Investments, the company name printed on the check Chip had given him. He called it and listened to a recorded message.

Thank you for calling EMR Investments. Our business hours are nine to five, Monday through Friday. You may leave a message at the tone, and an EMR associate will return your call as soon as possible.

Adam waited for the tone and gave his name and number, along with a request that Mr. Richards call him as soon as possible about an urgent family matter.

Next, he asked for listings for Lisa Richards, Lisa Weathers and, as a last resort, Charles P. Weathers. Nothing.

When he returned to the waiting room with a fresh cup of coffee for himself and a Diet Coke for Ellie, Phil entered the room from the other end.

Phil snatched the coffee from Adam's hand. "Thanks," he said as he took a seat next to his wife. "Adam, your friend is going to be all right. Naturally, there was some damage that'll need to be repaired. They're prepping him for surgery right now. We'll have to…"

Ellie swung her head toward Phil so abruptly it stopped him cold. "What do you mean *we*?"

Phil took her hand in his. "I'm sorry, El, but Dick Greenberg is shorthanded tonight. He asked if I could help out."

"And you couldn't say no?"

Phil gave her a helpless look. "What could I do?"

Ellie sighed. "It's my own fault for marrying a doctor. My mother tried to warn me."

Phil jerked his thumb toward Adam. "Actually, it's all his fault. Take it out on him."

"Oh, don't you worry," Ellie said. "I know whose fault it is. I just haven't decided on the appropriate punishment yet."

Adam's eyes darted back and forth between them.

Ellie pronounced sentence. "Adam, I'll go easy on you this time. *You* are taking me to dinner."

Adam smiled and winked at her. "Beats the hell out of boiling oil."

Phil kissed his wife on the cheek. "I have to scrub. I'll be through in a couple of hours. Meet you back here." He handed the empty coffee cup to Adam and stood.

Adam caught him by the arm. "Phil, there's something I need to know."

"What's that?"

"The exact location of the entrance and exit wounds. The angle might tell me where the bullet came from."

Ellie jabbed his arm with a finger. "You let the police handle it, Adam. It's their job, not yours."

"I know, I know. I just want to make sure they don't miss anything. I don't like the idea of having a sniper in my neighborhood."

Phil gave him a stern look, then shrugged it off. "Whatever. I'll have it when you get back." As he walked away, he said over his shoulder, "And keep your hands off my wife."

"But what if she comes on to me again?"

"Shoot her. We're running a special on bullet wounds tonight."

Phil left the waiting room as Nurse Dot Whiting walked in.

"Ellie," she sang out. "I love that dress. Hot date tonight?"

Ellie shot a quick dagger at Adam, but let it go at that.

"Thanks, Dottie. I just got it today. You remember Adam?"

"Sure do. We talked a little while ago. You guys hanging around to wait for Phil?" She smiled at Adam while talking to Ellie.

The way Nurse Whiting looked at him made Adam uncomfortable.

After they said good-bye to Nurse Whiting and were leaving the hospital, Ellie said, "She likes you, you know."

He gave her a warning look. "Don't start with me."

"I'm not starting anything, but it wouldn't hurt to ask her out sometime."

"She's too short."

"Dammit, Adam. You always say something like that. Too short, too tall, too this, too that. I miss Caroline, too, but she wouldn't want you to live like a monk."

"I don't live like a monk. My social life would fill a dozen tabloids."

"You're full of crap, Adam Kingston."

"And you're a nag, Ellie Russell."

CHAPTER

14

On his knees in the master bedroom of Suite 406, he released his grip on her neck and let her head fall back onto the carpet. Her bright red hair flattened into a fiery circle around her battered face. He flexed his fingers, stiff from applying pressure, and looked at her nude body.

Her eyes bulged out farther than he had thought possible. Her mouth was frozen in a silent scream. His blows had smashed her nose and broken most of her front teeth. A river of thick blood from her nose had filled her mouth before flowing down her chin and neck onto the carpet.

She lay on her back, her left leg straight, her right leg bent at the knee. Her hands were by her sides, her fingers clutched into the carpet. Her head had rolled to one side, away from him. He reached down with a beefy hand and turned her face toward him.

"It's your own damn fault, bitch," he said, sneering down at her. "I can get hard. I've done it lots of times. Guess you won't laugh anymore now, will you?"

He leaned across her, reached under the bed, found the strap of his nylon travel bag, and slid it out. He dug inside it and brought out a box of trash bags and a roll of duct tape. Reaching in again, he found a pair of surgical gloves and pulled them on.

Still on his knees beside her, he put his hands on his hips and wagged his head from side to side.

"Now see what you did, bitch? Made more work for me."

He removed six of the black plastic bags from the box, and doubled their strength by inserting one inside another. He slid her lower half into the first two, then her upper half into another pair. The last two were used to wrap around her middle, overlapping the others.

With the duct tape, he encircled her body twice where the bags overlapped at her breasts and did the same at her knees, then inspected his work. Satisfied he had done a good job, he struggled to a standing position. He was breathing heavily from his efforts, and perspiration ran off his scalp onto his face. He felt his anger returning when he had to swab his forehead with the back of his hand. He raised his right foot and slammed it down hard where he knew her face was and felt bone breaking under his weight.

"No-good bitch. A hundred bucks? Shit. You ain't worth two cents, none of you."

He knelt again and, pushing her ahead of him, scooted her across the carpet to the bed. He maneuvered himself around so he sat with his feet against her and pushed until she was as far under the king-size bed as his legs reached.

"Guess you'll keep under there for a while. Maids never clean under beds."

He went into the bathroom, flushed the surgical gloves down the toilet, washed his face and hands, and returned to the bedroom with a wet, soapy towel. After he had scrubbed her blood from the carpet, he tossed the towel under the bed and stood.

The clock on the nightstand read ten-forty. Still early. Still time to go after another one. After thinking about it, he decided it was too much trouble. He was tired. He'd watch a skin flick and do himself.

He went into the living room and switched on the TV.

Chapter

15

Adam and Ellie returned to the hospital at ten-forty-five to find Phil waiting with good news. Chip's internal injuries had been repaired, and the prognosis was good. Adam wanted to see his client, but Phil told him it would be at least twelve hours before Chip could talk.

Phil and Ellie drove Adam to the Colonial Towers. After they said goodnight at the side door, Adam started to go in, but changed his mind. He needed to unwind.

During the day, he thought of the Boardwalk as a thoroughfare for the hordes who trod its tireless planks and rode its shuttle trains in sun-bleached pursuit of their pleasures. He liked it better at night when the superficial noises of the day surrendered to the ageless voices of the sea and wind. He walked across it now with his hands deep in his pockets, listening as the soft lapping of cresting waves became gentle accents above their own rhythmic onrush and retreat into themselves, letting cool, salt-laden breezes tease him from one direction then another.

No stars were visible, and the moon was a hazy gray splatter on an endless, black canvas. Far out, beneath a barely discernible horizon, a brightly lit cruise ship slid past nodding pinpoint lights of small fishing boats. He watched a couple stroll barefoot along the surf, their pants legs rolled up, their hands linked, shoes and socks swinging in their free hands.

Watching them, he thought of other nights on the beach, of blankets spread on the sand, of chilled wine disguised in paper cups, of sitting with Caroline for hours, listening, feeling, touching.

At the edge of the Boardwalk, where it gave way to the beach, he decided to walk in the sand, maybe wade in the surf. When he reached down to remove his loafers, he saw a familiar figure where he had stood with Chip before the shooting. He watched Detective Stuart Wilson switch on a flashlight, aim it downward, and begin swinging it back and forth.

Adam had to admire Wilson's concentration. He walked to within three feet of him before the detective looked up and shined the small but powerful flashlight in Adam's face.

"It's you, Mr. Kingston."

"Yes, it is," Adam said, holding his hand in front of his eyes. "Do you think you can turn that thing off?"

"Of course. Sorry." The detective fumbled for a second, found the right button, and switched it off. "I'm surprised to see you here."

Adam jerked a thumb over his shoulder. "I live here."

Wilson glanced at the Colonial Towers. "Oh, yeah. I forgot."

"Tell me, Detective, did you confiscate the bullet?"

Wilson put his hands on his hips, lowered his head and shook it from side to side. He let out a small, nervous laugh. "You know what, Mr. Kingston?"

"What, Detective Wilson?"

"You and I got off on the wrong foot. I'll be honest with you. I only made detective two months ago, and I guess I've been a little full of myself since then. When I went back to the station, one of the other guys heard your name and told me about you. How you used to be an FBI agent and how you still work with them as a consultant. You must have thought I was a real piece of work, I mean, questioning what you said, explaining procedures, and...well, I want to apologize."

Adam held a serious expression. "Two months, huh?"

"Yeah."

Adam grinned. "Funny. I would've guessed three, maybe four." He extended his hand.

Stuart Wilson stared, then a wide smile grew, and he shook Adam's hand. It wasn't the movie-star smile this time, but the genuine smile of a sincere young man admitting he had a lot to learn.

"Now that we have that out of the way," Adam said, "I suppose you're here to find the bullet."

"Yes, as a matter of fact, I am. When I went back to the hospital, I looked for you, but they said you'd gone out to dinner. Anyway, when I asked about the bullet, they told me it went clean through. The position of the entrance and exit wounds, though, indicated a downward trajectory. I figured the bullet would've continued on a downward angle and might have lodged in the Boardwalk somewhere. That's why I..." He paused and shook his head. "There I go. Babbling again. You already knew that, didn't you, Mr. Kingston?"

Adam lied. "Never thought much about it. Nice work. And why don't we make it Stuart and Adam?"

"Fine by me."

"Good. Now, did you find it?"

"Not yet. I haven't been here that long. But I can tell you one thing. It won't be easy. I never realized how much of a beating these old boards take. Nicks and gouges all over the place. Like looking for the old needle in the haystack."

"Mind if I give it a try?"

"Not at all. I can use all the help I can get."

"May I?" Adam asked for the flashlight by reaching toward it.

When Stuart handed it over, Adam switched on the beam, and
in less than a minute, found a jagged circle two feet across where
the wood had been scrubbed several shades lighter. The city main-
tenance crew had done their job. It wouldn't do for tourists to see a
blood stain on the Boardwalk.

Adam stood in the middle of the scrubbed circle. He remembered the hole in the back of Chip's shirt being just above his hip
on the left side. Most of the blood on the Boardwalk would have
come from there. He took a step forward, then another one, and
brought his feet together. He was now standing in the same spot
where Chip had stood when he'd been shot. He looked around.

"Stuart?"

The detective was a few yards away, walking slowly with his
head down, studying the boards beneath his feet. He rushed back.

"Did you find something?"

"This is where Chip was standing. We were watching the kids
with the breadcrumbs who were…right over there." He pointed.
"I was about where you are now. Here, you stand where I am." He
stepped aside and guided Wilson into the spot where Chip's feet
had been. "Now, don't move."

Adam stood in front of him, raised his right hand, and pointed
his index finger at the detective's midsection.

Stuart stood still, but his eyes jumped from Adam's face to
the tip of the finger pointed at him, then back again. "What are
you doing?"

"Bear with me a minute."

Adam moved his finger forward until it touched Stuart an
inch below his rib cage, two inches left of the center of his stomach. Then he raised his finger to allow for the difference in height
between Chip Weathers and Stuart Wilson.

"There," he said. "Put your finger right there. That's where the bullet struck."

He stepped behind Stuart and positioned the exit wound the same way, directing Stuart to place a finger of his other hand there. Phil Russell had done the same exercise at the hospital using Ellie as his model.

Adam then stepped off to the side, leaving the bewildered detective standing with arms bent like a very thin teacup with two handles.

"I don't mind telling you, Adam, I feel like an idiot," Stuart said, looking around. "Now what?"

Adam suppressed a grin. "Hold what you've got for another minute."

He drew an imaginary line between Stuart's two finger points, then extended the line to the Boardwalk about six feet behind the detective. He walked to that spot, knelt, and found what he was looking for. Nearly invisible among the nicks and gouges from years of sturdy service, one of the boards had a fresh, round hole not more than a quarter inch in diameter.

He placed the butt of the flashlight on the bullet hole and aimed the beam at Stuart's back, adjusting the beam until it was centered on the exit wound position.

"You can move aside now," he said.

With Stuart out of its path, the beam of light carried to the wall of the Endicott House. Over that distance, the beam spread and diminished in power, but Adam saw its faint circle of light on the corner of the building, encompassing the third, fourth, and fifth floors. Within the circle, each floor had a small patio overlooking Thirty-fourth Street.

Something stirred in his memory, but Stuart interrupted his thoughts.

"Now I get it," the young detective said. "The line of trajectory."

He knelt beside Adam and looked up.

"The shot came from up there?"

"Maybe," Adam said, trying to remember something he'd seen earlier. "Would you happen to have a pocketknife on you? We may as well get this bullet out."

"No, I don't," Stuart replied. "Wait."

He reached into his pants pocket.

"I have nail clippers. Will that do?"

"That'll do."

Adam opened the clippers and with the pointed file, widened the bullet hole, being careful not to touch the small piece of metal buried there. After several minutes of digging, he inserted the file beneath it and pried out the spent bullet.

Stuart said, "I'll be damned. We found it."

"Yes, we did. Do you have a bag?"

"An evidence bag?"

"Yes, an evidence bag."

"Uh, in the car."

"Can you get it?"

"Sure. Be back in a minute." Stuart hurried away.

Adam studied the Endicott House, replaying the shooting and what happened afterward in his mind, trying to recall everything he saw and heard. Then it came to him. While waiting for the ambulance to arrive for Chip, he had a quick glimpse of a man on the fourth-floor patio with binoculars.

Stuart reappeared at his side. "Here's the bag."

Adam continued staring at the room on the fourth floor of the Endicott. No lights were on inside the room, but he saw the telltale flickering of a TV set. Adam couldn't be sure the shot came from the fourth floor, and it was hard to believe a shooter would stand in the open after shooting someone. But the man on the patio may have seen or heard something, or…

"Adam? I've, uh, got the evidence bag."

"Sorry. Just thinking about something. Here." Adam handed the bullet to him.

Stuart slipped it into the bag and sealed it. "Now we'll see what we can come up with from this. If we can identify the weapon, it might lead somewhere."

"Stuart," Adam said, "did you and your people talk to anyone in that building?" He nodded toward the Endicott House.

"No, we didn't. Remember? I told you about the confusion about where the bullet came from. We thought it came from somewhere on the beach. We haven't gotten to the buildings yet."

"How about you and I do a little door knocking right now?"

Stuart looked at the Endicott House. "I'm game. You mean, like, go door to door in there?"

"Just one door."

CHAPTER
16

He pushed himself out of the chair, pulled up his pants, and zipped his fly. The hand towel he had masturbated in lay on the floor between his feet. He kicked it under the chair. When he punched a button on the remote control, the TV screen switched from the adult movie channel to a local station in the middle of a news broadcast. He raised a finger to the Off button but stopped when he saw a familiar scene.

"...the shooting took place right here, Sally, on the Boardwalk at Thirty-Fourth Street, just outside the Colonial Towers Condominium complex. The victim, identified as Charles P. Weathers Junior, address unknown, was rushed to the hospital, but no further details are known at this time. The police have not ruled out the possibility of a drug-related motive for this shooting."

"Thank you for that on-the-scene report, Bill. Meanwhile, police in Baltimore have their own mysterious shooting to worry about. The nude body of an unidentified man was discovered today in the trunk of this car in the Westside Garage after..."

He clicked off the TV and walked to a window overlooking Thirty-fourth Street. He peered out between the vertical blinds, expecting to see a television crew with bright lights, cables, and cameras. When he saw only two men standing and talking, he realized they must have taped the segment earlier while he was out.

When the two men turned in his direction and began walking toward his building, he recognized the tall one. Kingston. The young one was there earlier, too, talking to people after the shooting. Cop!

Shit. They're coming in here.

Chapter

17

Adam stepped off the elevator and turned right. Detective Wilson followed two steps behind.

The Endicott House was built before architects decided brightly colored and well-lit corridors were a safety feature. Dark walnut paneling covered the walls and ceiling above dark green carpeted floors. The doors were slightly lighter than the walls. Halfway between each door, small light bulbs behind round, yellow plastic covers surrounded themselves with circles of soft light on the wall.

Ten feet from the fourth and last door, Adam stopped. The door of Suite 406 stood open. No light shone from inside the room.

Stuart halted beside him. "What's wrong?"

"A few minutes ago, someone was watching television in that room."

"Maybe they went to bed."

"And left the door wide open?"

Stuart reached to his waist and pulled out his service revolver. "Wait here," he said. "I'll check it out."

Adam obeyed. This was police business. He was retired.

Stuart stepped to the door and stopped beside it with his back pressed against the wall. He swung his head into the opening and out again. Adam watched the young detective take a deep breath, then rap his knuckles against the doorframe.

"This is the police," Stuart called. "Room 406. Anyone in there?"
The hallway was silent. Stuart rapped again.

"Police. Is anyone there?"

Silence.

With his back to the wall, Adam was surprised when a sudden image flashed across his mind. The shape was definite and unmistakable. A gun. Was he thinking about Detective Wilson's revolver? He could have been, but his instincts told him otherwise. More than once, they had kept him from turning the wrong corner… or entering the wrong door. He inched along the wall to where Detective Wilson stood. If he followed his instincts and was wrong, he knew he would look very foolish afterward.

"This is the police," Stuart shouted. "I'm coming in."

When Stuart slid around the doorframe into the dark opening, Adam decided to go with his instincts, rusty or not. He took two long strides forward and hurled himself against Stuart Wilson's back. In the same instant, he heard the first shot. Its sound, muffled, familiar. *Handgun. Silencer.* He heard a painful groan from Stuart. *He's hit!*

The two of them landed on carpet inside the dark room. Another shot from the right. The sound of glass breaking and falling from the left.

Adam's eyes searched the darkness. A large shape, close ahead. *Sofa.* He dragged Stuart's body behind it.

Another shot, followed by a soft thud. Adam's foot bumped against something hard on the floor. He groped for it. *Stuart's gun.* He jerked it over the top of the sofa and fired. Once. Twice. The shots from the snub-nosed .38 were like cannon fire in the dark room. When their echo died, the silence became as thick as the darkness. Dim light from the corridor framed the open doorway, but inside the room, Adam could barely make out the sofa in front of him.

Stuart groaned again.

"How bad is it," Adam whispered, watching the darkness for any movement.

"My arm," Stuart said. "My head. What happened?"

Adam heard a shuffling sound across the room and saw something moving in the darkness, going for the door. A large silhouette darkened the open doorway. Adam fired. Splinters flew from the doorframe as the moving shape disappeared into the corridor.

Adam scrambled to his feet, took two steps, and tripped over Stuart's leg. The .38 fell from his hand. He found it, regained his feet, and ran to the door. Without hesitating, he held the gun in both hands, arms extended, and swung into the corridor.

Fifty feet down the corridor, a large man stood in front of the elevator, turned so he was facing and staring right at Adam. In one hand he held a travel bag. In the other, a large handgun.

Before Adam could say or do anything, three things happened—a small, green light above the elevator door pinged and flashed on, the elevator door slid open, and the man raised his gun and fired.

Adam swung back into the room, saw the slug tear into the doorframe, then sprang out into the corridor, ready to fire. He caught himself in time.

An elderly woman with a cane stepped off the elevator in front of the man. Tiny and bent, she shuffled forward, intent on her steps and oblivious to the two armed men. Perspiration glistened on the man's head. His round, reddish face broadened into a sly, twisted smile. He held the smile on Adam and stepped into the elevator, safely shielded.

The door closed, and the old woman continued, one careful step at a time, toward the room opposite the elevator, aiming at it with a key in her hand.

From inside Suite 406, Adam heard Detective Wilson moan. There would be no chase. He had to see how badly Stuart was hurt.

CHAPTER
18

Adam tucked the .38 under his belt, found the light switch, and flicked it on. Detective Wilson sat on the floor, leaning against the back of the sofa, trying to wrestle out of his sport coat. His left sleeve was drenched with blood.

Adam knelt beside him. "How bad?"

"Arm hurts like hell. Head, too. Must've hit it when I fell. Guess I blacked out."

Adam examined the wound on Stuart's forearm. The blood flow had nearly stopped. The bullet had dug a trench along his arm for two inches without digging in. A deep flesh wound, painful and bloody, but not serious.

Adam gave him a reassuring smile. "I think you'll live."

Stuart winced, pumped his forearm up and down a few times and wiggled his fingers.

"Yeah, I guess I will. Thanks to you. If you hadn't pushed me out of the way…How'd you know?"

"An old friend."

Stuart's expression was half pain and half curiosity. "An old…"

"Give yourself a few years, and you'll know." Adam reached to his hip pocket, then remembered he'd used his handkerchief on Chip's wound. "Do you have a handkerchief?"

Stuart produced a clean white one and watched as Adam wrapped and tied it over his wound. "I heard the elevator. Guess he made it."

"I'm afraid so," Adam said. "Here." He handed the detective's gun to him.

"I watched you in the doorway," Stuart said as he holstered it. "You handle one of these pretty well."

"It's been awhile."

A voice behind Adam said, "What's going on here?"

Adam turned to see the head and shoulders of a thin gray-haired man leaning across the open doorway.

Wide-eyed and pale, the man repeated in a trembling voice, "What's going on here?" He slid his shoulders back so that only his face showed in the opening.

"This man's a police officer," Adam said. "He's been injured and needs help."

"I already called the cops. Man across the hall said he heard gunshots. I'm the manager here." His eyes darted around the room. "What's been going on?"

"Thanks," Adam said, ignoring the man's question. He heard Stuart grunt and helped him to his feet. Stuart wobbled a little, then leaned against the sofa.

"I'm Detective Stuart Wilson," he said to the manager. "Ocean City Police Department. I need you to close that door, then go downstairs, wait for the police, and bring them up here. And I want to see the registration record for the man who had this room."

"Yes, sir," the manager said. His eyes surveyed the room again as he reached with a shaking hand and pulled the door shut.

Adam was impressed with the way Stuart took charge. He checked the damaged room himself.

A dining area filled the right corner of the large room with a kitchen visible behind it. Next to the kitchen door, a hallway led, he guessed, to the bedrooms. On the other side of the hallway opening hung the remains of a full-length mirror. Shards clung loosely around the edges of the wood frame like shark's teeth. A scattered pile of mirror fragments lay on the floor. He remembered hearing glass breaking after the man's second shot. On the other side of the room, a loveseat sat at a haphazard angle to the wall. Drag marks in the brown carpet said someone had moved it recently. Something to hide behind. Two holes in the wall above the loveseat told Adam where his own shots had gone.

The sofa he and Stuart had hidden behind sat in the center of the room with a jagged hole ripped in its back cushion. The third shot from the man who had waited in ambush behind the loveseat.

Stuart said, "Looks like we made a hell of a mess here." He pushed away from the sofa. "I'd better give this place a once over."

"Maybe you should rest," Adam said, "until help gets here."

Stuart waved his good hand. "Nah, I'm okay."

Adam watched him disappear into the hallway leading to the bedrooms, then continued looking around the living room. He spotted something green on a table beside the door of the suite.

It was a purse, the kind women carry when they dress to go out. He remembered Caroline calling them evening bags. This one was well worn with bulging sides. Without picking it up, he undid the clasp at the top with two fingers and the bag fell open. He knew better than to touch it or root through anything that might be evidence. The police would do that. Besides, he didn't have to. The contents were in plain view. Some folded cash, loose change, a lipstick, half a dozen condoms, ballpoint pen, compact, tube of Binaca, several blank credit card charge tickets, a folded white envelope...

He had seen enough and closed the bag.

Stuart appeared beside him. "Nothing here. No luggage, no clothes, bathroom's clean. Looks like whatever he brought, he took with him."

Adam said, "He was carrying a large travel bag."

"I found this," Stuart said. He held up a roll of silver-gray tape skewered on a ballpoint pen. "Behind the love seat. Duct tape. You think our man left it behind?"

"Could be," Adam said.

"Then again," Stuart said, "it could have been left by work-men. Who knows?" He let the tape slide off the pen onto the table. "What's that?" he asked when it rolled against the evening bag.

"Our friend had company."

"Well, how about that?" Stuart said with a note of excitement in his voice. "She left her purse behind."

Adam didn't respond. His thoughts were on the evening bag. A hooker would never leave without her purse. "Did you check the kitchen?" he said.

"Not yet." Stuart walked away.

With Stuart conveniently occupied, Adam touched the evening bag and the roll of tape, not enough pressure to leave prints or disturb any already there, but enough to bring images.

A woman's face...red hair...makeup, heavy, bold...laughing...chang-ing now, fear, panic...a scream...a flat, black shape, rising, floating...another one, opening at one end, mouth-like, swallowing the first...more, rising, opening, swallowing...silver tape, unrolling, rerolling, forming circles...the black shapes changing, becoming her shape, silver circles at each end...moving, floating... entering a wide, dark opening...above the opening, flowers, pink and yellow... green leaves, swirling vines...

"The kitchen looks like no one's been in there," Stuart said as he again appeared at Adam's side. He checked his watch. "I think I'll go down and wait for the troops. They should be here any minute. Besides, I'm anxious to see who was registered in this room."

"Good idea," Adam said. "Mind if I stay here, poke around a little?"

"Help yourself. I shouldn't be long."

After Stuart left, Adam took another trip around the living room. Nothing tied in with the images he'd seen. In the hallway leading from the living area, he found a utility room, a bathroom, and two small bedrooms. Everything clean, neat, and orderly. Nothing clicked. He heard sirens on the street below as he reached the master bedroom at the end of the hall.

He stood in the doorway staring at an irregular circle of wetness on the carpet five feet from the bed. Someone had either spilled something or cleaned up a mess. His eyes followed a path on the carpet. Drag marks, like something had been pushed or pulled.

The bed was made but rumpled as though someone had rolled around on it. Instead of the simple bedspread he'd seen in the smaller bedrooms, this bed was covered with a comforter. Beige with a swirling floral pattern, pink and yellow flowers amid green leaves, intertwined with delicate vines. Down the side of the bed, the comforter ended a foot from the carpet, leaving an opening under the bed.

A wide, dark opening…above the opening, flowers, pink and yellow…green leaves, swirling vines…

Adam heard a crowd entering the living room. He walked toward the noise as Stuart entered the hallway from the other end.

"The cavalry's here," Stuart said. "Now we'll give this place a good going over."

"Start in the master bedroom," Adam said as he brushed past the detective. "Under the bed."

CHAPTER
19

He reached the rented Mercury Grand Marquis out of breath, bathed in perspiration, and close to hyperventilation. He had walked as fast as he could without attracting attention. He fumbled with the keys, unlocked the door, tossed his bag on the passenger seat, and climbed in.

He looked back the way he had come. A few people strolling, half a dozen cars, a man and woman on a tandem bike, a handful of grungy, long-haired punks sitting on the curb across the street. No one chasing him.

He unzipped the bag, pushed aside the box of trash bags and his handgun, and pulled out the first piece of cloth he found. He didn't care that it was a clean shirt. He wiped his face and scalp with it. The sweat was driving him crazy.

He started the engine, flicked on the air conditioning, and let his head rest against the seatback. He continued wiping himself, waiting for his breathing to slow.

He thought of something. He threw the shirt to the floor and began searching in the bag with both hands.

The duct tape.

"Shit." He slapped his palm against the steering wheel when he realized it must have fallen out of the bag when he removed his handgun. He thought for a minute. They'd find his prints on the tape.

Hell, he'd left prints all over the room. No problem. He'd be long gone before they made the connection.

A familiar sound grew and made him freeze. Sirens, swelling to earsplitting level, coming at him from behind. He sat perfectly still as they reached him, screamed by, and turned onto Thirty-fourth Street half a block further on. Flashing red, blue, and white lights turned the night around him into the Fourth of July. Three patrol cars, an ambulance, another patrol car. A fire truck lumbered up, hit its brakes as it passed the Mercury, screeched its way to the corner, and turned.

A fire truck, for Christ's sake. What'd Kingston and that puny cop do, set the place on fire?

He grinned and listened to the sirens diminish to a steady whine and pictured all those vehicles jammed up at the end of the street by the Endicott. After a moment, cool air filled the Grand Marquis, and he breathed normally. When he crossed Thirty-fourth Street, he saw it as he'd pictured it.

Two blocks later, he began searching for a place to spend the night. He liked the thought of that cop and Kingston being up half the night filling out reports while he got a good night's sleep. Tomorrow, he'd take care of unfinished business.

He was relaxed by the time he pulled into the parking lot of a Comfort Inn. He liked Comfort Inns. Not as luxurious as the Endicott, but nice. He knew he would have to use another name. Albert Cookson was probably hot by now. Maybe he would use Vernon Michaels. The thought of using that name made him laugh out loud.

CHAPTER

20

Adam saw the clock above his kitchen stove and groaned. Ten minutes past two. Seeing it made him feel twice as tired. He had begun to think it would take the entire night to get away from the circus at the Endicott. When no one was looking, he left and walked across the street to the Colonial Towers and home. A long day.

He thought about a cup of coffee, but decided against it.

Too late for coffee. Orange juice.

With a cold glass of juice in hand, he stepped into the dining room, leaned against the wall and stared across the table to the portrait of Caroline and him. He left the drapes open on the patio door and stood in this spot at the end of each day. He liked the picture best in the soft wash of moonlight.

Caroline's smile reached across the room to him, relaxing his tired body, warming him as it always did.

"Hell of a day, babe," he whispered. "A new client who may be a murderer, a psycho next door, shooting and strangling people. Can't wait to see what comes tomorrow. And Ellie's trying to set me up again. A nurse this time. What do you think? Maybe it's time? Maybe. I'll think about it." He raised his glass and drained it in one long swallow. "Miss you."

After rinsing the glass, he slugged his way through the dark, silent apartment to the bedroom. During the day, the light and noises of the busy world outside filtered in. When it was late, and

he was tired, his home was an empty, soundless tunnel. The alone-
ness surfaced then. He plopped on the side of his bed and rubbed
his face with both hands. Maybe Ellie was right.

*Take down these pictures, get some new furniture, something modern, get
some bright colors on the walls. Put some life in here. Get yourself a pet.*

A little painting and new furniture wouldn't hurt. A pet? Not a
dog or cat. He was away from home too much. Goldfish? Naaahhh.
All they do is swim around in circles. Birds might work. Two, maybe
three or four, in a cage in the living room. Two or three cages. Yes,
birds. Birds make noise. Birds need to be taken care of, cleaned up
after. He could give Henry, the doorman, a few bucks to feed them
when he went out of town.

He also remembered his promise to Ellie at the hospital to
check on his enemies from the old days, find out if one of them was
gunning for him and hitting Chip instead. Not likely. A lot of the
people he had arrested and helped put away made threats, but no
one at the Bureau took them seriously. Besides, he had been retired
for more than twelve years. Ancient history. Still, he promised Ellie.
Tomorrow morning, he'd make a list.

Although he was dead tired, through the ritual of brushing
his teeth and undressing for bed, he couldn't keep his mind from
adding more to the list of things to do the next day.

Check on Chip. Need to talk to him as soon as possible.

Try Eric Richards's number again. Really need to talk to him.

Find a place that sells birds.

Call Leo Jackson.

CHAPTER

21

Brenda McCort reached both arms high above her head, enjoyed a good long stretch, and took a slow, sweeping look around.

Desks cluttered with computers, keyboards, loose papers, and coffee cups filled the squad room end to end. Some desks were occupied by friends, others by people she couldn't stand for one reason or another, all going about the daily business of being Baltimore's Best.

The windows on her side of the room admitted precious little morning light through frosted glass, and barely softened the traffic noise from Pratt Street one floor below. Screeching brakes, blaring horns, and groaning blasts from city buses blended with the constant ringing of telephones and the shouting of busy cops.

Occasionally, at home alone in her apartment after work, Brenda let her mind wander to thoughts of returning to school, getting her degree, and becoming a teacher. Maybe get married again. It was what her parents wanted. Now, sitting here in the noise and clutter, she smiled with the realization that those thoughts were a way to pass time and nothing more. This was home. She'd been on the force for fifteen years, a homicide detective for the last five, and divorced for four. At thirty-eight, she had no serious thoughts of changing professions. Or getting married again.

Brenda had been at her desk for more than an hour, wading through piles of e-mail and phone messages. E-mails answering e-mails, messages returning messages, a few crank calls. The usual.

She turned her attention to her new case, the man found yesterday in the trunk of a car in the Westside Garage. He was no longer a John Doe. His fingerprints taken at the morgue identified him as Albert J. Cookson, fifty-seven years old, from Linglestown, Pennsylvania.

Brenda closed the file. She needed more information on him before she could do any more with it.

Next, she went through her In basket. She'd been waiting for two reports on her other new case, the young woman found in the Century Street basement. Both were in the pile.

First, the forensics report. She'd been dead fifteen years, it said, give or take a year or two. Petite, five-one or five-two. Hair samples confirmed she had been a blonde. Probable cause of death, multiple skull fractures. Three hard blows.

Brenda had withheld the hair color and cause of death from the media. Cranks who called with an uncontrollable need to confess to something would guess strangulation or gunshot. If one of the callers knew her hair color and how she was killed, she would have a valid suspect.

She had also received the city tax record showing ownership of the three-story row house at 834 Century Street. A family named Lear owned it until twenty-one years ago when Charles P. Weathers bought it. At the same time, the classification changed from single-family dwelling to multi-family. Weathers had converted the house into an apartment building, a common practice with large row houses in older neighborhoods.

Eight years later, the owner's name changed to EMR Investments, Inc., and according to the records, EMR still owned

it. Brenda opened a desk drawer and pulled out her telephone directory. She found no listing for Charles P. Weathers, but there was
one for EMR Investments with an address in Hunt Valley. She
dialed the number.

"Good morning. EMR Investments. How may I help you?"

From the friendly voice, Brenda pictured a plump, gray-haired
grandmother in her sixties.

"Good morning. This is Detective McCort with the Baltimore
City Police Department. I'm investigating..."

"Oh, my," the woman said. "You must be calling about that
poor young woman they found at the Century Street property.
It was such a terrible thing. I feel awful every time I think about it.
I hope you find whoever did such a thing. A young girl like that.
It was so terrible."

"Yes, it was," Brenda said, grateful for the chance to speak.
"We were hoping you could help us in our investigation. We're
interested in getting past records of tenants of the house."

"Past records of tenants? We have that, I'm sure, but you'll have
to speak to Mr. Richards. I can't give out information, but I'm sure
he'll want to help you any way he can. He was very upset when they
found that poor girl."

Brenda noted the name. Richards. As in R of EMR, she guessed.

"Is Mr. Richards in?"

"I'm so sorry, but he's away on business this week. But I
know he'll give you anything you need when he returns. Such a
terrible thing. A young girl like that. There's so much crime these
days. Why, you can't pick up a newspaper or turn on the TV
these days without..."

The lady went on, her voice becoming almost tearful as she
talked. Brenda waited for an opening. Her chance came when the

lady paused to catch her breath after asking, "Why do people do such things?"

"I wish I knew, believe me," Brenda said. "Are you certain Mr. Richards is the only one who can give us the names of tenants?"

"Oh, yes. Mr. Richards takes care of everything like that. Ever since Mr. Weathers died, Mr. Richards has taken care of everything."

"Mr. Weathers? The previous owner?"

"Yes, when Mr. Weathers died, we didn't know what to do, but Mr. Richards took care of everything. Mr. Weathers was his father-in-law, you know. He was such a nice man, Mr. Weathers. If it hadn't been for Mr. Richards taking over, I just don't know what we would've done. Mr. Weathers's son didn't stay around after he got in that trouble, you know, and his daughter moved away. We never even see her. If her husband, Mr. Richards, hadn't stepped in, who knows what would've happened to the business. It was just terrible the way those children turned out, and Mr. Weathers being such a nice…"

"When will Mr. Richards be back in the office?" Brenda knew she had to interrupt or spend the rest of the morning listening to the Weathers family history.

"He said Monday morning, but sometimes his schedule changes. He's so busy, you know. We have properties in Philadelphia now. Mr. Weathers only had properties in Baltimore for all those years, but Mr. Richards has expanded the business."

"Thank you very much. You've been very helpful."

"Would you like to leave your number? I can have Mr. Richards call you as soon as he comes back."

"That's all right. I'll call back on Monday." Brenda thanked the lady and hung up.

It could be a break, Brenda thought. Even though the company name changed, the business stayed in the same family. That could make it easier to get the information she needed. She scribbled a note to call Richards first thing Monday. With a little luck, he would tell her who lived in the house when the girl died. Once she knew that... .

Her thoughts were interrupted by Timmy Kaminski bursting into the Squad Room and sauntering toward her with papers in one hand and a Dunkin' Donuts bag in the other. Kaminski traded greetings with two officers by the file cabinets and did a high five with another at a desk before he reached hers and stopped.

"You remembered," she said with a quick smile when he dropped the bag on her desk.

"Of course I remembered. I never forget when it's my turn." He grabbed the back of his chair at the desk in front of hers, swung it around to face her, and plopped in it. "You're the one who forgets."

"I do not." She held the bag open and looked in. "Where's the chocolate frosted?"

"They only had two left."

"So where are they? There's nothing in here but glazed." She looked up, saw his silly grin and answered her own question. "You ate them."

"What can I say?" he said with a palms-up shrug. "Traffic was slow. I got hungry."

She pulled out a glazed donut and took a bite. With her mouth full, she mumbled, "Selfish hog," and wrinkled her nose at him.

"Well, maybe you won't be so quick with the insults when you see what I've got." He held up a sheet of paper and waved it back and forth.

Brenda took another bite. "Depends on what it is."

"Our man from the garage yesterday. Albert J. Cookson, from Linglestown, Pennsylvania."

"Yeah, what about him? By the way, where's Linglestown?"

"Outside Harrisburg. But wait'll you see this. An APB on him from Ocean City."

"Really?" Brenda shoved the last piece of donut into her mouth and snatched the paper from his hand. "Well, well," she said as she scanned it. "Our Mr. Cookson strangled a woman in Ocean City before he got himself killed."

Timmy Kaminski shook his head. "Uh-uh. After. Cookson's body was found yesterday morning, remember? The woman was killed in Ocean City last night. Read it again."

She read more carefully this time and picked up her phone. "Kaminski," she said as she punched in numbers, "thanks and get lost. I've got work to do."

"You got it," he said, spinning around in his chair to face his own desk. He looked back over his shoulder. "Oh, yeah. Beth said come for dinner Sunday."

She gave him a thumbs-up and a wink as she listened to the second ring at the Ocean City Police Department. Halfway through the third ring, a female voice answered.

Brenda read the name of the investigating officer on the APB. "Detective Stuart Wilson, please."

CHAPTER
22

Adam rolled over and tried to focus on the red splotch, but his eyes didn't cooperate. He rubbed them and tried again. The shape of his clock radio materialized, and the glowing red smear shrunk into recognizable numbers. 9:22.

He remembered it being nearly three-thirty before he fell asleep. He'd wanted to get up earlier, but had been too exhausted to think of setting the alarm.

He rubbed his eyes again, stretched long and hard, shook the room with a bellowing yawn, and made it to the side of the bed. From there, a major effort got him on his feet and moving toward the bathroom.

When he arrived in the kitchen twenty-five minutes later, showered, shaved, brushed and dressed in sweats, he was functional enough to put two and two together. If he'd been alert enough last night to set the alarm in the bedroom, it might have occurred to him to set the coffeemaker on automatic.

He filled it with five scoops instead of the usual four, and went to his den where the monster waited—the treadmill. He took one look at it, shook his head, promised to make up the time another day, and returned to the kitchen.

The coffeemaker gurgled promises of a clear head and enough energy to do all the things he wanted to do today. By the time he finished his second cup, he had compiled a list of everyone he could think of who might take shots at him. He knew it was a waste of time, but he promised Ellie. He came up with six names of men he helped put behind bars who swore revenge. He called an old friend at the Bureau who promised to check on them.

Next, he called EMR Investments, using the number he'd obtained from Directory Assistance the night before. A friendly, older woman's voice answered.

"Good morning. EMR Investments. How may I help you?"

"Eric Richards, please."

"I'm sorry, sir. Mr. Richards is not in. Could one of our associates help you?"

"No, I have to speak to Mr. Richards. When will he be in?"

"I don't expect him until Monday, but he calls in for messages. Can I have him return your call?"

"Yes, please. And please tell him it's very important that he call me as soon as possible."

"I certainly will. And what is your name, please."

Adam recited his name and phone number.

"Oh, yes, Mr. Kingston, you left a message for him last night. It was on the machine."

"Yes, I did. Did he get my message?"

"No, I'm sure he didn't, or he would have called you. Are you sure one of our associates can't help you?"

"I'm sure," Adam said.

"May I tell him what you're calling about?"

"He'll know. Tell him it's the fortune teller."

Adam could almost see the curious look on the lady's face as he thanked her and hung up.

Phil Russell at the hospital was next. He got lucky. For a change, Phil was not in surgery, not with a patient, and not in a meeting.

"He's still out, Adam, and I'd say it'll be at least this afternoon before you'll be able to talk to him."

"Last night you said twelve hours."

"I said at least twelve hours. It's not like he was in the best of health when we got him. We've got him full of IVs to build his strength, but it takes time. Have you located any of his family?"

"Not yet. That's one of the reasons I'm anxious to talk to him. I've had no luck reaching the brother-in-law and don't have the first clue where to start looking for the sister."

"Too bad," Phil said. "Want me to call you when he's able to talk?"

"That'd be great, Phil. How's Ellie this morning? Still mad at me?"

"A little. When she thought you'd been shot...well, you know how she is."

"Yeah, I know. I felt bad about that. And, Phil..."

"Yeah?"

"Thanks for being there last night."

"Forget it. We're just glad it wasn't your sorry hide I had to patch up."

"Don't worry. I don't do that stuff anymore." As soon as he said it, his escapade in a dark room at the Endicott House flashed through his mind. "Talk to you later," he said, hanging up.

No need for them to know about last night. And no need to be pulling crazy stunts like that again. Right? Right. Let the police handle it.

Leo Jackson was last on his list. If Leo still headed Homicide in Baltimore, he might divulge information without asking too many questions. Maybe. It was worth a try. He needed to know if they had identified the woman found in the basement and if they had any suspects—Chip Weathers, for instance. If they didn't know about Chip, he wouldn't tell them. They'd haul Chip in, IVs and all, and until he knew the full story, he wanted Chip close at hand.

CHAPTER
23

Brenda gathered her notes and files and hurried to the rear of the squad room. She stood in the doorway of her captain's office and waited for him to notice her.

Leo Jackson was on the phone. In his late forties with a broad, ruggedly handsome face that smiled easily, he had a full head of dark brown hair Brenda would kill for. It was so thick and wavy she suspected it never needed combing. He was six-four and carried two-hundred-and-sixty pounds on a large frame. The men said he looked like a retired linebacker. Brenda thought of him more as a giant teddy bear.

After a few seconds, he looked up and waved her in. Brenda sat and listened to his side of the conversation.

"Great to hear from you, Adam," he said in a voice that seemed too soft for a man his size. "It's been way too long...Oh, Lil's fine, feisty as ever."

He laughed, that rolling belly laugh of his that told Brenda it was a personal call. She wondered if she should leave.

"So what've you been up to, Adam? Keeping your nose clean?"

Brenda stood to leave, but Jackson waved her back down. His expression and tone of voice were serious when he spoke again.

"That's an ongoing case, Adam. You know I can't give out details, even to you. All I can tell you, and only because it's you, is this. No, we haven't identified the victim and, no, we have no valid leads or suspects...No again. There's no evidence that says it happened somewhere else. As far as we know, she got it in the basement where she was found."

The word "basement" made Brenda suspect they were discussing her Century Street case.

"Now, old friend," Jackson said, "you tell me something. What's your interest in this case?"

Amusement spread across the captain's face as he listened.

"You *can't* tell me?" he said. "You mean you *won't* tell me." He winked at Brenda and grinned. "I know you, Adam. You wouldn't be calling if you didn't have something going on. I should haul your bony ass in here and sweat it out of you."

His grin faded after he listened a few seconds more.

He said, "If that's the way you want to play it, okay for now, but listen to me. You know where the line is. Don't go too far over it. You hear what I'm saying?...I know you will. I'll count on it... Yeah, we'll come down again soon. Lil would love to see you, asks about you all the time. Great hearing from you. Bye, Adam."

The captain stared at the hand piece before he slowly put it in its cradle. Then he stared a moment longer before looking across the desk.

"What's up, McCort?"

She wanted to ask why someone named Adam called him about her Century Street case, but first things first.

"Captain, I have to go to Ocean City. It looks like we may be onto a serial killer."

She told him everything that had happened since Albert Cookson's body was found in the trunk of a car.

Jackson nodded. "Have you made the car?"

"Not yet. I'm still waiting for Pennsylvania to come back. Should be soon."

She added the results of a call she'd made to the Linglestown police.

"Cookson's wife reported him missing two days ago when he didn't return from a trip to the convenience store."

She told him the Ocean City Police suspected the man posing as Cookson shot and wounded a man from a window of the Endicott House. She didn't get the name of the man who'd been shot.

He looked at her, appearing deep in thought, then his eyes drifted to his telephone. "You said the Endicott House. I've seen that place. Isn't it right on the Boardwalk?"

Brenda checked her notes. "Yes. Boardwalk and Thirty-Fourth Street. Why?"

His eyes came back to her, but he ignored her question.

"So this guy does Cookson, goes to Ocean City with Cookson's ID, plays sniper from his window, then does a prostitute in his room. Any connection between the victims?"

She shook her head.

"None we know of. His choice of victims seems to be as random as his methods. Cookson shot at point blank range, the other man from a window, the woman beaten and strangled, but the way he wrapped the bodies in trash bags and duct tape... . Captain, this guy's a psycho. I can smell it. And I have this sick feeling there are other victims. Pennsylvania, here, Ocean City, anywhere in between. We just haven't found them yet."

"But if he's moving around so much, what makes you think he's still in Ocean City?"

"He may be gone by now, but we can't be sure. All I know is that's where he was last night. Maybe I can get a lead, a description, anything. I talked to a Detective Wilson at Ocean City PD, and he's anxious to work with us on this. I think I should get there as soon as possible."

"Okay," he said. "Go to Ocean City. And be careful."

He reached for his phone, but when she hadn't moved, he said, "Is there something else on your mind?"

"Yes. That phone call. Was it about my Jane Doe from Century Street?"

He leaned back. "As a matter of fact, it was. Why don't you fill me in."

When she finished bringing him up to date, he rubbed his chin. She'd known him long enough to know what that meant. He was weighing what he was about to say.

"Let me ask you something," he said. "How do you feel about psychics?"

His question caught her off guard, but she blurted, "They're quacks."

He grinned.

"I'm not talking about the three-dollar-a-minute kind you see in TV ads. I'm talking about genuine psychics, people with special gifts, the kind who work with law enforcement agencies."

Brenda took time to reposition herself in her chair. It was a sore subject with her. A few months earlier, her mother got hooked on a telephone psychic and ran up a bill of over six hundred dollars.

"Same answer," she said, wondering where this conversation was going. "I've heard of cases where they were helpful, but I've also heard most of their so-called visions turn out to be useless."

"Have you worked with one?"

"No. Are you suggesting I work with one now?"

"Possibly."

"Captain," she said, looking him squarely in the eyes. "I'd rather not."

He leaned forward. "I thought you'd feel that way, and I won't force you to do anything you're dead set against."

"Thank you." She rose from her chair again. "Now, I'd better be..."

"But..."

She sat down again.

"...Give me a few more minutes."

Leo Jackson rose from his chair and stepped around it to the window behind his desk. With his back to her, his hands clasped behind him, he spoke quietly.

"Eight years ago, before I came here, I ran the Vice Squad in Dayton, Ohio. Dayton's smaller than Baltimore, but we had a good-sized syndicate operating there. Drugs, prostitution, gambling, a little of everything. We spent two years on it and had them nailed. But when we started hauling them in, they came up with a scheme of their own."

He sat on the corner of his desk close to her.

"They kidnapped my wife and son."

"Lil and Dwayne? My God."

"The deal was simple. I screw with the evidence enough to get the case thrown out, and I'd get them back. You know how easy it is to do. An illegal search, lose a few documents, forget to Mirandize somebody. Simple. They gave me twenty-four hours. The Feds were working with us since our case involved interstate charges, so I talked to one of the agents I'd gotten to know pretty well. He leveled with me. The chances of getting my family back were practically zip, no matter what I did. I knew he was right."

Brenda knew, too. She had worked a few kidnappings. In many of them, the victim was dead before the ransom was paid.

"What happened?"

"The agent gave me the name of a man they'd used themselves, a psychic investigator, a former Fed. At the time, I thought the same as you do now, but I was desperate. I called the man, and he flew out to Dayton. After he was there only a few hours, just by talking to me, walking around our house, sitting in the car they grabbed Lil and Dwayne from, he told us where they were. We took the place and recovered them safely."

"Thank God," Brenda said. She touched her hand to his. "But what a terrible thing to go through."

He smiled. "No one else around here knows about this. It's not something I enjoy talking about. I'd like to keep it that way."

"Of course. I won't mention it."

She was thinking the so-called psychic had only made a lucky guess, but she said nothing.

Jackson took his time sliding off his desk and returning to his chair.

"I told you about it for a reason. I don't disagree with the way you feel about psychics—most of them, anyway—but Adam Kingston and a few others like him are the real thing."

Brenda repeated the name. "Adam Kingston." She glanced at the telephone. "Adam. The man you were talking to when I came in."

He nodded.

"And you want me to work with him on the Century Street case."

He nodded again. "I'm only suggesting you talk to him."

Brenda raised her arms in a gesture of defeat. "All right, I give up. I'll talk to him, but..."

"But you're still not convinced about psychics."

"Sorry. I guess it's the hardheaded Irish in me."

He put his hands together as if praying and closed his eyes. "Lord, please save us from the hardheaded Irish of the world."

Brenda chuckled. "So where do I find this psychic of yours?"

He scribbled on a notepad before he answered. "That's the easy part. Here's his address and phone number." He tore off the page and handed it across the desk.

She read it. Then she read it again.

"Wait a minute. He lives in Ocean City? Boardwalk and Thirty-fourth Street?"

Jackson's face held a wide grin.

"That's right. The Colonial Towers. I've been there a few times. It's right across the street from…"

"The Endicott House. But…that's where the man posing as Cookson killed the woman…He called you about my Century Street case, not Cookson."

He was still grinning. "Uh-huh."

"That's one hell of a coincidence, Captain."

"Uh-huh."

Brenda cocked her head and studied his face.

"Are you thinking what I think you're thinking? That this qua…sorry…this Kingston might know something about both these cases?"

"You're the detective, McCort. Check it out. Then you tell me."

Brenda snatched up her files and started for the door. "You can bet on that."

"Have a safe trip," he said as she practically ran out of his office.

CHAPTER
24

Adam thought his conversation with Leo had gone well. He'd found out what he needed to know, and Leo hadn't pressed him about it. The Baltimore police didn't know the young woman's identity or about Chip's involvement. They also didn't know she had been killed in a bedroom, not in the basement where she was found. Leo was a good friend. He'd invite him and Lil for a weekend soon.

It was time for a break. He had been on the phone for nearly an hour. With a chocolate donut and a fresh cup of coffee, he headed for his patio.

He made it as far as the door when the phone rang. He hurried back to the kitchen and answered on the third ring.

"Good morning," a cheerful voice said on the other end. "Stuart Wilson. How are you this morning?"

"Fine, Stuart. How's the arm?"

"Sore as hell. I'll be wearing a bandage for a few days, then I'll be good as new."

"I'm glad. We were lucky last night."

"You don't know how lucky. Wait'll I tell you the news. Turns out our guy at the Endicott is real popular. I got a call from Baltimore Homicide. They picked up our APB this morning and tied him to a victim they found yesterday in the trunk of a car."

Now Adam knew why there was excitement in Wilson's voice. Young cops get that way when they're involved in a big case. After enough of them, the feeling becomes dread, and you think of questions to ask.

"A prostitute?" Adam asked.

"No. Middle-aged man."

"Strangled?"

"Shot."

"Did the shells match?"

"They didn't find any. The one we dug out of the Boardwalk came from a rifle. The ones from the room were .44 Magnum. I know this much already, our guy is well-armed."

"Are you sure it's the same man?"

"Absolutely. I haven't told you the clincher. The man they found in Baltimore was IDed as Albert Cookson, and get this, our guy checked into the Endicott as guess who?"

"Albert Cookson."

"Right on. The real Cookson was bagged and taped the same as our hooker. It's the same guy all right. We're just holding our breath, waiting for more victims to turn up. Baltimore's really hot on it. They think he might be a serial killer. They're sending someone to work with me."

"Thanks for letting me know, Stuart. Good luck with it, and you be careful."

"I will, and thanks again for last night. I mean it. You saved my buns. Oh. One more thing. We need you to sign a statement about last night. Can you come by today?"

"Sure. What time?"

"Well, let's see. The detective from Baltimore said she'd be here around three-thirty. Three? Shouldn't take long."

"Three, it is."

This time, Adam, with his coffee and donut, made it to the patio.

On the Boardwalk, six floors below, the exercise walkers, wired for sound with radios and CD players bouncing on their hips, weaved through the casual browsers who ambled along at a slower pace to work off their breakfast.

The beach was a splattered rainbow. Early sunbathers had staked their claims with beach umbrellas, blankets, towels, and folding chairs of every color and stripe. Above the beach, seabirds zipped back and forth, voicing loud complaints to the intruders on their foraging ground. Their squawking, the shouts of beach revelers, and the never-ending sound of the surf, heralded the beginning of another summer day in Ocean City.

It would be hot and humid, Adam decided, surveying the familiar scene, with a clear sky and just enough breeze to make it bearable. As he swallowed his last piece of donut and washed it down with a gulp of lukewarm coffee, his telephone rang again. He hurried to the kitchen.

"Hello."

No one answered.

"Hello. Is someone there?"

Still no answer, but he heard breathing.

"Hello! Who's there?"

A woman's voice, soft and tentative, said, "Mr. Kingston?"

"Yes."

"I'm sorry to bother you, but I wanted to know if…uh…if you were the one with the man who was shot on the Boardwalk."

An alarm went off in Adam's gut. Who would be calling him about Chip? And why is she so hesitant, almost as if she's afraid to speak?

"Yes, I was with him," he said. "Who's calling, please? Do I know you?"

"No. You don't know me. I just wanted to know if he's…going to be all right."

"Do you know him?" Adam asked.

When she didn't respond after several seconds, he tried again. "Are you a friend of his? A relative?"

He heard her take a deep breath before she replied.

"My name is Lisa Weathers Richards. Chip is my brother."

Lisa.

Adam's pulse quickened. "I'm glad you called, Lisa. I need to meet with you, to talk about Chip."

"No, no," she said in a rush. "That's not possible. I just wanted to know if he's…all right."

"He's going to recover, if that's what you mean. But there's more to it than that. We really need to meet. Are you here in Ocean City?"

"No, it doesn't matter where I am. I…I can't meet with you."

She sounded more nervous by the second.

Easy now. Don't lose her.

Adam spoke calmly. "How did you get my name and number?"

"I called the hospital. They told me you were with him, and I looked you up in the telephone book. I wanted to know if he remembers what…what happened to him."

She has a local phone book. Can't be far away.

"About getting shot? I think so. He was conscious for a few minutes after it happened."

"No. I mean…from before."

From before? She's pumping me, fishing for something. Play dumb.

"I'm not following you. Before what?"

"Didn't he tell you about his amnesia?"

"Yes. He told me about that."

"Does he remember how it happened, what happened in that apartment on Century Street?"

Apartment? Don't lose her now.

"He told me some of it, but he still needs to sort it all out. He needs your help."

"How much has he told you? About me. And about Eric."

"Lisa, I want to discuss it with you, but not on the phone. If you want to help your brother, let's…"

A *click* cut him off.

"Dammit."

He slammed the phone into its holder on the wall, but before he could take his hand away, the images began. He gripped the phone, closed his eyes, and concentrated. The images grew stronger.

Somewhere dark, a room…bedroom…figures, moving in darkness, violent movements…loud, angry voices…how many figures? two? three? more? too dark…the gray flat shape again, rising, falling, rising, falling…stairs…someone coming down, carrying something, no, someone…her…blonde hair, wearing white, blue stripes…

Adam gripped the phone, hoping more would come. Nothing did. The images had been scenes from the house on Century Street, and they'd come from the other end of the line. From Lisa. That could only happen if she'd been thinking about those things. And how would she know what happened in that bedroom unless she'd been there?

He had to find her. But how? Her number wasn't showing, which told him she had Caller ID blocked.

Wait. A few months ago, a young lady called, phone company, selling something. Sure, why not. Automatically call back anyone who calls me. A code. What was it? Star something. Sixty? No. Sixty-something. Sixty-nine? Yes! Star sixty-nine.

He punched in the code. It rang once, twice, three times, four... "Come on, come on. Answer it."

The fifth ring began and abruptly stopped. She'd picked up. He didn't wait for her to speak.

"Lisa, this is Adam Kingston. I have to talk to you. Please don't hang up. It's very important."

He heard her breathing, felt her anxiety. After several seconds, she asked in a guarded voice. "What do you want?"

"Not on the phone. We have to meet in person. Chip needs your help. You could be the only one who can help him."

"There's nothing I can do. I...I have to go."

"Lisa, wait, please."

Don't lose her. Say something. Anything.

"Chip did tell me about what happened."

Think! Anything.

"He told me some things about you. And about Eric. And about money. A lot of money. That's why we have to meet in person. It's not something I can discuss on the phone." He held his breath and hoped.

"About Eric?" After a pause that seemed like forever, she said, "All right. I'll meet you."

"Good. Where are you? I'll come right away."

"No. Not here. There's a shopping center, Solomon's Landing, on Ocean Highway, before you cross into Delaware."

"I know it," he said. "What time?"

"One o'clock. In the parking lot by that big store. Kmart. How will I know you?"

Adam told her to look for his car and described it. She hung up.

He stepped away from the phone and dropped into a chair at the dinette table. Why had she called him? If she only wanted to know Chip's condition, the hospital would have told her that. She was his sister, his nearest living relative. Why didn't she simply go to the hospital?

She had another reason for calling. She wanted to know if Chip had regained his memory, how much Chip had told him.

He knew one thing. She knew more about what happened in that house than the Baltimore police. She definitely said *apartment*, not *basement*.

CHAPTER
25

At noon, Adam left his building by the side door and walked half a block down Thirty-fourth Street to the parking garage reserved for tenants. It was a separate building, four stories high, separated from the Colonial Towers by a small alley. He took the stairs to the third level where he kept the ruby red Buick LeSabre that had once been Caroline's. He bought it for her on their tenth anniversary, a year before she died. A few minutes later, he was driving north on Ocean Highway toward Delaware.

Solomon's Landing, a strip mall anchored by Food Lion at one end and Kmart at the other, was a mile or so before the state line, a forty-minute drive in heavy, in-season traffic. He pulled into the parking lot, drove to the front and turned right between the first and second rows of parked cars stretching toward Kmart.

He wondered what Lisa would look like. Chip said she was five years older than him. That would make her forty-one. Chip also described their mother.

...small, on the frail side, classy, like a queen.

He wondered if Lisa would resemble her mother.

Driving slowly past souvenir and beachwear shops with SALE signs in their windows and a restaurant offering the *Best Crab Cakes in Maryland*, he checked out the women he saw. None were petite and fortyish with a regal air.

He chose a spot in the second row near Kmart and backed into it so he would be facing the stores. As soon as he turned off the ignition, it occurred to him she might be sitting in a parked car. He got out and stood by the LeSabre's door.

In the first row, facing the stores, two cars had people sitting in them. Both were men.

Typical. Women shop, men wait

In the second row, the one he was in, he saw no one sitting in any of the cars. At the far end of the row, a dark blue sedan backed into a slot. Adam squinted through sunlight bouncing in waves off the cars between them and saw that the driver was not Lisa. A heavyset man wearing a baseball cap and sunglasses.

He looked in the other direction, the way he had come in, to see a gold two-door rolling slowly toward him. A Mercedes two-seater. It looked new. Sixty grand plus, he guessed. He had to wait until it drew closer before he could see the driver. A woman, blonde, right age.

Lisa.

The Mercedes slowed to a stop in front of him. He watched her lean across the passenger seat and give a look of recognition to the car he'd described on the phone. After a quick glance at him, she drifted by and pulled into a space four cars ahead in the first row.

She sat in the car, staring straight ahead, turning her head once to look back at him, before she opened the door and stepped out. She stood barely more than five feet tall. Her silky yellow blouse, tightly belted at the waist over beige slacks, displayed well-developed breasts and well-rounded hips. Not overweight, but full-figured for her height. A gold headband pulled her pale blonde hair back from a round face nearly half hidden by oversized sunglasses.

She walked as far as the bumper of her car, looked his way, then turned in the other direction and moved away.

Three bulky, wood picnic tables topped with red umbrellas sat one behind the other on a grassy plot at the end of the parking lot. Beyond them, a kiosk with soft drink vending machines offered relief from the summer heat. She had chosen the site for their meeting.

He followed, studying her as she moved ahead of him. Chip's description of their mother as on the frail side didn't fit. Her generous figure drew passing glances from both men and women. She moved in short, quick steps with her head bowed as though examining the surface beneath her but not really seeing it, the walk of a person deep in thought about something unpleasant.

At the end of the row of parked cars, two preschoolers, a boy and a girl, nearly ran into his legs. He jumped aside, bumping into the side of a parked car to avoid the collision. Their parents rushed by him in frenzied pursuit, tossing him an apologetic look before each of them grabbed a small arm and began the lecture.

"You want to get run over?"

"You have to hold Daddy's hand or no ice cream."

"Next time you're staying home."

"I thought you were watching them."

"I thought you were."

Adam smiled. Then he looked at the car he had bumped into, the dark blue sedan he had watched back in a few minutes ago, and called out, "Sorry," to the man behind the wheel. He only saw the man from the chest down, and he seemed preoccupied with rooting through a large travel bag in the passenger seat. Adam returned his attention to Lisa.

She had gone past the three picnic tables and was buying a soft drink at one of the vending machines. A man sat reading a newspaper at the first table. The second and third were unoccupied. Adam stopped beside the third table as she came toward him.

She didn't look at him until she had selected the chair across the table from where he stood, wiped the seat with her hand, and eased herself into it. As he sat in one opposite her, he had the feeling that if the table had been long instead of round, she would have chosen to sit at the far end.

Her skin was smooth and tanned. From a spa, he guessed, rather than sunbathing on the beach. The little he could see of her face behind the large designer sunglasses told him she had been a beautiful girl who matured into an attractive woman. Her lips were full but colorless, and her jaw was tight with tension.

"So you're the man Chip came here to see." She spoke with firmness in her voice, but he detected a trace of the nervousness he'd heard over the phone.

"Yes, Chip came to me for help. I'm glad you called. I've been anxious to talk to you."

She pulled the tab on her Diet Pepsi and took a quick swallow. "He's going to be all right, you said, and he remembers some things from before."

"He'll be fine," Adam said.

He would let her go on thinking Chip's memory was returning. It might prompt her to tell him things he needed to know.

"He'll spend a few days in the hospital, then he'll need a lot of rest. It would do him a lot of good to see you."

"What did he tell you about me? Me and Eric?"

"He told me he hasn't seen you for a long time, and that he didn't know where you were. Do you live near here?"

"Delaware. Bethany Beach. When Eric and I separated, I moved into our house there."

She took another drink, this time turning her head away from him, giving him a quick glimpse behind the rim of her sunglasses. Her eyes were an unusually pale shade of blue. He hoped she would remove the sunglasses. Eyes told him as much about people as their words. He wanted to know what was going on inside Lisa Weathers Richards, why she was so nervous and upset about meeting with him, why she was so concerned about what Chip told him.

"Nice area, Bethany Beach," he said in an attempt at casual conversation. "Quiet, away from the vacation crowd."

Her shoulders rose and fell in a shrug of disinterest. "It's all right." She held the Diet Pepsi can between her palms and rolled it slowly back and forth, watching it as though its movement was more important than the conversation. "What did he tell you about losing his memory, how it happened?"

So much for chitchat.

"He told me almost everything, but a few things are still a little hazy. That's the way amnesia works. It comes back in bits and pieces." He was making it up as he went along but, what the hell, she was fishing, too. "He said you could fill in some of the blanks."

"Blanks? Like what?"

"Like exactly what happened in the apartment on Century Street."

The can stopped moving. She turned her head toward him for an instant, then quickly away.

"He doesn't know what happened?" Her voice had lost all traces of firmness.

"Not all of it, but it'll come back to him soon," he said, hoping she bought it. "It's a matter of time. That's where we need your help. You can make it easier for him."

"What makes you think I can help?"

"I think you know something about what happened that day. Help me, Lisa. Help your brother get his life back."

"I...I can't tell you anything." The hesitation was back in her voice now, as strong as it had been over the phone. "I don't know anything about it. I can't help you."

Adam sensed she was on the verge of leaving. He decided to change the subject. "At least tell me this much." He pulled the check Chip had given him from his pocket and held it out for her to see. "Chip gave me this as a retainer. Two thousand dollars from a fund in his name, administered by Eric. Why does Chip live the way he does? Like someone who's penniless and homeless?"

She glanced at the check, but showed no reaction. "It was his own fault. He would've thrown it all away if Eric...if we hadn't stepped in."

"Stepped in? What do you mean?"

"His inheritance. Our parents left each of us a certain amount of money. After Chip lost his memory, Eric and I did everything we could for him, but he couldn't get his head together. He acted funny, strange. He'd sit around for days at a time, staring at old pictures, not saying a word. Then he'd go on wild spending sprees, buying gifts for people he hardly knew, throwing his money away, giving it away. We had to go to court to save it."

"The court gave you and Eric control of his inheritance? Is that why he left home?"

She shook her head. A half smile appeared, more like a smirk. "No. That's not why. He didn't care about the money. He didn't care about anything." She drummed her fingernails on the table. "The doctors called it some kind of withdrawal...psychosis...or something. I don't remember. It was too long ago."

"What happened to his inheritance?"

"It's all there. Every penny. I don't know what he told you, but no one took it, if that's what you're thinking. It's closely monitored by the court. All he has to do is prove he's responsible and it's his."

Her nails drummed faster on the tabletop. She crossed her legs, then uncrossed them. Suddenly she stood up.

"I don't want to talk about it any more. I have to go."

Adam rose with her and spoke softly.

"Lisa, please. A woman died in that apartment. Chip is involved in it, and he needs your help."

She shook her head and raised a hand as if to push away his badgering.

"I'm sorry, but I can't tell you anything. I'm sorry he got shot, and I'm sorry he's so messed up, but I can't help him. I have to go now."

She walked away quickly. Adam caught up with her beside the first table. He took her by the arm and stopped her.

"At least tell me about Eric," he said. "How can I get in touch with him?"

"Let me go."

She jerked her arm from his grip so suddenly it threw him off balance and back against the table. The man sitting there looked up, dumbfounded.

"Leave me alone," she shouted. "All of you. Leave me alone."

She looked around like she wanted to run, but didn't know which way to go.

He wanted to say something to calm her, but a movement behind her grabbed his attention. The man in the blue sedan he'd bumped into a few minutes earlier now sat in the passenger seat with the car window down. The baseball cap and sunglasses were gone but the smile was there—the same twisted smile he'd had on his sweaty face when he stepped into the elevator at the Endicott House the night before. In his hand, he held the same gun, pointed, ready to fire.

CHAPTER

26

In one leap, Adam was on Lisa, both arms wrapped around her, picking her up, falling to the grass, rolling with her in his arms behind the picnic table, yelling "Get down!" to the man sitting there, all as the first shot ripped into the thick table top spewing splinters in the air. The shot was loud. No silencer this time.

He heard the man from the table muttering, "Ohmygod, ohmygod," as he ran to safety beside Kmart's wall. The second blast tore through the chair the man had been sitting in and struck a table leg six inches from Adam's head.

Adam heard Lisa gasping for breath in his arms, struggling to get free. He released her. "Don't move."

He gripped the edge of the table above him with both hands and shoved. The table upended and stood on its edge in time to take the third shot. He heard people shouting, running. He looked at Lisa. Her sunglasses hung on one ear, cracked in the middle, her hands clutched over her eyes.

He leaned to the edge of the table and looked around it. Over its flattened red umbrella, he saw the man scrambling across the seat of the car to the driver's side. He was giving up.

Adam brought his feet under him and crouched over her. "Stay right here," he said. "I'll come back for you."

"Wh…where are you going?" Her lips quivered. Her hands still covered her eyes.

"To my car. That son of a bitch is starting to tick me off. Stay here."

He kept low until he was around the table and saw the car pull out and turn away from him, moving fast. He ran full speed toward the LeSabre, watching as he ran. The car struck a van that pulled in front of it. It backed up, wheeled around the van and continued on, picking up speed toward the lane that would take it to the highway.

Adam reached the LeSabre with his keys in his hand. He unlocked the trunk quickly, reached in and pulled out a metal box with one hand while his other hand fingered for the small key that unlocked it. Seconds later, he was running through rows of parked cars toward Ocean Highway with his nine millimeter Beretta in his hand, safety off, ready to fire, watching the blue sedan reach the highway, hoping it would turn north.

It did. Without stopping, it sped out of the parking lot, across the southbound lane forcing another car to fishtail around it, then turned sharply into the northbound lane.

Adam ran faster, watching the car come toward him. He threaded his way through the last row of cars as the speeding blue car came abreast of him. He reached the sidewalk in time to fire and see glass shatter behind the driver, then see the car disappear behind a motor home coming the other way. When it reappeared past the motor home, it was too late to fire again, too much risk of hitting another car. He watched the sedan race toward Delaware.

"Dammit."

The motor home sailed by with a very pale driver frozen behind the wheel.

Adam heard a loud voice behind him.

"Freeze, mister! Right there. Drop your weapon. Hands behind your head. Do it now!"

Breathing heavily and drenched in perspiration from running in the midday heat, Adam tossed the Beretta so it landed on grass, not concrete. Then he raised his hands and turned toward the state trooper behind him. The young man stood with his legs spread wide, his gun leveled in both hands, his face flushed.

Over the trooper's shoulder, he watched a gold Mercedes turn from the parking lot into the southbound lane of Ocean Highway and meld into traffic.

Terrific.

As the trooper approached him, Adam repeated two license plate numbers to himself until he had them memorized.

CHAPTER
27

Detective Wilson looked across his desk.

"There's no doubt in my mind. It's him."

He'd been strictly business in their exchange of information since Brenda McCort arrived, but he couldn't help wondering if the attractive homicide detective from Baltimore was involved with anyone. She wasn't wearing a wedding ring and she wasn't that much older. Thirty-seven, thirty-eight, tops. Dressed nice. Conservative, but nice. Dark blue blazer, gray skirt, white blouse.

She nodded. "I hope we can stop him before he fills any more trash bags." She sat with her legs crossed, holding an attaché case on her lap.

"We'll get him," he said, thinking she had great legs.

He smiled at her, making it a smile of confidence and determination, nothing arrogant or cocky. He could ask her out to dinner. Professional courtesy and all that.

Brenda looked at her watch. "It's nearly four o'clock. Didn't you say Kingston was coming in?"

"He said he'd be here at three," Stuart said, wondering if he'd used the wrong smile. "He must've been detained. I'm sure he'll show, but I don't think he can tell you any more about last night than I already have."

"Oh, I'm sure he can't," she said. "It's about another case. He may have information on it."

"Anything I can help you with?"

"No, but thanks, anyway. Tell me, though, what do you know about him?"

"Adam Kingston? To tell you the truth, I didn't know anything about him until last night. Some of the older guys heard me mention his name and filled me in on his background. We even have a file on him."

Brenda's eyebrows raised. "Oh?"

Stuart waved a hand and chuckled.

"Not that kind of file. Not a perp file. He's a consultant, a psychic investigator. He works mostly with the Feds, but our department called on him once to help find a missing child. As a matter of fact, he was an FBI agent himself. One of the best, they say."

"So one day he decided to give all that up and buy himself a crystal ball?"

"I'm not sure how that came about," Stuart said, curious about the sarcasm in her voice. "The way I heard it, a few years ago, his wife was diagnosed with cancer. Terminal. He took a leave of absence from the Bureau to take care of her, and they moved here full time. They had a condo."

"I know," she said, "Boardwalk and Thirty-fourth."

"Anyway, when his wife died, he took it hard. Started drinking, big time. One night his car took out a utility pole and he was nearly killed."

"You got all this from a consultant's file?"

He shook his head. "No. From Martha."

"Martha?"

He laughed. "Yeah, Martha, the lady who runs Records. She's been here forever. Martha knows everything and forgets nothing. With her around, we don't need a computer."

He laughed again, hoping she would laugh with him. When she didn't, he continued.

"Anyway, when I asked Martha to bring up his file, she told me the story behind the story, as they say. When Kingston hit the utility pole, some electrical wires came loose and, according to her, he took enough volts to kill an elephant. They didn't expect him to live through it. He did, but he never went back to the Feds."

"Maybe he decided being a psychic was more lucrative."

"Martha's into things like that—UFOs, paranormal stuff, ESP—and she said things like electric shock can sometimes bring out special abilities. Me? I don't know anything about it. But...why do I get the feeling you're not a big fan of psychics?"

"Let's say I had a bad experience. But let me ask you something, Detective Wilson..."

He held up his hand. "It's Stuart." He tried the smile again.

She smiled back. "Okay, Stuart, tell me the truth. Do you believe in it, that psychic business?"

"To be honest, I've never thought much about it one way or the other." He was thinking she had a great smile and wondering if it was too late to get a dinner reservation at the Del-Mar Inn. "But I can tell you this much—you remember that multiple homicide in Arizona a few weeks ago?"

She nodded. "The FBI cracked it. A tough one."

"He was in on it, and they gave him practically all the credit. You know the Feds. They don't usually give credit to anybody."

Brenda's smile was gone. "Everybody gets lucky once in a while." She checked her watch again. "So where is he?"

Stuart shrugged. "I wish I knew." He examined his own watch and decided to go for it. "By the way, if you don't have any plans for..."

The ringing of his telephone cut him off.

"Excuse me." He picked it up and said, "Wilson." He listened for a moment, then looked at Brenda. "It's the state police—about Adam Kingston."

Brenda leaned forward.

"Okay, Wanda, put it through." He waited for the connection and said, "This is Detective Wilson."

He listened for a full minute before he covered the mouthpiece with his hand and told Brenda, "Adam had a run-in with our man. Traded shots with him. The State Police have him."

Brenda uncrossed her legs and scooted to the edge of her chair. "They have the killer?"

Stuart shook his head. "They have Adam. The killer got away." He spoke into the phone. "Yes. Absolutely. He's working with us. Baltimore Homicide is here too. We'll take full responsibility." He eyed Brenda, and she nodded. "We're on our way and thanks for your cooperation."

He hung up. "So. Feel like taking a ride?"

CHAPTER
28

Adam was anxious to get out of the state police barracks. It had taken time to convince the young trooper he had a license to carry a firearm. The trooper let him get it from the box in the trunk of the LeSabre, but still hauled him in, along with the box. It then took a while to get the state police commander to listen to the whole story and agree to call Stuart Wilson. He had to admit they did everything by the book. Very professional. Still, he was anxious to get the hell out of there.

The door opened and Commander William T. Truesdale came into his office carrying two Styrofoam cups of coffee in one large hand. He handed one to Adam, then sat behind his desk. He was near sixty, but appeared rock solid inside a uniform that fit perfectly. He had been courteous, but did not exude friendliness.

Adam set his cup on the commander's desk and smiled. "Thank you. Anything from Delaware on the car?"

"Not yet, but they're on it. We passed the plate number and description to New Jersey and Pennsylvania. Maryland's covered in case he doubles back. If nothing turns up in a couple of hours, we'll go farther—New York, Virginia, West Virginia."

"What about the gold Mercedes?"

"Same. We're on it." The commander moved a stack of papers from the side of his desk to the middle and glanced over Adam's head to a clock on the wall. "OCPD should be here in a few minutes. You can wait outside if you like."

Adam rose from the chair. He'd been dismissed. He asked, "Did you get the registrations on the two cars?"

Truesdale was reading. Without looking up, he said, "Detective Wilson will get them. Your weapon's outside, too. Soon as he signs, you're free to go."

Adam walked to the door.

"By the way, Kingston."

Adam turned back. The commander was looking at him, and a bare hint of a smile showed on his weathered face. "I followed that case in Louisiana. That little boy you found? Good work."

"Thank you, sir."

The commander nodded, and what might have developed into a genuine smile disappeared.

"Just don't go shooting up any more parking lots," he said and returned to his paperwork.

Adam left the office thinking if he ever needed a cop, he'd want one like Truesdale. A hard-nosed, old-line professional who would never accept the idea of anyone owning a gun unless they wore a police uniform. But he probably wouldn't invite the commander to any parties.

He carried his coffee to the entrance lobby. Two troopers chatted by the front door. A large middle-aged sergeant shuffled papers at a desk against the far wall. Wooden chairs lined the other walls. He didn't see the trooper who'd brought him in, but he'd committed the young man's name and badge number to memory and would write a complimentary letter to the state police.

Ten minutes later, he'd finished his coffee and Stuart Wilson came through the front door followed by a woman in a blue blazer.

"You're too much," Stuart said as he walked across the lobby grinning. "I let you out of my sight for a few hours, and you get yourself in trouble."

Adam grinned back. "It wasn't my fault. Honest."

"So I heard." Stuart's expression turned serious. "Too bad you didn't get him." He rubbed his injured arm.

"Next time." Adam glanced around Stuart at the woman behind him.

Stuart stepped aside. "Oh, I'm sorry. This is Detective Brenda McCort, Baltimore Homicide. Adam Kingston."

Adam smiled. "It's a pleasure, Detective McCort."

She gave him a quick nod and said flatly, "Kingston." To Stuart, she said, "Are we going back to your office to talk?"

"I have to see the sergeant," Stuart said. "You two can wait here and get acquainted." He walked away.

Brenda turned sideways to Adam and crossed her arms.

Attractive, Adam thought, but not very friendly. He decided to give it another try. "I assume you work with Leo Jackson. I spoke with him this morning."

She twisted toward him long enough for a glance. "I know. I was in his office when you called. This killer has top priority, but while I'm here, I want to know why you're so interested in my Century Street case."

So that's Leo's game. He didn't press me himself, but he sicced Miss Stone Face on me. Cute, Leo.

"I've already discussed it with your captain," he said in the same firm tone she used. "We have an understanding."

She glared. "Well, you'd better understand this, Kingston. It's an ongoing homicide case, and I intend to find out how you're involved in it."

So much for getting acquainted, Adam thought. He was grateful that Stuart interrupted the discussion at that point by rejoining them. He didn't want to discuss her Century Street case and learn she knew about Chip's involvement. Now that he'd spoken to Lisa, it was even more important that he have more time with Chip.

"Well, that's it, Adam," Stuart said. "You're a free man again. I believe this is yours."

He handed Adam's metal box to him.

"Thanks." Adam opened the box, took a quick look, then tucked it under his arm. "Sorry I put you out."

Stuart smiled. "After last night? Forget it. Whattaya say we get out of here? How about a bite to eat? I'm thinking the three of us can put our heads together and see what we can do to catch this guy."

"Lunch sounds good to me," Adam said, "if Detective McCort feels like it. A chocolate donut is hardly enough to get through a whole day."

Brenda said, "It wasn't chocolate, it was…" She stopped, a confused look crossing her face. "How did you know I had a donut this morning?"

Stuart laughed. "The man's a psychic, remember?"

She continued eyeing Adam, but said nothing.

Adam ignored it. He meant the donut he ate that morning on his patio, but what the hell. If she's impressed, so what.

"Well, I'm starved," Stuart said. "Let's go."

In the parking lot, Stuart unlocked his car. "Where would you like to eat? There's plenty to choose from."

Brenda shrugged. "Doesn't matter to me."

"My car's at Solomon's Landing," Adam said, "and there's a place there that claims to have the best crab cakes in Maryland."

"That'll work for me," Stuart said. "You have to get your car anyway. Have you eaten there?"

"No, but let's give it a try. Besides, I'd like to pick up a couple of things."

"Like what?" Stuart asked.

Adam climbed into the back seat. "A pair of sunglasses and a Diet Pepsi can."

Chapter
29

The ride to Solomon's Landing took fifteen minutes. In the front seat, Stuart and Brenda chatted about the differences between police work in a large city and a resort town.

Adam sat in the back seat, thinking about his meeting with Lisa. She seemed ready to leave as soon as she found out Chip didn't remember what happened on Century Street. But why did she seem so nervous and frightened?

"All of you," she said. *"Leave me alone. All of you."*

All of who? And why did that lunatic gunman show up? Following me? Some kind of sick vendetta for last night? Something didn't fit. It bothered him all the way to Solomon's Landing.

Stuart parked in front of Captain Tommy's Crab House.

"Adam, if these crab cakes aren't the best in Maryland, you're paying."

"Fair enough. Why don't you get us a table? I'll be there in a few minutes."

Stuart asked, "Where you going?"

Adam held up the box containing his Beretta.

"To put this in my car. I won't be long."

After he stored the box under the front seat of the LeSabre, Adam walked to the end of the parking lot. The first of the three wood tables was gone. The state police may have recovered a bullet from it, maybe not. It didn't matter. It would match the ones found at the Endicott House. The slugs were useless unless they had the gun.

The Diet Pepsi can and broken sunglasses were nowhere in sight. With any luck, a cleanup crew had picked them up. He spotted a plastic trashcan by the vending machines, another one on the sidewalk beside Kmart. He decided to check the one by the vending machines first.

He removed the lid and tipped the trashcan on its side on the grass. About a dozen soft drink cans rolled out. Two were Diet Pepsi. One had lipstick on the rim. Lisa had not been wearing any. Someone had crushed the other can. A man thing. He put the trashcan back as he'd found it and went to the other one.

This can was three-quarters full. A little rooting through the top layer uncovered the broken sunglasses and, beside them, a Diet Pepsi can. No lipstick, half full. After emptying what was left of her drink into the trashcan, he rooted a little more and found a wrinkled brown paper lunch bag. He dumped out a half-eaten apple and put the sunglasses and the can in it.

On his way back to the restaurant, Adam pulled his cell phone from his pocket and called his home number. Phil said he would let him know when Chip could have visitors. No messages. He then called the hospital only to be told Phil was in surgery.

After a quick stop to wash his hands, Adam joined Stuart and Brenda. His meal awaited him. He sat the lunch bag on the floor beside his chair.

"Looks like you ordered for me."

"I hope you don't mind," Stuart said. "The special sounded so good, we ordered it all around."

He waved a hand over his plate with the flourish of a magician, then pointed.

"Ta-da. Captain Tommy's Secret Recipe Giant Crab Cake Sandwich."

"Sounds good to me," Adam said. "Thanks."

He lifted the top of the sesame seed bun. A truly giant crab cake, covered with lettuce, topped with a generous slice of tomato.

"Sorry I took so long. I called to check on Chip."

"Oh, yeah," Stuart said with his mouth full. "I meant to ask. How's he doing?"

"Good, but weak. As of this morning anyway. I'm still waiting to talk to him."

Stuart looked across the table at Brenda.

"The man our guy shot on the Boardwalk yesterday. Adam was with him when it happened."

Brenda said, "I'm sorry. I hope your friend will be all right."

"Thank you." Adam was surprised by the sincerity in her voice. *Maybe she's not totally made of ice after all.*

He watched her cut her sandwich in half. Caroline used to do that. Most people he knew used both hands and ate them whole. Like Stuart. The hand on his injured arm was fine, and the injury didn't interfere with his appetite. He'd devoured half his sandwich already.

Stuart swallowed. "We were talking while we waited, Adam, trying to figure out why this guy came after you today." He paused to take a gulp of iced tea. "We figure he's after you for running him out of the Endicott last night. You'd better watch your back from now on. We think we've got a real psychopath on our hands, and it looks like you're at the top of his list."

"Maybe," Adam said.

"I have to agree with Stuart," Brenda said. "He's probably sociopathic as well as psychopathic. He may feel he's on a mission which justifies anything he does, no matter who gets hurt. He eliminates anyone who interferes. We think that's how he sees you now. Stuart's right. His kind doesn't go away."

She knows her stuff, Adam thought. But she wasn't there when it happened. And she didn't have the nagging feeling that had bothered him since they'd left the state police barracks. He decided to try his theory on them.

"You could be right, but I'm not sure it fits. If he'd wanted me, he didn't have to wait until we got to the shopping center. He would've been watching where I live, waiting for me to come out. He could have made his move then, but he didn't."

Brenda said, "So he followed you. Why?"

"Maybe it wasn't me he was after."

Stuart, looking confused, asked, "Then...who?"

"I think you have her name," Adam said. "Did the state police give you the registrations on the plates I gave them? I came to meet the driver of the Mercedes."

"Got it right here."

Stuart pulled two folded sheets of paper from his inside coat pocket.

"Let's see." He scanned the first one. "Okay. The Mercedes belongs to Lisa J. Richards, 303 Oceanview Terrace, Bethany Beach, Delaware."

When Stuart said the name "Richards," Adam saw Brenda sit upright. He watched her open her attaché case, pull out a file folder, and begin leafing through it.

"So," Stuart said, "you're saying he was after this Lisa Richards. But why? And how did he know you were meeting her?"

"I don't know. Not yet."

Adam watched Brenda select a sheet of paper from the file folder and lay it on the table in front of her. Even upside down, he made out *EMR* and *Richards* scrawled at the top.

Any second now, she's going to put it together.

He turned to Stuart. "What about the other car, the blue sedan?"

"Right here," Stuart said. He looked at the other sheet of paper. "It's a rental. A Mercury Grand Marquis."

He ran a finger down the sheet.

"Mmmm, those state boys work fast. According to this, it was rented yesterday morning on Lombard Street in Baltimore with a VISA card belonging to our old friend, Albert Cookson."

Brenda looked up from her notes. "Cookson's body was found in a garage on Lombard Street in the trunk of a car."

Adam asked her, "Do you know whose car it was?"

She found another paper in her file and held it up.

"Came in a few minutes before I left. It's registered to Susan M. Michaels, Linglestown, Pennsylvania. No luck contacting her, and it's not on the hot sheet. Does that name ring any bells?"

She looked at Stuart.

"Not to me. Where's Linglestown?"

"Outside Harrisburg," Brenda replied.

Stuart asked Adam, "That name mean anything to you?"

Adam knew where Linglestown was. He worked on a kidnapping and murder case there a few years ago. The name sounded familiar, but Susan and Michaels were common names. He shook his head. No bells were ringing.

"So where does that leave us?" Stuart said.

Brenda laid her papers on the table. She answered Stuart's question, but looked at Adam.

"That brings us back to the name Richards."

Adam was facing Stuart, but he sensed her eyes on the back of his head.

"Does that name mean something?" Stuart asked her.

"It could," Brenda said. "That other case I mentioned to you earlier? It involves someone named Richards. It could be coincidence, but I don't think it is. I think Mr. Kingston knows more than he's telling us."

Stuart looked at Adam. "I, uh, think I'm missing something here. How about it, Adam? What's going on?"

Adam pushed his plate aside and wiped his hands with a napkin. "Detective McCort is right. I don't have all the pieces yet, but..."

"Can I get you guys anything else?"

A waitress stood at Adam's shoulder. He ordered a coffee, and Stuart asked for a refill of iced tea. Brenda shook her head.

Adam thought about Leo Jackson's warning.

You know where the line is. Don't go too far over it.

Withholding anything now would put him way over that line.

CHAPTER
30

After the waitress walked away, Adam told Stuart and Brenda everything that had happened since Chip showed up at his door.

When he finished, Brenda spoke first.

"You should've advised him to turn himself in. I'm sure you knew that, Kingston."

Adam felt a warm tingling on the nape of his neck. He always felt it when he was scolded. He forced a polite smile.

"That was my first thought, detective, but sometimes there are extenuating circumstances. Sometimes you bend the rules a little."

"The rules, maybe, but not the law," she snapped.

With an effort, he held his smile. "Maybe even the law should be, let's say, relaxed a little when you have a man who's lived like a ghost for nearly half his life, who only wants to know who he is. Or was."

Brenda's cheeks flamed. "Well, maybe this so-called ghost of yours killed an innocent young woman in cold blood and buried her under a basement floor."

"I think, detective," Adam said, losing the smile but holding his patience, "the operative word is maybe, don't you?"

"Excuse me, guys." Stuart said. "But can we please play nice here and get back on track? How about it? You two can sort your thing out later."

"You're right," Adam said. He flashed the polite smile at Brenda. "Sorry."

She stared at him a moment longer before she returned her attention to the papers on the table in front of her and began rearranging them.

Adam watched her, wondering what she was thinking. Was she a strictly by-the-book cop? Lock 'em up and worry about the facts later? He thought he'd seen something in her eyes before she turned her head, but couldn't be sure.

"Okay, now," Stuart said, "let me see if I can get up to speed here." He looked at Brenda. "You have an unidentified woman who was killed and buried under a basement floor a long time ago."

She nodded.

"You," Stuart said, pointing at Adam, "have a man who says he was there and maybe he killed her, but he can't remember."

Adam nodded.

"Next, we have a man who shot your client and—you think—followed you so he could do the same to his sister." His head swiveled between them. "Am I getting it right so far?"

Adam nodded again.

Brenda looked at him. Not a glare this time. A thoughtful look. Finally, she gave Stuart a quick nod of her head.

"All right," Stuart continued. "I've also got a dead prostitute and you," he pointed at Brenda, "have a man who was left in the trunk of a car from Linglesburg, Pennsylvania."

"Linglestown," she said.

"Whatever. Why them?"

"Maybe," Adam said, "he grabbed Cookson because he wanted a false identity. He also would've expected Susan Michaels to report her stolen car, so he needed another one. Cookson's ID and credit card provided that." He spoke to Brenda. "I wonder why Susan Michaels didn't report her car missing."

"So do I," she replied. "My partner's trying to run her down."

Stuart said, "Let's hope he doesn't find her bagged and taped. But that doesn't tell me where the prostitute fits in."

"It could be she simply picked the wrong customer," Brenda suggested, "and something went sour."

"Okay." Stuart's eyes again moved from one to the other. "Now that I've got all that straight, the big question—if you're right about this, Adam—is why is he after Chip Weathers and his sister? Can you tell me that?"

Adam shook his head. "Not yet."

"You mentioned money," Brenda said. The hard edge was gone from her voice. Her expression was one of deep thought. "That check he gave you signed by Eric Richards. He runs EMR Investments. I made a couple of calls this morning. It's a big business. Apartment houses, half a dozen office buildings and shopping centers. Maybe it comes down to money."

Stuart turned to her as though he'd been betrayed, his head cocked to one side. "Sounds like you're going along with Adam's theory."

She shrugged. "We have to consider all the possibilities."

"Sure we do," Stuart said, "but now you're telling me this homeless man, Weathers, is worth a lot of money, and that's what this is about." He shook his head. "Maybe I could buy into some of what you're saying, Adam, but I can't..."

A beeping noise interrupted Stuart. He reached to his waist, unclipped a cell phone, and studied the screen.

"I have to take this, but for the record, I'm staying with the serial killer theory."

He rose from his chair and walked a few feet away from the table.

Adam said to Brenda. "Now you know why I called Leo about your Century Street case."

She placed her elbows on the table and laced her fingers together. "Uh-huh. Did he kill her?"

"I honestly don't know. I wish I did. Gut feeling? No, he didn't do it."

She leaned back in her chair. "Don't you mean a psychic feeling?"

So that's her problem. A skeptic.

"No," he said. "Pure gut."

"Has your gut ever been wrong?"

"A few times. What're you going to do?"

"About Chip Weathers, you mean?"

"About Chip Weathers."

She gathered her papers. "I think you know what I have to do. I don't have the luxury you have, of being able to bend the law. I have to question him and, most likely, I'll arrest him. He was there, he was injured and bleeding from a fight. That makes him a valid suspect in a homicide. I have to do my job."

He watched her busy herself with notes and files and remembered times when, as an FBI agent, he hadn't liked what the job required him to do. He wondered if she, now that she'd heard how Chip had shown up at his door pleading for help, could be disliking the idea of arresting him.

"And then?" he said.

She put her files in the attaché case on the floor beside her.

"Then," she said, raising her eyes to meet his, "I think we have to find Eric and Lisa Richards."

This time her eyes gave her away.

She's not so tough.

Stuart Wilson came toward the table. Before he reached them, he called out, "They found the Mercury."

Adam and Brenda said together, "Where?"

"He abandoned it in a supermarket parking lot in Milford, Delaware."

Brenda said, "Not another victim, I hope."

"Close. He tried to grab an old lady, but she threw her groceries at him and got away. He made off with her car."

"Good for her," Adam said. "Did she see which way he went?"

"This way. Back to Maryland. We've got a description out on her car, but I have to run up there and check out the one he dumped. You two want to ride along?"

"I can't," Adam said. "I have something else I have to do."

"So do I," Brenda said. "At the hospital." She looked at Adam. "If I can get a ride back to my car."

Adam gave her a polite, professional smile. "Sure."

CHAPTER
31

In the foyer of the restaurant, Adam set his brown paper bag on the counter and handed the check to a muscular redheaded woman. As she punched numbers into the cash register, he pulled out his wallet. Brenda had given him fifteen dollars, Stuart had given him a business card with his phone numbers on it.

Brenda reached into a pocket of her blazer, brought out a cell phone, and walked away from him.

"I hope everything was okay," the woman behind the cash register said with a big smile. "That'll be thirty-four sixty-five."

He handed her two twenties. "Everything was fine. The crab cakes were delicious."

Smiling again, she said, "Best in Maryland."

"I believe it. By the way, who's Captain Tommy?"

This time he got a sly grin. "I am."

"Really?"

"Captain Thomasina just wouldn't cut it, would it?" She counted his change into his hand. "You come back again now."

He matched her grin and told her he would. With his bag in hand, he approached Brenda, who was still on the phone.

"Thanks very much," Brenda said. "You've been very helpful."

She folded her phone and said, "EMR Investments. Eric Richards called in around noon today to get his messages. His secretary told him I called this morning, so he knows I'm trying to reach him."

"Then he got my message," Adam said, "but he hasn't called me back."

"She said he's been in Philadelphia since Tuesday. He told her he'd be there a couple more days and back in the office on Monday. She gave me his hotel number in Philadelphia and his home number."

"Try the hotel."

She called the number, asked for Eric Richards, listened a moment, then said, "Thank you" and closed her phone again. "He checked out this morning."

"So he changed his plans and lied to his secretary. Try the home number."

She did, but got no answer. She put her phone away. "Can you take me to my car now?"

Adam glanced at the lunch bag in his hand. "Not yet. I'd like to try something first if you don't mind."

She gave him a cynical look. "A psychic thing?"

"A psychic thing," he replied.

CHAPTER
32

Outside, Adam led the way to the end of the parking lot and across the grassy plot to the table where he talked with Lisa earlier. He sat in the same chair she used. Brenda sat across from him. He placed the Diet Pepsi can and the broken sunglasses on the table in front of him and grazed his fingers over them.

Shapes, colors, turning, revolving...three red circles—the table umbrellas? ...three more, surrounded by smaller white circles...a rectangle—a window, broken glass...a long, thin cylinder, white bottom, blue top...a room...the floor, littered, piles of debris...chairs, tables, sofa, overturned...a box, old, metal... inside, thin straps, crisscrossed on something flat, foot-shaped—a sandal, a woman's sandal...something else in the box...a book...no, more like something folded, like leather—a wallet...a shovel now, digging, tossing dirt...red circles again, six of them, small white circles all around them...

The images disappeared. Adam leaned back and studied the underside of the red umbrella above the table. The red circles he'd seen were different. They were flat, and there were six of them. He thought about the broken window and the littered room. The images involved Lisa.

Her house in Bethany Beach? What was the blue and white cylinder?

He remembered it now. The white cylinder with a blue top was a lighthouse. It was visible from the highway, and he'd noticed it many times on his way up the coast. It was Lisa's house he'd seen. And it had been broken into and ransacked.

"Well?"

Adam looked across the table at Brenda.

"Well?" she repeated.

"There was a sandal in the picture in the paper. Was another one found?"

Brenda shook her head. "No. Why?"

"How about a wallet, a leather wallet?"

"No. Everything we found was in the picture. Why?"

"We have to go to Delaware."

"Why?"

"I'll tell you on the way."

"But...what about the hospital?"

"I'll take care of that," he said, "as soon as we get to my car."

As they walked toward the parking lot, past where the first table had been, something sparkled in the grass. The sun glinted off something small, and Adam nearly stepped on it. He picked it up. A pale blue contact lens.

"What's that?" Brenda asked.

He held it in the palm of his hand for her to see.

"It's a colored lens," she said. "Looks like someone didn't like the natural color of their eyes and wanted to change it. Do you think it's hers?"

"Right color, but it could be anyone's. It's the old-fashioned hard kind, could have been here awhile." He dropped it into his shirt pocket and walked away.

"Wait," she said from behind him.

He stopped and looked back. She hadn't moved except to fold her arms.

"What?" he asked.

"I have to say something."

He was impatient, anxious to go, but tried not to show it.

"Okay, what?"

"This psychic thing you do. I'm sorry but...I'm trying to go along with you because what you said in the restaurant made sense. Leo's always telling me I have to be more open-minded, and I'm trying, but...I have a job to do at the hospital. You know that. I can't run off chasing psychic visions, or whatever you call it. You have to give me something, anything."

His first thought was to call her a cab. His second was that she was making an effort to work with him, not against him. The least he could do was meet her halfway.

"Fair enough," he said.

He took her arm and guided her to the table behind them. When they were seated, he said, "I'll tell you what I know so far. First, Chip was in the house when the woman died. I can't say for sure if he did it or not. If he didn't, he may know who did—if he gets his memory back. She was buried in the basement, but she was killed somewhere else—an apartment, a bedroom, probably in the same house—then carried to the basement. And I think there were more than two people in the room when she died."

"Can you prove any of that?"

"Not yet."

She leaned back and studied him with narrowed eyes and pursed lips. "How did she die?"

"Head injuries, I think. Bludgeoned. With what, I don't know."

"Her description. What did she look like?"

"She was small and she was a blonde. That's all I know."

She nodded. "Not bad. We didn't release the cause of death or her hair color. But why did you ask about the sandal and wallet?"

"You have one sandal. Somewhere, there's another one, and there's a wallet."

He watched her eyes, could almost see little lights coming on in them, wheels turning behind them. "Someone has the wallet and sandal tucked away in an old metal box and..." He waited for her to pick up his train of thought.

It took her only a second. "And there could be prints, or some kind of ID in the wallet, or..."

He prompted again. "If the wallet belonged to the victim..."

"It might tell me who she was."

Their eyes locked for several seconds.

"You think," she said, "that Chip's sister, Lisa, knows something, is involved somehow, and she may have the wallet and the sandal."

"Maybe."

"And that's why you want to go to Delaware?"

"That, and something else."

"What?"

"Someone broke into her house and tore it apart."

"Looking for the box?"

"Maybe."

"And you got all that from an empty can and a broken pair of sunglasses, that psychic thing."

"Some of it."

She studied him again. "How sure are you about this?"

He grinned. "It's not an exact science."

Brenda rolled her eyes. "Okay, let's go to Delaware."

As they stood, she shook her head. "I must be crazy."

He smiled. "Welcome to the club."

She returned his smile, the first real smile he had seen from her, and it caught him off guard. He normally didn't pay much attention to smiles and didn't know why hers caught his attention. Or why he had the sensation of having swallowed something warm that got caught halfway down his gullet. Probably because he hadn't expected it from someone so serious, so stone faced. No, that wasn't it. It was because when she smiled, she was quite…what was the word he was reaching for? Pretty.

Pretty? Damn, Where in hell did that come from?

He shook it off and walked toward the parking lot at a fast clip.

She fell in step beside him. "If this is a wild goose chase, and Leo takes my badge…"

"I'll break his legs."

"Fair enough," she said.

CHAPTER

33

With the LeSabre headed north toward Delaware, Adam called the hospital again and asked for Phil Russell. He waited several minutes before Phil came on.

"Should've known it was you," Phil said. "As usual, your timing is perfect. I was on my way out the door. Dinner's waiting."

"Sorry, Phil, but you were supposed to call me."

"I did."

"When?"

"Thirty minutes ago. I left a message."

"I didn't get it. What'd you say?"

Phil mumbled something about cold dinner and something that could have been "pain in the ass" before he said, "Okay. He's still weak and sleeping most of the time, but he's coming along. I left instructions to give him soft food at seven. You can see him after that. Eightish. Now, can I go home and eat?"

Adam looked at his watch. Five-twenty. "Not yet. I want you to post armed security guards outside his room."

"Armed security guards? You're kidding."

"That's right. Two of them."

"Two's all we have, Adam, two old men, and they're not armed. They're a hundred years old, for Christ's sake."

"Yes. And give them specific instructions. Chip is not to leave the hospital."

"Leave the hospital? He can't even stand up!"

"He's officially in the custody of Detective Brenda McCort, Baltimore Police Department. No one sees Chip until she gets there."

"Adam, what the hell is this, some kind of game?"

"That's right, Phil. McCort. Detective Brenda McCort."

"You're nuts."

"Thanks, Phil. Enjoy your dinner. Love to Ellie."

Adam put his phone away and looked at Brenda who was staring at him.

"We can't see Chip until eight o'clock, but he'll stay put until we get there. Okay?"

"Okay," she said. A wavy grin played across her lips.

After they had gone another mile, she said, "By the way, I've met a few hospital security guards in my time. As a matter of fact, I had an uncle who was one. He was seventy-six years old and never held a gun in his life."

"Really? Imagine that."

CHAPTER
34

Forty minutes after crossing into Delaware, Adam turned off the highway between two square brick columns. Ornate white script letters spelled out "Oceanview Estates" across each one.

The entrance road wound through a quarter mile of pine forest before it curved left. Street signs identified it as Oceanview Terrace. They saw the blue and white lighthouse a half mile ahead. He drove toward it, catching glimpses of the water and an occasional sailboat between large ranchers and two-story colonials. Manicured lawns, shrubbery, and expertly shaped shade trees stated that old money lived here. Expensive cars in each long driveway emphasized the fact.

The driveway of 303 was empty. Lisa's house was one of the long sleek ranchers, beige brick with white trim. Adam turned into her driveway and parked in front of her double garage doors.

"Looks like no one's home," he said.

"Looks that way," Brenda said, scanning the front of the house. "You said someone broke in. No signs of it from here."

"There should be a busted window. Probably in back." Adam got out and walked to the garage. He stood on his tiptoes and peeked in. He never understood why garage door windows were always six feet from the ground.

"No cars," he said to Brenda, standing behind him. "Let's go around to the back."

"Let's try the doorbell," she said firmly. "There are procedures, you know."

"Right. Procedures."

He followed her along the sidewalk to the front door. He passed a large picture window and looked in to see a formal dining room, a hutch with drawers pulled out, and shelves emptied. Through an opening in the dining room wall, he saw kitchen cabinets, their doors hanging open, cans and boxes cluttering the counters beneath. He couldn't see the floor of either room, but he could imagine the mess.

Brenda reached the front door and pushed the button. Chimes echoed inside. Adam reached around her and tried the doorknob. Locked. She gave him a sharp look.

"Let's try the back," he said.

"Wait." She pushed the button again.

Before the new chorus of chimes faded, he walked away. "You coming?"

Instead of going toward the garage, he went the other way, to another large window. Through narrow slats of horizontal mini-blinds, he saw a thoroughly tossed bedroom. The bed was bare to the frame, its mattress and box spring leaning against a wall. Drawers dangled loosely from a dresser. Items of clothing littered the floor.

Brenda cupped her hands against the window and looked in. Adam left her there, walked to the corner of the house and turned. She followed.

The rear of the house opened onto a sunken patio with neatly arranged lawn furniture and a redwood hot tub. At the edge of the patio, a well-kept lawn began and extended some fifty yards to the Atlantic Ocean. A walkway of round, red, concrete steppingstones in a bed of gravel led from the patio to the beach. Tall, trimmed hedges bordered the yard on both sides.

Adam walked down two steps onto the sunken patio and over to a busted window. A lawn chair sat beneath it. So easy, he thought. Smash the glass, reach in, unlock the window, raise it, and use the chair to climb through. The house apparently had no alarm system. Why did people in rich, secluded communities think they were immune to break-ins?

Through the window, he saw the living room he had seen in the images at Solomon's Landing. Stuffing from a slashed sofa and chair cushions covered the floor, books and pictures lay in piles beneath shelves, paintings and wall decorations were shattered and bent where they landed after being ripped from walls.

Beside him, Brenda looked in, then took two steps back. "You were right about someone breaking in," she said. "I hope you're not thinking of going in there."

He looked at her. "Actually, I was thinking of going in."

"We can't do that."

"Why not?"

"Because, for one thing, if someone sees us go in, they could call the local police. I have a badge, but you don't, and I'd be in trouble for letting you do it. For another thing, we could disturb a crime scene, destroy evidence, and not only that...what am I doing?" She waved her hands in the air, turned and walked away, shaking her head. "Why am I wasting my breath? You know the drill as well as I do."

Adam put on a serious, frowning expression. "You're right, detective. You're absolutely right. What we should do is call the local police, then find a judge willing to issue a warrant. Then we can go in and look around. If we really push it, we should be able to get all that done by next Tuesday."

"That's better," she said. "We can..." She saw his face and stopped. Adam grinned.

She glared at him. "You're going in there, aren't you?"

He nodded. "Uh-huh."

"How? Through that window?"

"No. Through that door." He pointed to French doors a few feet away.

"And if the door's locked..."

"It's not."

"How do you know?"

"I can see you never worked Burglary," he said. "Burglars may use windows to get in, but they use doors to get out, and they don't bother to lock them when they leave."

"And how do you know they used that door?" she said, still eyeing him furiously. "And how do you know they're not still in there?"

He walked to the French doors, crooking his finger over his shoulder for her to follow. Beside the door, he knelt and pointed to a thin path of small white particles leading across the patio. "He walked through the mess he made when he slashed the cushions, and left a trail when he came out."

"Okay, okay," she said. "You made your point. And for the record, I worked Burglary for three years, but it's been a while, and..."

"And you're thinking about what Leo will do if we get caught in there."

"Right. But I can see I can't talk you out of it, so let's get it over with."

He opened the door and entered the house with her a step behind.

Halfway across the large living room, Adam stopped. At his feet were several pictures that apparently had been on shelves along the wall to his right. He slid them carefully out of his path with his foot. One was a wedding picture. Chip's parents. There were three of young Chip. Little League. Boy Scouts. High school graduation. Looking around the floor, he saw more. Chip and his father surf fishing, his mother and father on a cruise ship, smiling and sunburned, Chip and his mother wading in the surf with the lighthouse in the background. There were others of Chip by himself, the parents together, and Chip with his parents. He recalled Chip talking about his family's pictures when they were sitting on his patio.

I must have worn them out looking at them...my parents. And I didn't even know them.

"I don't see any of her." Brenda's voice came from behind him.

"What?"

"No pictures of Lisa here. She must have been camera shy."

Adam was deep in thought. "Maybe."

They examined the rest of the house, touching and disturbing nothing. They found every room, closet, and drawer ransacked. Even the garage.

In the bathroom of the master bedroom, Brenda pointed at a grouping of items on the counter by the sink.

"Hair dye, cotton balls, all the essentials. Looks like she touches up the gray."

Adam shrugged. "Let's not hold that against her. All women do it."

She shot him a look. "Not all of us." She walked away. "Are we about finished here?"

Adam grinned when he was sure she couldn't see it.

He stepped over the clutter on the bathroom floor—boxes, bottles, and plastic containers strewn from the medicine chest and cabinets—to the sink. He pulled several strands of hair from a brush and wrapped them in toilet tissue from a roll lying on the floor.

She waited for him in the hallway. "Are you about finished? We're really pushing our luck."

"I think so."

"Besides," she said, "it's obvious whoever searched this place didn't find what he was looking for."

"You're right. He didn't. Every inch of this place has been tossed. He would've stopped when he found it."

"Then it's not here, that metal box you talked about."

"Not in the house anyway."

As they made their way through the house and returned to the patio, Adam thought about the images he'd seen at Solomon's Landing. Was there something in those images that might tell him where the metal box was hidden?

He had seen a shovel. It could have been the one used in the basement on Century Street. He thought about the red circles surrounded by smaller white ones.

The walkway leading from the patio to the beach drew his attention.

...*red circles, six of them, tiny white circles all around them...*

The steppingstones. Round, red circles of concrete. Surrounded by white gravel.

"We should get out of here," Brenda said.

"Not yet. Wasn't there a shovel in the garage?"

"Actually, it was a spade," she said, looking at him with a mixture of curiosity and impatience. "Shovels have square ends. A spade is rounded. Wait a minute. I hope you're not thinking about digging up the yard."

He almost said something about calling a spade a spade, but the furious expression on her face changed his mind. Instead, he walked toward the garage.

"I'll be right back."

CHAPTER

35

With the tip of the spade, he worked the first red steppingstone loose, picked it up and laid it aside. He pushed back several inches of the gravel bed beneath it and was down to sandy soil. After digging down nearly a foot, he decided nothing was there.

"I mean it," Brenda said. "This is ridiculous." She stood behind him, shifting her weight from one foot to the other, crossing and uncrossing her arms, looking around as though she expected them to be discovered any minute. "Do you realize how many of those things there are?"

He looked down the length of the walkway leading to the beach. She was right. There had to be at least forty.

Six. There were six of them in the image.

"I'm serious, Kingston. We have to get out of here."

"Call me Adam," he said, deep in thought.

"I should call you crazy. Are you coming or not?"

He walked away from her, past the next four slabs to the sixth one.

"Just one more," he said.

After removing the stone, he'd dug only a few inches when the tip of the spade hit something solid. Less than a minute later, he lifted a faded, dirt-encrusted towel. When he peeled away the towel, he held a rusty, metal box twelve inches square and four inches deep. A small padlock dangled on its front.

"Well, I'll be damned," Brenda said. "You were right."

He laid the box at his feet. "Do you think we should open it, detective, or are there procedures to follow?"

She fell to her knees beside the metal box and looked up at him with a coy grin. "Stop wasting time and bust that damn lock off. And call me Brenda."

One sharp stab with the spade sent the lock flying. Adam knelt beside Brenda and raised the lid of the box. Inside they saw a sandal with thin straps, the mate to the one found in the basement grave, and a leather wallet. Mildew sprouted on both. Untouched by mildew was a stack of white envelopes. There were at least a dozen of them, tightly wrapped in clear plastic and tied with string.

Without taking his eyes off the contents of the box, Adam asked, "You know what I think?"

"What?"

"I think we'd better get the hell out of here before we get caught."

*   *   *

He drove south toward Maryland for ten minutes before they came to a Burger King. With a large coffee for himself and a Diet Sprite for Brenda, he parked in the shade of an elm tree in the corner of the parking lot.

"Well," he said, looking at the metal box on her lap, "let's see what we have."

Brenda hesitated. "You realize nothing in here can be used as evidence because of the way it was obtained. Plus, we could get in a lot of trouble."

"Right. I'll take the wallet, you take the envelopes."

She sighed and mumbled something about directing traffic for the rest of her life as she opened the box.

Adam gingerly lifted the mildew-spotted wallet and laid it on a napkin he had spread on his lap. He used his coffee stirrer to pry up the snap that held it closed, then pushed the top half of the wallet open. In the first pocket of a glassine picture section in the center of the wallet was a posed portrait of the Weathers family. Chip and his father stood with broad smiles behind a high-backed chair. Chip mentioned his father the day before.

I looked like him. He was tall, powerful looking, the kind of man a boy could look up to.

A good description, Adam thought. Chip, a shorter, thinner version of his father with the same dark brown hair, brown eyes, and square, solid features was probably in his late teens.

Chip's mother sat in the chair, her hands folded in her lap.

…small…frail…like a queen…

Pale blue eyes sparkled from her thin tapered face, framed by hair the color of corn silk. The young woman sitting at her feet with hair a shade more golden, but the same blue eyes, fair skin, and slight frame was an image of her mother twenty years earlier.

Adam went through the rest of the pictures. In one, three teen-aged girls posed like fashion models on the hood of a car, Lisa in the middle. Two more were of the family, followed by one of a pre-teen Lisa and her father in swimsuits lounging on the sunken patio. Next, Lisa, Chip, and their mother waved at the camera from the entrance to Disney World. The last picture was a posed portrait of Lisa and a handsome, broad-faced, dark-haired man smiling like newlyweds. Eric.

The rest of the wallet was empty except for a scrap of paper in the bills section. In a thin, feminine hand, someone had written, *Julia, 834 Century, Apt. A.*

Adam looked at Brenda. "Now we know what Eric looks like."

"Hmmm?" She was engrossed in reading.

"A picture of Lisa and Eric together. What've you got?"

"Love letters."

"Love letters?"

"Yes," she said. "From someone using the initial C to someone called J." She handed it to him. "Whose wallet is it?"

"Lisa's."

"Lisa's? Why would she bury her own wallet?"

"Good question," Adam said. "Who are C and J?"

"Good question," she said. "Let's trade."

After the trade, Adam scanned the three letters Brenda had removed from their envelopes and unfolded. Each one was addressed to J and signed by C. The letters were written in large bold handwriting. A man's hand, he thought, as he read about how much C loved J, how their time together was so wonderful, how he couldn't wait until they could be together forever. The envelopes were addressed to Miss Julia White, 834 Century Street, Baltimore, Maryland, 21226. He squinted to read the faded postmarks on the envelopes. Some were too far gone, but the ones still legible told him they were mailed in Baltimore over a period of three months, March through May, sixteen years ago.

"Did you notice the handwriting?" he asked.

"It slants backward," Brenda replied. "Whoever wrote them was probably left-handed. By any chance, is Chip Weathers a southpaw?"

Adam thought. Had Chip held his fork in his left or right hand? "I don't recall."

"Did he wear a watch?" she asked. "Left-handed people usually wear their watch on the right arm."

He shook his head. "No watch."

Brenda returned her attention to the wallet.

"This is strange," she said. "She removed the driver's license, credit cards, insurance cards, all the usual IDs, but left the pictures in the wallet."

"Strange," Adam agreed.

He examined each of the envelopes. All were addressed the same and mailed during the same time period. Between the last two he found something else.

"Look at this."

It was a check, made out to Julia White and signed by Eric M. Richards, dated May 29, sixteen years ago, in the amount of ten thousand dollars.

Brenda glanced at it. "But…it looks like it was never cashed."

"It wasn't."

They both stared at the check.

Brenda spoke first. "She didn't cash it because she died before she got the chance. Lisa kept the check and all the rest of this. Why?"

Adam didn't answer. He stared out the windshield, deep in thought.

She joined him. After a moment, she asked, "So what do we have?"

"We have a hot romance between J…"

"Julia."

"…and C…"

"Chip," she said.

"And we have Miss Julia White…"

"Living in the apartment on Century Street where she was killed and buried in the basement. I finally know her name."

"Maybe."

"Maybe?" she said. "It's obvious what happened. We have the letters Chip wrote her. They had a lover's quarrel, and it got out of hand. I don't know where the check fits in, but you have to admit, it makes sense."

"It doesn't explain why that lunatic is trying to kill Chip and Lisa after all this time. And it doesn't explain why someone kept all this stuff."

"Someone? You mean Lisa."

"Maybe." He started the car.

"We're going to the hospital now?"

"No. My place."

"Why?"

"I have to do something."

"Another psychic thing?"

"No," he said, noting the lack of skepticism in her voice when she said *psychic* this time. "A hair thing."

CHAPTER
36

They arrived at Adam's apartment at 7:15. Brenda volun-
teered to make coffee while Adam went into the small bedroom
he'd converted into a den. From the bottom drawer of his desk, he
removed a microscope he borrowed from Phil Russell and never
returned. He placed the hair samples between glass slides. When
Brenda entered the room ten minutes later with two coffees, he was
leaning back in his chair, his hands locked behind his head, staring
at the wall.

"I don't mean to be picky," she said setting the cups on his
desk, "but you're supposed to clean your coffeemaker once in
a while."

Deep in thought, he muttered, "Ruins the flavor of the coffee."

She made a face and shook her head.

"By the way, your answering machine's blinking."

"Thanks," he said, still without looking at her. "I'll get it in
a minute."

She lodged a hip against his desk and nodded at the microscope.

"You seem grim. What've you been up to?"

"See for yourself."

He rose to let her have the chair and stood beside her while she
adjusted the scope.

"I see blonde hair," she said.

"Check the roots."

She looked again.

"Okay, I see blonde hair with dark roots. You can barely see it, but it looks brown, maybe closer to auburn. Where did you get it?"

"From her hairbrush."

"From the house in Bethany Beach? I didn't see you take it."

"You were out of the room."

Her thoughts came out slowly. "Then...she's not a natural blonde...but the old pictures of her in the wallet...she had the same hair as her mother. You're saying she's..."

"She's not Lisa Weathers Richards."

"Then...who is she?"

"I'd say her name is Julia White."

"My God, Adam. If she's Julia masquerading as Lisa, does that mean my Jane Doe is..."

Adam looked at her for the first time since she had entered the room.

"Lisa."

Brenda slumped in the chair and turned her head away. He heard her take a deep breath and let it out slowly.

He picked up his coffee and raised it to his chest. The dark brown liquid stared up at him. He recalled Chip sitting on his sofa the day before, looking at him through tear-filled, dark brown eyes.

I think I killed that woman...that's why I'm here...to find out who she was.

Adam sat his cup on the desk and left the room.

CHAPTER 37

The first message on his answering machine was from Phil, the one telling him he could see Chip at eight o'clock.

The next message was also from Phil.

"Adam, after I talked to you, I found out a man came into the hospital earlier this afternoon and tried to see Chip. Said he was Chip's legal guardian and made a big scene when they told him Chip was flagged for no visitors. Threatened to bring his lawyers down on us. Just what the hospital needs, a lawsuit. Thanks a lot. Anyway, I thought you'd want to know."

Adam said to Brenda, who stood behind him, "Eric's in town." She nodded.

The last message was Stuart's voice.

"Adam, I thought I'd catch you up. We picked up the Grand Marquis and we're checking it for prints. We also found the other car, the one he grabbed from the old lady in Delaware. He ditched it at the Jolly Roger Amusement Park, right here in town. We've got it staked out. He's in town, bud, so watch your rear, okay? I'll call you if anything develops. If you need me, I'll be at the station for a while, then you've got my beeper number. Oh, yeah. What'd you think of Brenda McCort? A real babe, huh?"

Adam turned his head far enough to see Brenda roll her eyes. He checked his watch. 7:45.

"Time to go to see Chip," he said.

On their way to the hospital in the LeSabre, Brenda asked Adam why he took hair samples from the house in Delaware, why he was suspicious about the hair color.

He told her he expected Lisa to be small and frail like Chip's description of their mother, not the well-rounded woman in the Mercedes. Daughters don't have to grow up to look like their mothers, of course, so it was only a small surprise at the time.

Then there was the blue contact lens he'd found in the grass at Solomon's Landing. Lisa kept her sunglasses on, perhaps fearing he might detect the false eye color. She also covered her eyes after he pulled her down behind the table when the shooting started. It might have been a reflex action, or she could have realized she'd lost the lens and didn't want him to see the true color of her eyes.

"Interesting," Brenda said. "But flimsy."

"Very flimsy. I didn't think much about it until we were in the house. Remember when you said something about her touching up the gray?"

Brenda nodded. "We were in her bathroom."

"We'd been through the whole house by then. There were pictures of Chip and his parents, but none of Lisa.

"So she touches up to keep the blonde, not to get rid of gray," Brenda said, "and there should've been pictures of her around the house with the rest of the family. The only ones of her were the ones hidden away in the wallet. Julia White got rid of them so no one would see the real Lisa. It might have blown the masquerade. Still pretty flimsy, but..."

"Flimsies add up," Adam said as he steered the LeSabre into the hospital parking lot.

While he looked for a parking space, Brenda said, "That explains why the driver's license and other IDs weren't in the wallet. She needed them to carry it off."

Adam found a spot and parked. "Something else bothered me. She called me to check on Chip's condition instead of going to the hospital. Now I understand why. She was afraid of seeing him face to face until she knew if he had recovered his memory."

"That makes sense," Brenda said. "If he had, he would've known she wasn't the real Lisa."

"Come on," he said. "Let's go see Chip."

In the hospital elevator, Brenda asked the question Adam had wrestled with since they left his apartment.

"Are you going to tell him?"

"That the woman he thinks he might have killed was his own sister?"

"Yeah, that."

"We don't know what happened in that apartment, and as long as his memory is locked up, neither does he. He knows a woman died, and he thinks he was responsible for her death. I don't know a lot about amnesia or how the human mind works, but I'd hate to think what it might do to him if he thought he killed his own sister. No. I'm not going to tell him yet."

The elevator doors opened. Adam followed Brenda out and fell in step beside her. As they walked down the corridor, he wondered what the homicide detective with a strong sense of responsibility to the letter of the law would say to Chip.

When he saw the two guards stationed outside Chip's room, Adam remembered how Phil Russell had exaggerated their ages.

They're a hundred years old, for Christ's sake.

He didn't think either of them was a day over eighty.

The tall thin one leaned against the doorframe with his arms crossed, his head down, and his eyes closed as if sleeping upright. In a chair beside him, a short heavyset man focused on a paperback held in both hands at chest level. Adam saw his lips moving from halfway down the corridor. He winced at Brenda's whispered remark about the Earp brothers being on the job.

The echoing clicks of Brenda's high heels on the tiled floor must have broken the guard's concentration on his novel. He looked up as they approached, swiped the book against his partner's leg, and struggled out of his chair. When Adam and Brenda reached them, both guards were standing at stiff attention with stern expressions.

With his book tucked behind his back in one hand and his other hand held out in a stop gesture, the short one announced in a gruff, official voice, "No one allowed in. Police orders."

Brenda showed her badge. "Detective Brenda McCort," she said, "Baltimore Homicide."

Without lowering his hand, the guard leaned forward and examined her badge for several seconds, then nodded to his partner. The tall one leaned over stiffly and opened the door to Chip's room. The two guards resumed rigid stances as Adam followed Brenda in.

CHAPTER
38

Chip's bed was raised, and he sat propped by pillows under his arms, staring out a window on the far side of the room. His head rolled toward them as they entered, and a weak smile grew through his thick beard and mustache. His eyes were sunken, and his face was colorless.

"Adam." His voice was a hoarse whisper. "Good to see you."

"Good to see you, too, Chip." Adam stopped at the foot of the bed and smiled. "You look a little better than the last time I saw you. How do you feel?"

"Like a pin cushion." Chip's smile dissolved into a grimace of pain. He squeezed his eyes shut. When he opened them, he looked at Brenda.

"Who's that? Not another doctor with a needle, I hope."

"No," Adam said. "She's not a doctor." He hesitated, dreading the thought of telling Chip who she was and why she was there. "This is Brenda McCort. She's…"

"I'm a detective," Brenda said in a voice as soft as the smile she gave Chip, "with the Baltimore Police Department. The man who shot you is a suspect in a homicide. I have to talk to you about him, but I don't think this is a good time." She paused long enough for a glance at Adam. "It can wait."

Adam gave her a quick wink.

"Guess what, Adam." Chip's voice was stronger. "I have something to tell you. Good news."

"Good news?" Adam said, "That'd be a novelty. What is it?"

"I remember some things. Not a lot. Just stuff from when I was a little kid, but it's a start. It's coming back. My memory."

Adam saw a glimmer of excitement in Chip's eyes and felt some of it himself. He moved to the side of the bed.

"That's great news. But are you sure you're up to talking about it now? I mean...hell, I don't know what I mean. How did it happen? When? What do you remember?"

"Whoa. Slow down," Chip said. "I said a few things. The shrinks said it might take another shock to bring it back. Maybe the guy who shot me did me a favor."

"I'll be sure to express your gratitude when I see him. Now, talk to me. What do you remember? Do you remember your parents? How about the house in Bethany Beach? Do you remember..."

"Adam," Brenda interrupted with a chuckle. "Maybe if you'd let him talk, he could tell us. Here." She pulled a chair over behind him. "Sit down and shut up."

Chip managed a weak laugh.

Adam raised his arms in compliance and sat. "Okay, okay. Let's have it. Tell us what you remember."

"Like I said, it's only a few things. You said a house in...where?"

"Bethany Beach."

"Yeah, that's it. First thing this morning, I thought about that house. At first, I thought it was a dream, but it was real, a real memory. It's on the water, right?"

"Right on the ocean."

"A lighthouse. There was a lighthouse."

"White, with a blue top," Adam said. "A little way up the beach."

Chip's voice trembled.

"Lisa and I used to play there, on the big rocks around the lighthouse. We weren't allowed to, but we'd sneak off. One time, Lisa slipped on the rocks and cut her foot. I ran home to get help, crying like a baby."

"Your parents," Adam said. He felt uncomfortable with Chip talking about Lisa. "What do you remember about them?"

Chip frowned. "Not much. Not yet. Like I said, just a few things. I keep dozing off—all that junk they pumped in me, I guess—but every time I wake up, there's more. Like dreams, but real. We had a big black car. I remember Lisa and me riding in the back seat. We played games and sang dumb songs, like *Old MacDonald Had a Farm*. Mom used to sing, too. She had a beautiful voice. Sometimes Dad would try to sing with us, and it was so bad we'd all break up. Mom said he sounded like a frog with a toothache."

Adam and Brenda listened as Chip recounted what he remembered of his early years. He seemed to be gaining strength from the exhilaration of recalling what had been lost for so long. His memory appeared to be returning in small pieces in no apparent sequence, but in none of them was he more than ten or twelve years old. The memories were happy ones of a close family.

Was that the way amnesia worked? Adam wondered. The early years coming back first? The good stuff?

Chip became quiet and turned his head toward the window.

"Adam," he said in a small voice. "Lisa. Have you talked to her? Does she know I'm here?"

"No, I haven't spoken to her."

He heard Brenda shift her position in the chair behind him.

"But," he added quickly, "I expect to talk to Eric soon."

It was the best he could think of to change the subject.

Chip turned back from the darkness outside the window. "When I was in the hospital before, Eric was great. I did a lot of sleeping then, too, but it was like every time I opened my eyes, Eric was there, asking me if I needed anything and if I remembered anything. After I left, he hired Cueball to check up on me."

Adam had looked toward Brenda. He swung back to Chip when he heard the strange name. "Did you say Cueball?"

"I thought I told you about him."

"You told me Eric hired someone, but you never mentioned his name."

Chip yawned. "Never knew his name. I called him Cueball because he was fat and bald. Like a billiard ball. Cueball. Get it?"

Adam stood. "I get it. Listen, you're tired. We'd better go."

Chip nestled his head into a pillow. "Bet old Cueball is wondering where I am right about now."

"You get some rest," Adam said. "I'll come back tomorrow."

Chip said, "You too, detective...uh...what was it?"

"It's Brenda," she said. "And, yes, I'll be here tomorrow, too."

They walked to the door and had it open when they heard Chip's sleepy voice. "Brenda?"

"Yes, Chip."

"You married?"

"No. Why?"

"Adam makes a darn good omelet."

Brenda started to say something, but Adam took her by the arm and pulled her toward the door. When she gave him a questioning look, he put a finger to his lips and whispered, "Let's go. He's asleep."

Outside Chip's room, Brenda shook hands with the two guards and complimented them on the job they were doing. Her professional manner made them stand taller, and her farewell smile left them looking forty years younger.

In the elevator, Adam said, "Thanks for what you did."

"You mean what I said to the guards?"

"No. What you didn't say to Chip."

She shrugged. "No point in questioning him about Lisa until the rest of his memory returns. You realize it's only a matter of time, don't you?"

"I know, but thanks anyway."

"It can wait. He's not going anywhere in his condition."

"That's not why you did it."

"What do you mean?"

"You're a softie."

"A what?"

"A softie," he repeated. "Under that hard-nosed cop exterior, you're a marshmallow."

"Marshmallow? Look who's talking, the big tough ex-Fed. You'd buy any hard luck story that comes along."

"Not me. I'm hard as nails."

"Yeah, right."

Without looking at each other, the two of them grinned all the way to the first floor.

Coming off the elevator, she asked, "I wonder what he meant, about the omelet."

"Nothing. He was delirious."

"Uh-huh."

CHAPTER
39

In the hospital lobby, Adam stopped and pulled out his cell phone.

"I want to see if Stuart called again. He said he would if he developed anything more on the shooter."

"Tell me something," Brenda said. "You think Eric is connected with the shooter, don't you?"

He started toward the exit door as he pushed numbers on his phone.

"Maybe."

He froze when he heard her voice behind him.

"Oh, no, you don't, Adam Kingston. Hold it right there."

He turned back to her. She stood rigid, her arms crossed, her cheeks on fire. "Now what?"

"I'll tell you what. Every time you say *maybe*, you're holding something back. What is it this time? It has something to do with Eric and that…that man Chip talked about, doesn't it? The one he called Cueball."

He started to speak.

"If you say *maybe* again, I'll punch your lights out."

"Okay, okay," he whispered, his hands up.

He glanced around the hospital lobby to see if anyone was watching their scene. The lobby was empty.

"I'll tell you if you calm down."

Her hands were on her hips now.

"I'm calm, dammit. Tell me."

They sat on a padded bench across from the hospital gift shop. He told her about the man Eric hired to keep track of Chip and described the man he had traded shots with at the Endicott House and at Solomon's Landing. She agreed it could be the same man.

With her satisfied, Adam called his answering machine. There was only one message. A woman's voice.

"Mr. Kingston, it's Lisa Richards. I...I need your help. Someone broke into my house. It was Eric. I know it was him. Please, I have to talk to you. I'll tell you what you want to know, what he did to that girl on Century Street. But I can't go back to my house. He might come back there. I'll...I'll call you later and tell you where to meet me."

After he related the message to Brenda, she said, "She doesn't know we know who she really is. She doesn't know we have the box."

"She must've been at the house before we got there," Adam added. "As soon as she realized Eric had searched the house, she probably checked to see if he found the box. No, she hasn't seen the holes in her yard. She thinks her secret is safe."

"From us anyway," Brenda said. "Eric knows she's not Lisa. It would take both of them to pull off the impersonation all these years."

"Yes, it would," Adam said.

"So, where does that leave us?"

Adam leaned back on the bench and rested his head against the wall. "Let's do a little supposing."

"Okay."

"Let's suppose Eric killed Lisa."

"Okay. Go on."

"And let's suppose Chip was there. He witnessed it, but his amnesia blocked it out."

"I'm listening."

"Then, somehow," Adam continued, "Eric persuaded Julia White to impersonate Lisa."

"Why?" Brenda asked.

"I don't know."

"Why would Julia do it if she was Chip's girlfriend?"

"I don't know that either, but we're only supposing here."

"Go on," she said.

"Sixteen years later, Chip sees the picture in the paper and knows he was involved in what happened. He tells Eric he's coming here…"

"To see the great Adam Kingston."

He gave her a harsh look. "Don't interrupt. Eric gets worried that Chip will remember what happened and decides it's time to get rid of everyone and everything that can tie him to Lisa's death."

"By everyone, you mean Chip and Julia. So he hires a shooter."

"Right."

"And by everything," Brenda continued, "you mean what was in the box. It's not enough to convict him, but enough to make him a prime suspect."

"Right. Julia went along with his plan, perhaps fearing for her own life, perhaps for money, but she kept the goodies in her box as her insurance policy."

Brenda said, "Eric sends his man, Cueball, to kill Chip, and he almost succeeds. Then the man follows you to Solomon's Landing to get a shot at Julia. How am I doing, professor?"

"Fine. Keep going."

Brenda leaned against the wall beside him.

"All right. Eric sneaks into town and searches the house in Bethany Beach for the box. That scares the hell out of Julia, so she decides to tell you everything to save her own skin. Which brings us to where we are right now."

Adam nodded. "I've got to make another call."

"Who to?"

"Stuart Wilson. I want to see if he can arrange for a couple of uniforms to replace the hospital guards upstairs. If we're right about Eric and the shooter, Chip needs real protection."

"What do you mean if we're right? It all makes sense."

"A couple of things don't fit."

"Like what?"

"Let me call Stuart first and see if he'll arrange for the protection."

"You want me to call Stuart? My badge might add clout."

He grinned. "Maybe."

She gave him an elbow in the ribs and snatched the phone from his hand.

While Brenda called Stuart, Adam reached into his pocket. He'd brought along the picture section from Lisa's wallet, thinking he might show the pictures to Chip. He'd forgotten about it in the excitement of Chip regaining some of his memory.

He fingered through the pictures, seeing a family that went places together, played silly games, sang together and laughed together.

He and Caroline used to sing on car trips. How did that one go?

...with Gilligan, the Skipper, too. The millionaire and his wife...

And looking for license plates with letters of the alphabet and coming up with words to match.

There's one. B-S-F. Big Smelly Feet.

His thoughts moved to his client. Chip lay in a hospital bed desperately reaching into a dark hole, retrieving memories that would make him smile and laugh as they reappeared. Until he came to the last one. The day his sister died.

He stared at the final picture in the wallet, the one of Lisa and Eric. They were a handsome young couple, all smiles, looking into their future. Lisa's would come to a tragic end, he knew that. But why? How? What happened in that house?

Where the hell are you, Eric Richards?

As he held the picture in his hand and the question repeated itself, images swirled in his mind.

Semi-darkness, outside…dark shapes, forming squares, rectangles… evolving, coming into focus…they're cars, in rows…blue, gray, black, a red one—the LeSabre…a movement behind the cars, a shadow, coming forward…a man, tall, broad-shouldered, stopping, turning, walking away, fading into darkness…

He heard Brenda saying, "Stuart said there's nothing new on the shooter, but he'll arrange for uniforms to…"

Adam leapt to his feet. "He's here."

"Who's here?" Her eyes darted around the lobby.

"Eric."

"Eric? Where?"

"The parking lot. Come on."

CHAPTER
40

They ran through the revolving door to the sidewalk. Adam walked slowly to his right, scanning the rows of parked cars for the shape of a man, any movement. Brenda went left.

When they were thirty yards apart, Adam saw a black car move out of its space five rows back. With its headlights off, it turned into the lane and rolled slowly past the LeSabre. He saw one person in the car.

He shouted, "Over here!" in Brenda's direction and sprinted toward the moving car. Its headlights came on, and it increased speed.

Adam reached the LeSabre and within seconds brought the big sedan to life and steered out into the lane. He hit the brakes long enough for Brenda to snatch the passenger door open and leap in, then floored the accelerator, his eyes locked on the black car as it reached the end of the parking lot and turned south on Ocean Highway.

Out of breath from running to the car, Brenda gasped, "Was it him? Could you tell?"

"It's him. Hold on."

Adam sped to the end of the parking lot and wheeled onto the highway. They were twenty car lengths behind Eric's car. He watched it pick up more speed and weave through the sparse traffic. He did the same, and in less than a mile, cut the lead in half. A quick glance at the speedometer told him he was pushing seventy and climbing. He pulled his emergency blinkers on and leaned on the horn when he neared a car he had to dodge.

Brenda watched both sides and yelled "Clear," at intersections. They made it through three red lights, gaining ground to four lengths behind the black car.

"Look out!" Brenda shouted. "Incoming!"

A white pickup hauling a camper inched its way across the highway. Adam hit the brakes hard, a second or two before Eric did. The black car fishtailed into a ninety degree spin, bumped across the median strip, skidded sideways across two lanes and smashed its passenger door into a lamppost on the far sidewalk. The LeSabre slid to a stop ten feet from the camper.

Adam saw Eric Richards climb out of his car. Richards looked directly at him for a second, then ran to the corner, turned, and disappeared into a side street.

Adam jumped from the car, calling to Brenda. "Circle around. Cut him off."

He ran off as she scooted into the driver's seat. When he reached the corner, he spotted Eric running in the middle of the street.

Adam dug in and ran after him. He had only gone a few strides before the slap of shoe leather on asphalt was drowned out by war whoops raining down from above. From the balconies of tall wood-frame rooming houses on both sides of the street, clusters of young tank-topped revelers hoisted their drinks and yelled encouragement to both runners.

Halfway down the block, Richards veered out of the street and ran between two houses. Adam reached the narrow opening in time to see him straddling a board fence six feet high at the end of a backyard, then sliding down the other side and out of sight.

Adam ran through the tunnel-like breezeway and across the backyard. He gauged his strides and leaped onto a trash can by the fence, grabbed the top of the fence with both hands, and vaulted over. He landed in a crouch in a dark alley that ran the length of the block. He looked right, then left. Eric was nowhere in sight.

He swept both ways again. On the left, he saw the back end of a pink minivan parked by the fence. A topless green Jeep sat ten feet up on the right. Eric had to be hiding behind one of them.

Adam stepped toward the minivan and knew he'd guessed wrong when he was hit from behind. A pair of arms encircled his chest, lifted him nearly off his feet, and shoved him forward, straight at the minivan.

He struggled to keep his feet beneath him and managed to plant one foot and twist his body at the last second so that Eric hit the minivan first with a loud grunt and gush of air.

Adam felt the arms around him go limp and threw his left elbow back, striking Eric's midsection. He pivoted and swung his right fist into the side of Eric's face, then stepped back to let the man who'd jumped him crumple to the ground gasping for air.

Adam's lungs burned, forcing him to bend forward with his hands on his knees and take giant breaths. He didn't see Eric rise and lunge, knocking him off balance and into the fence head first. He threw his hands up in time to break the impact, then spun to see Eric push himself along the side of the minivan and break into a wobbly gait down the alley.

Damn!

He'd had enough running.

He sucked in a huge breath and yelled, "Stop or I'll shoot! Freeze right there or I'll blow your head off."

Eric stopped and stood with his back turned, slouched over and panting rapidly. Adam walked toward him, matching him pant for pant. Halfway there, he ordered, "On your knees. Hands behind your head. Don't make me shoot you."

Eric followed instructions. Adam stepped around in front of him and stood with his hands at his sides.

Eric raised his head, stopping for a second at the level of Adam's empty hands.

"You...you don't have a gun."

Adam stared into bloodshot eyes set deep in a flushed face. "I lied. You want to run some more?"

Eric shook his head and dropped his chin to his chest.

Good. I'm beat.

Adam heard a car behind him and turned to see his LeSabre race up the alley and skid a sudden stop. Brenda jumped out, leaving the headlights on and the door open.

She trotted toward him. "Are you okay?"

Between rapid breaths, he said, "I'm fine. What the hell kept you?"

"What do you mean? I circled the block twice." She glanced down at the crumpled shape on his knees between them. "Besides, looks like you did all right for..."

"For an old man?"

She smiled. "For a psychic."

He couldn't hold back a grin. "Thanks."

Another car entered the alley from the other end, gunned toward them and screeched to a stop. A blond-haired man came out of it and walked into the area now lit by two sets of headlights. "Adam, what the hell've you been...who's that?"

"Stuart Wilson, meet Eric Richards, then arrest him."

"For what?"

"Reckless driving."

*   *   *

Brenda rode with Stuart to the Ocean City Police station with Eric handcuffed in the back seat. Adam followed in the LeSabre. He considered going home to wait for Julia White to call about meeting him, but talking to Eric was more important. Besides, with Eric in custody, she was safe, and he couldn't be sure she would call at all. He hurried inside and found Stuart and Brenda at Stuart's desk. "Where is he?" he asked.

Stuart said, "I put him in the interview room."

"Is he all right?"

"He's fine. You tagged him pretty good, but he waived a medical exam."

Brenda touched Adam's arm. "How about you?"

Adam sat in the chair beside hers. "I'm fine," he said, "but I need to work out more often." He looked across the desk at Stuart. "I want to talk to him."

"Okay by me," Stuart said, "but you'd better hurry. We can't hold him. He'll be hit with a hefty fine for taking out a lamppost, get a few points on his driving record, but that's it."

"Where's the interview room?"

Stuart nodded to his right. "Down that hall. Second door. We're going through the usual routine—license, priors—but that'll only take a few minutes. He'll walk out with a handful of traffic tickets."

"Can you drag your feet a little writing up those tickets, give me a little time with him?"

Stuart shrugged. "I suppose we can slow the wheels of justice a little. By the way, witnesses at the scene said there was another car chasing the one he crashed. An older sedan, they said. One said it was maroon, another said candy apple red." He winked at Brenda. "I don't suppose you'd know anything about that, would you?"

"Sorry," Adam said. "My car's ruby red. You said the second door?"

He started to rise, but stopped when he felt Brenda's hand on his arm.

"What are you going to do?" she asked.

He looked at her. "I was thinking of playing a little poker."

Brenda said, "You mean run a bluff and see if he folds? You think you have enough aces?"

Adam shrugged. "We'll find out."

Stuart stood. "C'mon, Brenda, let's take a little walk."

"Where to?"

"Door number three. I want to see this."

Adam led the way down the hall and stopped at the second door. Brenda followed Stuart to the next one.

CHAPTER
41

The box-like interview room was clean, stale, and except for a gray metal table and two chairs, empty. Adam glanced at the dark window of one-way glass in the wall to his right. He closed the door behind him and took his first good look at Eric Richards.

Eric was across the room, standing sideways, leaning one shoulder against the wall, scrutinizing his manicured fingernails. Under different circumstances, Adam could see how the handsome, well-built man might be an impressive figure, the picture of a successful businessman. But not tonight.

Eric's thick black hair was an unkempt bush, his face pale and drawn beneath sunken, shadowed eyes. The sweat-stained collar of his white dress shirt sagged low on his neck. His dark gray pants, half of an expensive suit, were wrinkled and creaseless, and Adam guessed he hadn't shaved or changed clothes in at least two days. Eric threw him a glare that demonstrated cockiness and self-assertion. Beneath the facade of being composed and in control, Adam saw a man on the edge of a thin precipice. Yet, even in Eric's dilapidated condition, Adam smelled his arrogance. The odor became stronger with the first word out of Eric's mouth.

"Kingston," he said without taking his eyes off his nails.

It wasn't a greeting. It was a challenge from a desperate man trying to run a bluff of his own.

Adam responded in the same tone. "Richards." He enjoyed a
challenge and looked forward to this one.

"Funny," Eric said as he casually used one fingernail to flick
something from beneath another one, "when Chip told me he was
coming here to see you, I told him he was wasting his time."

Eric's baritone voice was loud. His tool of intimidation, Adam
guessed. But it was a pitch too high, too forced.

"But you gave him the money anyway."

"Chip's like my own kid brother. I'd do anything for him."

"Even give him money to throw away on a fortune teller? A
con man?"

Eric looked at Adam for the first time. A grin pulled up one
side of his mouth. "He told you I said that?"

"Sort of."

Eric tossed a so-what shrug and walked to the table. "I have to
admit, that's how I felt at first. But Chip showed me a magazine,
Newsweek, I believe, with an article about you. I was impressed."

"Really?"

"You have quite a reputation, Kingston."

"Thanks."

Eric pulled out a chair at his end of the table and sat. "I always
wonder about magazine articles like that," he said, a facetious
tone in his voice. "They always tell about a person's successes, but
seldom mention the failures. I suppose you've had your share of
those, too."

Adam grinned. "Haven't we all?"

Eric turned sideways in his chair, crossed his legs, and took time
to brush something off the knee of his expensive wrinkled pants. "So
tell me. How is Chip? Is he going to be all right?"

"He'll be fine."

"Good." After a slight pause, Eric added, "Do they know who shot him?"

"Not yet."

"Damn shame." Eric searched his pants for something else to brush off. "People aren't safe on the streets any more."

Adam decided he'd wasted enough time with this smartass. It was time to ante up.

"Let's be honest, Eric, that's not what you really want to know, is it?"

Eric flashed a smile, an innocent one he probably used to charm people. "I'm afraid I don't know what you mean."

"I mean the real reason you were lurking around the hospital tonight."

"Lurking?" Eric tossed out a small laugh, one as plastic as the smile. "Really, now. I wasn't lurking, as you put it. I went there to find out how Chip was. I was concerned about him."

"What you were really concerned about was whether or not he'd regained his memory, if he remembered what happened on Century Street sixteen years ago."

"Of course I'd be concerned about that. That poor woman was found in one of our buildings, and Chip had the crazy idea he had something to do with it."

"Maybe it's not so crazy. He was there when it happened."

Eric pointed an index finger across the table. "Let me make something clear to you, Kingston. If Chip was there, if he killed that woman, I'll see that he has the best lawyers, the best doctors money can buy. We'll prove he wasn't responsible for what he did." He lowered the finger but held a firm stare.

Adam stared back. "Very touching."

Time to raise the pot.

"But he wasn't the only one there, was he?"

He held Eric's eyes, hoping for a reaction.

Eric broke eye contact and looked at his watch. "I'm afraid I can't help you there," Eric said. "I have no idea what you're talking about." He fingered the watch, moving it back and forth along his right arm.

Adam watched him play with the watch. "You're left-handed."

Eric looked up. "Yes, I am. What does that have to do with anything?"

"Nothing. But I'm curious about something else. How did you know Chip was in the hospital, that he'd been shot?"

"Why would you ask that? It was on the news."

Adam leaned forward. "It was on the news here, but in Philadelphia? Not likely. Are you sure your wife didn't tell you?"

Eric hesitated. "Lisa? I'm sure you're aware we've been separated for years. I haven't spoken to her in quite a while." His voice had jumped another pitch higher. "What are you getting at?"

"Then I suppose I had it figured wrong. You told your office you were staying in Philadelphia, but you checked out of your hotel and came here. I thought it was because Lisa told you Chip was alive and in the hospital. I even thought you had her call me this morning to find out if Chip had regained his memory."

"I don't know what you're talking about," Eric said in a forced tone. "I told you I haven't spoken to Lisa."

"I'm talking about the woman who lives in Bethany Beach, Eric. You had her call me. You even had her meet me to find out how much I knew."

"I came here out of concern for Chip." He fingered the watch again, turning it round and round on his arm. "I wanted to see Chip, then I was going to contact you."

"Really? You were going to contact me? Then why did you run when I spotted you at the hospital?"

"How did I know it was you? A strange man chased me in a dark parking lot, and I ran. For all I knew, you could've been the man who shot Chip and tried to shoot Lisa at that shopping center."

"The shopping center?" Adam leaned back in his chair and crossed his arms "Now I'm wondering how you happen to know about that. I'm quite sure that didn't make the evening news. Did the shooter tell you?"

"Don't be ridiculous."

"Then you must've heard it from her."

Adam watched Eric's eyes and saw the pupils move back and forth. It was what he'd been waiting for. That little movement of the eyes when a player realizes he's holding a losing hand.

"I...I told you," Eric stammered. "I haven't spoken to Lisa."

Now. Last card. Down and dirty.

"It would be a little difficult to speak to her, wouldn't it? She's been dead for sixteen years."

Eric's pupils moved rapidly, then froze when realization of what Adam had said struck home. His brows dipped into a frown. He turned his head away. The smell of arrogance was gone.

Adam waited.

Eric kept his head averted, staring at the wall. In almost a whisper, he said, "Chip must have told you about Lisa. Then he does have his memory back."

"Some of it," Adam said. "We also got quite a bit from her."

Actually, from a hole in her backyard.

Eric turned his head slowly back to Adam. He looked both surprised and confused. "From...her?"

"From the woman who's been masquerading as Lisa. Julia White. As a matter of fact, she called me a little while ago, asking for help."

"She...called you? Your help for what?"

"She was frightened. She's been shot at, her house has been torn apart. She wants protection. From you."

Eric slammed his hand on the table. "That bitch! That lousy bitch!"

He sprang from his chair, skidding it backwards, shrieking against the floor. He stomped to the wall and smacked his palm against it hard. It sounded like a rifle shot in the closed room.

"That lousy, lying bitch!" Eric smacked the wall again. "She turned on me. That bitch turned on me to save her own ass."

Eric faced the wall for several moments. When he turned around, he tried to appear calm. Beads of perspiration on his forehead made it impossible. His voice was weak.

"You can't prove anything. You have no proof of anything."

"We have the check you gave her for ten thousand dollars. We also have the letters you wrote. By the way, why did you sign the letters with a C? Some kind of pet name she had for you?"

Eric ignored the question. "You have nothing. So what if I wrote her letters, gave her money? It proves nothing."

"We have more," Adam said, "but I won't go into that now. What you should really be worried about is Julia's testimony. You said she'd do anything to save herself. What would her testimony do to you?"

Eric paced the room. When he spoke, it was to himself.

"She'd do it. That scheming bitch would testify against me, put it all on me."

Adam said in a calm tone. "I suggest you call a lawyer before you say anything else."

Eric stopped pacing and sat at the table again. His voice was a mumble. "That blackmailing little slut called you, turned against me, gave you the letters, the check, everything."

"No, Eric, she didn't give them to us. It's all in knowing where to look. Do you want to call a lawyer? I hope you know a good one. They're putting together a long list of charges against you right now."

Speeding, reckless driving, leaving the scene of an accident.

"You might want to consider making a statement before they drop the charges on you. Tell your side of it. It might help."

Adam locked his eyes on Eric's. He'd played all his cards. It was time for Eric to call or fold.

Eric sat, hunched forward, his elbows on his knees, playing with his watch.

"Kingston."

"Yes?"

"You're right. I want to make a statement, set the record straight. I'm not taking the blame for everything."

"Good idea."

"It was an accident, you know. I don't know what she told you, but Lisa's death was an accident. And the rest of it? It was all her idea. Did she tell you that? Did she tell you she forced me to go along with it? She said I did it, didn't she?"

"I can't divulge the contents of her statement, Eric, but I'll let them know you want to tell your side of it."

Adam walked to the door and reached for the knob.

"It was Cuddles," Eric whispered.

"What?"

"It was Cuddles. The C. She called me Cuddles."

Adam took one last look at Eric Richards before leaving the room. He had expected more of a challenge, but Eric was a pathetic disappointment. And a lousy poker player. And he sure as hell wasn't clever enough to engineer a sixteen-year masquerade.

CHAPTER

42

Stuart identified himself, stated the date, the time, and read Eric his Miranda rights. When he reached the end, he said, "Eric Richards, are you making this recorded statement voluntarily?"

Eric sat with his head bowed, his shoulders sagging forward.

"Yes," he mumbled.

"Please speak a little louder, Mr. Richards. Are you aware that you can have an attorney present?"

"Yes," Eric replied, only slightly louder than before.

Stuart shook his head and moved the small tape recorder across the table.

"Speak up, please. Do you wish to have an attorney present while you make this statement?"

Eric raised his head.

"Is this necessary?" There wasn't a trace of arrogance left. His baritone voice was now a pitiful whine.

"Answer yes or no, please. Do you wish to have an attorney present?"

"No."

"Do you wish to consult with an attorney before making this statement?"

"No. Can I have some water?"

"Later. Are you aware that anything you say can be used against you in a court of law?"

"Yes."

"State your full name, please."

"Eric Michael Richards."

Stuart pushed the recorder closer to him.

"Now, Mr. Eric Michael Richards, you may give your statement regarding the death of Lisa Weathers Richards."

Adam watched from the next room as Eric took a deep breath and ran the fingers of both hands through his thick uncombed hair. Brenda sat in the chair beside his with her legs crossed and her arms folded. She'd wanted to take Eric's statement herself, but deferred to Stuart since they were in his jurisdiction.

After another deep breath, Eric wiped a hand across his mouth.

"I'm making this statement to set the record straight regarding the death of my wife." He spoke into the recorder, watching it as though it were alive. "In spite of anything that's been said by Julia White, my wife's death was an accident, and everything that happened afterward was Julia's idea. Everything I did that day and everything I've done since then was because she..."

Stuart interrupted him.

"Save your excuses for the trial, Richards. Just tell us what happened."

Eric nodded.

"Yes, okay. Well, the day it happened, I was in Julia's apartment. I had gone there to settle a, uh, personal matter between us." He paused and wiped his mouth again. "I might as well say it. It'll come out anyway. Julia was blackmailing me. She threatened to tell my wife about our affair."

He looked at Stuart.

"An affair I'd already ended, by the way. Did she tell you that? Did she tell you I broke it off, that I wanted to save my marriage?"

Stuart pointed to the recorder.

"Just tell your story, please."

"It's the truth. I wanted to end it. That's when she threatened to tell my wife. I was already paying the rent on her apartment, but that wasn't enough. She wanted money. Ten thousand dollars. She said she'd return my letters and go away, get out of my life once and for all, if I gave her the money. I had no choice. That's why I went to her apartment that day. I gave her the check, and she went into the bedroom to get the letters. She kept them under her bed in a metal box."

Eric stopped talking and slapped his forehead.

"Those damn letters! Stupid. How could I have been so stupid?"

"You'll have to figure that out on your own time," Stuart said. "Please go on. You said Julia went into the bedroom to get a metal box."

Eric shook his head and mumbled, "Stupid," again.

He took a deep breath.

"As soon as Julia left the room to get the letters, Lisa burst into the apartment. Chip was with her. I don't know how she found out about Julia or the apartment, but she was hysterical. I'd never seen her like that. Before I knew what was happening, we were all four in the bedroom, and everything went crazy. Lisa attacked Julia, screaming and yelling like an animal. Chip was behind Lisa, trying to pull her off of Julia. I tried to get between them. It happened so fast. Julia had the metal box in her hands, using it like a shield."

Eric raised his hands in front of his face and held them apart, pantomiming what he was describing.

"Then she pulled it back and..." His hands moved back over his shoulder. "...swung it as hard as she could." He brought his hands around in a baseball swing. "She hit Chip instead of Lisa, and he stumbled backward."

As he listened from the next room, Adam pictured Chip behind Lisa, trying to pull his sister away from Julia, then falling from the blow to his head with the ripped pocket of Lisa's shirt clutched in his hand. The piece of cloth he'd carried with him for sixteen years.

Eric raked his hair again and continued his story.

"Julia fell onto the bed, and I managed to pull Lisa aside. She was still hysterical, screaming at the top of her lungs. She hit me, punched at me, tried to scratch my face. I did the only thing I could do. I slapped her. I wasn't trying to hurt her, you understand, it was only a slap, to bring her to her senses, but she fell. It was more like she tripped—our feet had tangled—and there was a dresser against the wall. Her head hit its corner. Next thing I knew, she was on the floor, holding her head and moaning. Then she called Chip's name. 'Chip, help me,' she said."

Eric spoke straight at Stuart.

"I only slapped her, like this..."

He pantomimed again, making a gentle slapping motion in the air. "...just to calm her down, and she fell and hit her head on the dresser. When she moaned and called Chip's name, I assumed she wasn't seriously injured."

His eyes searched Stuart's face as though waiting for Stuart to agree with him.

A look of disappointment slid across Eric's face when Stuart said, "What happened next?"

"I remembered Chip, but he wasn't in the bedroom. I heard noises in the living room and went to see if it was him. It was. Blood was gushing from his forehead, and he was thrashing around the room, bumping into furniture, like he was blind, out of his head. I tried to help him, to calm him, but he pushed me away and stumbled into the hallway. I followed, but he made it to the front door and ran from the house. I started to go after him, but that's when I heard a scream, so I ran back to the bedroom. The scream made me think Lisa had gone after Julia again. But Lisa lay on the floor by the dresser. Julia was kneeling beside her. Julia looked up at me and said she was dead."

Eric paused. "What was your name again?"

"Wilson. Detective Stuart Wilson."

"Wilson, this room is stuffy. I need a drink of water."

"Later. What did you do then?"

Eric wiped a hand across his mouth and cleared his throat.

"Julia said Lisa tried to get up, but couldn't make it and fell back on the floor. Julia went to her, to help her. That was the scream I'd heard, I guess. Julia screamed when she realized Lisa wasn't breathing. That's when I saw the blood in Lisa's hair and on the floor under her head. She had seemed all right when I left the room to find Chip, but she must've had a concussion, brain damage or something, from hitting her head on the dresser. There's no air in this damn room, Wilson. Is it too much to ask? A little water?"

Stuart punched the Stop button on the tape recorder.

"Water. Right."

Through the one-way mirror in the room next door, Adam watched Stuart leave to fetch water for Eric.

"I'll be right back," he said to Brenda. When she gave him a questioning look, he added, "I want to see if I've had any interesting phone calls lately."

At Stuart's desk, Adam called his answering machine. No new messages. Someone had called and disconnected. It could've been Julia. It could also have been a wrong number—or a telemarketer.

He leaned against the desk. He remembered seeing a forensics report among the papers in Brenda's file at Captain Tommy's Restaurant. There was a big hole in Eric's story, but he wanted to double check before he said anything. He'd have to go to his car. The file was in Brenda's attaché case in the trunk of the LeSabre along with Julia's metal box.

"Adam." Stuart walked toward him carrying a pitcher of water and a Styrofoam cup. "Any more calls from Julia White?"

Adam shook his head. "Anything on the shooter?"

"Not yet. We're still watching the car he ditched here in town, but I don't think he's dumb enough to go back for it. We got plenty of prints from the room at the Endicott and from the car he abandoned in Delaware. Should have a match by tomorrow morning." Stuart looked in the direction of the interview room. "In spite of the fairy tale he's weaving in there, I'm convinced he sent his hired gun to kill Chip and Julia."

"Maybe," said Adam.

Something else bothered him. Eric's reaction during the poker game—when he'd been tricked into believing Julia agreed to testify against him—didn't fit.

"Oh, I'm sure of it," Stuart said, "and I'm going to get it out of him before I'm through." He walked toward the interview room. "Ready for round two?"

"Ready." Adam fell in step behind him. "One more thing, Stuart. Ask him where Julia's metal box was when he ran into the bedroom after the scream?"

"Will do."

CHAPTER 43

Eric drank the first cup of water in loud gulps, then poured another one. He took a mouthful and swished it around in his mouth before swallowing.

Stuart watched with one finger poised over the tape recorder on the table between them. "Any time, Richards."

Eric yawned and rubbed his eyes with his knuckles, then nodded.

Stuart pushed a button and watched the tape spools begin to turn.

Eric cleared his throat. "Where was I?"

"You'd just returned to the bedroom because you heard a scream. Julia White told you your wife was dead."

"Yes, right. She hit her head on the dresser. That's what killed her."

"That metal box you talked about. Where was it when you reentered the bedroom?"

Eric frowned as if in deep thought, then shook his head. "I don't remember."

"Okay. Go ahead. What did you do then?"

"I picked up the phone to call the police and get an ambulance, but Julia grabbed the phone out of my hand. She said I needed to pull myself together before I did anything. Then she asked about Chip, where he was. I told her what had happened in the other room, how Chip was delirious and ran out the door. That's when we heard the commotion outside, tires screeching, people shouting.

We looked out the window and saw Chip lying in the street. He'd been hit by a car. A few minutes later, a police car pulled up. I don't know if someone called them or they were just passing by. They sure got there fast. Then an ambulance came and took Chip away. We couldn't tell if he was breathing or not.

"That's when Julia said she needed a drink, and I should have one, too. We went into the living room and she fixed them. We might've had a couple. I don't remember. We talked about what had happened, how Lisa's death had been an accident, but we didn't know about Chip. We didn't know if he was dead or not. If he was still alive, she said, we didn't know if he would back us up and say it was an accident. Julia said we should find out about Chip before we did anything else. We waited a while, maybe an hour, then she called the hospital.

"They said he was there, but when she asked how he was, they said they could only give out information to relatives. Julia lied and said she was his sister. After she got off the phone, she said they didn't know how badly he was hurt, but he didn't remember what happened to him. He didn't even know who he was. They found his identity by going through his wallet. They asked her if she could come to the hospital. They needed a relative to sign papers and whatever.

"I thought it was a crazy idea, her going to the hospital posing as Lisa, but she said we had to, we had to know if Chip was going to be all right and what he was going to say. I thought it was crazy, but she pulled it off. She was quite a little actress, you know. She had this collection of wigs in different colors and styles and liked to make herself up as different people. Sometimes I'd go to see her, and she'd be Elizabeth Taylor or some other movie star. Marilyn Monroe was my favorite. Sometimes, she would…"

"I'm sure it was a real turn-on," Stuart said, "but some other time if you don't mind. Can we get back to your going to the hospital?"

"Sure. Anyway, that's what she wore to the hospital, her Marilyn Monroe wig, and she kept her sunglasses on all the time we were there. Lisa had this very distinctive eye color. Light blue. That's why Julia kept the sunglasses on. Her eyes are brown. She even took Lisa's wallet to the hospital in case they wanted to see identification. They didn't, but she was prepared for anything.

"We saw Chip, but he didn't recognize us. When Julia talked to the doctors, pretending to be Lisa, they said he would survive his injuries, but they didn't know how long his memory loss would last."

Eric picked up his cup of water. He drank it, then slumped back in his chair staring at the ceiling. "She fooled them all right. If I'd known what it was going to lead to, what she was going to put me through for the next sixteen years, I wouldn't have gone along with it. I couldn't do a thing without her approval. Calling me every day, telling me do this, do that, while she's living the good life. Vacations in Hawaii and Europe, a new Mercedes every other year. You know what she did? She made me buy a condo in Jamaica. Business expense, she said, clients could use it. Shit, no one used it but her. And that's not all…"

"Save your pity routine for the jury, Richards," Stuart said, "and get on with the story."

In the next room, Brenda turned to Adam with an expression of sarcastic amusement. "Poor Eric," she said.

Adam nodded and grinned. It was the first remorse he'd seen from Eric Richards. No remorse for Lisa or Chip, only for himself, for what he'd gone through. Poor, pathetic Eric.

Adam found himself growing more anxious to get to his car and confirm his suspicions.

CHAPTER

44

For the next ten minutes, Eric told on tape how Julia had her plan in place by the time they returned to her apartment from the hospital. She convinced him that if Chip didn't regain his memory, he wouldn't be able to back up their story about Lisa's death being an accident. The police could charge Eric with killing her.

Then there was the money to think about. With Lisa dead, Eric would get her inheritance and her share of the family business. But if Eric went to jail for killing her, he wouldn't get a penny.

"I didn't like any of it at first," Eric said. "But she convinced me it made sense to keep Lisa alive. She was sure she could pull it off. She'd already proven it at the hospital. She could get contact lenses the color of Lisa's eyes, dye her hair the same color, learn to duplicate Lisa's signature, even copy Lisa's voice. She would stay in the background, keep her distance from people who knew Lisa, move out of town. She would sign Lisa's name on checks and other documents and talk to people on the phone in Lisa's voice. Eventually, I agreed with her plan. Hell, anyone would have done the same thing under the circumstances, wouldn't they?"

Eric looked at Stuart for a response.

Stuart said, "Do you need more water?"

Another look of disappointment crossed Eric's face. He leaned away from the table.

"No, I'm fine, and that's all I have to say. No matter what that lying bitch told you, you know the truth. Lisa's death was an accident, and everything that happened after that was her idea. I only went along with it because I had no choice. So that's it. You can turn that thing off."

Stuart said, "I'm afraid that's not quite it, Richards."

"What do you mean? I've told you everything."

"Not quite. You haven't told us about the man you hired to follow Chip Weathers, to keep track of him and report to you. Do you admit that you hired such a man?"

"Yes, I hired him. Chip insisted on living like a homeless bum. Even the shrinks couldn't straighten him out. I wanted to make sure he was all right."

"I want that man's name," Stuart said, "and I want to know where he is."

"Why? I don't understand why you'd want that. That has nothing to do with…"

Stuart cut him off.

"Why? I'll tell you why. I don't think you hired that man because you wanted to take care of Chip. I think you hired him because you and your accomplice, your little actress, were afraid Chip would remember things. Like what his sister looked like, and what happened in that apartment. You wanted to make sure if he got his memory back, you'd be the first to know. Oh, you'd take care of him all right. I can imagine how you two would've taken care of him."

Stuart leaned far across the table.

"I think when Chip came here to see Adam Kingston, you got worried. You were afraid Adam would live up to his reputation and find out what happened to Lisa. So you sent your bloodhound here to take care of Chip. You know what else I think?"

Stuart was on his feet and moving slowly around the table toward Eric.

"I think you and Julia White had a falling out. You wanted the box and everything in it that would tie you to Lisa's death, but she wouldn't give it to you. After you searched her house and came up empty, you put her on your hit list along with Chip. But that's where it went wrong, isn't it? She realized what you were up to and turned against you to save herself."

Stuart stood over him now, shouting, his face inches from Eric's.

"That man has already killed at least two people, Richards. He tried to kill Chip Weathers and Julia White, and he's still out there. I want his name, and I want to know where to find him. Have I made myself clear?"

Eric cowered from Stuart's angry face.

"But...that's ridiculous."

"His name, Richards. His name."

"You want his name? Sure, I'll give you his name. His name was Roland Sommers. And you want to know where he is? He's dead, that's where. Roland Sommers died of pneumonia six weeks ago."

CHAPTER
45

While Stuart and Brenda made plans to return Eric Richards to Baltimore where he'd be charged with his role in Lisa's death, Adam went outside to the LeSabre. Learning the man Chip knew as Cueball was dead and couldn't be the shooter had been a surprise, but it would have to wait. Other things were more prominent in his mind.

After retrieving Julia White's metal box and Brenda's attaché case from the trunk, he climbed into the back seat. In Brenda's file, he found the medical examiner's report and the information he was looking for.

Cause of death—multiple fractures to the skull. Three hard blows, weapon unknown.

He replaced the report in Brenda's file and raised the metal box onto his lap. As his fingers moved lightly over the lid and around the edges, he hoped what Julia White had buried in her backyard would fill in the gaps in Eric's story. After several seconds, the images began.

The bedroom...dark...three, no, four figures...voices, loud, angry... violent movement...arms flailing, grabbing...the flat gray shape, rising, falling sharply, striking one of the figures...Chip...running away, red flowing over him...outside now...cars, traffic noises...the bedroom again... someone on the floor, blonde hair—Lisa...reaching out, moaning...another figure crouched over her...the gray shape, rising, falling...Lisa screaming...

rising, striking…striking again…blond hair turning red…spreading, cover-
ing the floor…fading…

Adam opened his eyes and looked at the box, rusty and discol-
ored after sixteen years underground. Now he knew what the gray,
flat, rectangular object he had seen several times in his images was.
And he knew who killed Lisa Weathers Richards.

He hurried inside. Stuart and Brenda were at Stuart's desk.
Adam handed the attaché case to Brenda and placed the metal box
in front of Stuart.

"Well," he said, "so this is what she hit Chip with. This inno-
cent-looking box caused his amnesia and started this whole mess.
Now if we only had the dreaded dresser that did poor Lisa in, our
collection of weapons would be complete."

He laughed at his little joke but stopped short when Adam and
Brenda stared at him.

"What?" he asked.

"The dresser didn't kill her," Adam said.

Brenda grinned at Adam. "I was wondering if you picked up
on that."

Stuart's head swiveled between them. "You guys know something I don't know?"

"Show him," Adam said.

She pulled the report from her attaché case, laid it on the desk,
and pointed to a paragraph in the middle of the page.

"Forensics on Lisa's head injuries," she said. "Multiple fractures. She was hit three times with a blunt object, not once by the
corner of a dresser."

Stuart read, then slumped, his face flushed with anger. "He
lied. The bastard lied. All that stuff about hitting her head on the
dresser was garbage."

Brenda said, "Looks that way."

"Maybe," Adam said.

Brenda turned to him. "Uh-oh. What is it, Adam?"

"I think Eric told the truth," Adam said, "as much as he knew of it. He slapped her, she fell against the dresser, and he left the room to find Chip."

"And then," Stuart said, still angry, "he came back, saw she was alive, and finished her off."

"Or..." Adam took a deep breath. "It happened while he was out of the room."

He looked first at the puzzled expression on Stuart's face, then at the thoughtful one on Brenda's. She was putting it together.

"The scream Eric heard," she said, "while he was in the hallway..."

Adam nodded. "Lisa, not Julia."

"Jesus." Stuart appeared to be catching up. "She did it. She killed Lisa while Eric was out of the room. Then, when Eric came back, she..."

"Played him like a violin." Brenda finished his sentence. "She let Eric believe Lisa died because he slapped her and knocked her against the dresser."

"Well, I'll be damned," Stuart said. "That poor dumb son of a bitch. But he'll get no sympathy from me. He's still a rotten bastard, and when you get him back to Baltimore, I hope you pile enough charges on him to put him away for a long time. She's the one, though. She's the one who goes down for murder. The question is, can we prove it? How about a murder weapon? It'd be nice to have that, at least know what it was."

"We have it," Adam said.

Stuart wore a puzzled look again. "What? Where?"

"Right in front of you," Adam said, nodding at the metal box on the desk between them. "She used it as a shield when Lisa

attacked her and used it as a weapon when she hit Chip. While Eric
was out of the room, she used it again."

Stuart leaned forward, staring at the box. "Okay," he said.
"We'll…we'll send it to the FBI lab. They'll find her prints. They
can find prints on a gnat's hair."

"Which would only prove," Brenda said, "that it was her box."

Stuart hesitated. "Right. Okay. They'll find blood, Lisa's blood,
with skin and hair fragments."

"Or Chip's," Brenda said. "Even if they do find Lisa's, it only
proves it was the murder weapon, not who hit her with it."

Stuart slouched in his chair. "Yeah, right. So we've got squat
to prove Julia killed Lisa. She'll say Eric did it and forced her to go
along with it. Her story against his. She gets accessory, co-conspir-
acy, fraud. Couple of years, and she's home free. It sucks. It really
fucking sucks." He looked at Brenda and flushed. "Sorry. That
slipped out."

"Forget it," she said. "I've heard it before. But let's not forget
the man with the gun."

Stuart shot forward with renewed energy.

"Yes. Even if it's not the same man Eric hired to keep track
of Chip—what's his name, Sommers—that just means he found
another hit man. If we nail the shooter for killing Cookson and
the prostitute, he might make a deal and give us Eric for the
attempts on Chip and Julia. We may not get Julia for killing Lisa,
but she'll go down for conspiracy along with everything else. I
could live with that."

Brenda's disappointment showed on her face. "It's not what I
wanted, but it may be the best we can do."

Stuart nodded at the metal box. "What about this?"

"I'll take it with me," Brenda said. "It's useless as evidence, though, because of the way it was obtained." She turned to Adam with a sly, teasing look.

Adam responded with a shrug of innocence. "It served its purpose, gave me aces to play."

Her look melted into a smile. "Okay, no argument. Eric's statement covers it. We'll forgive you—this time."

Adam winked at her. "Thanks."

Brenda's expression became serious again. "All right. We have Eric where he belongs, but Julia's still out there, and so is the shooter."

Adam said, "Stuart, can you put out a description on her and the gold Mercedes?"

"Way ahead of you. Did it while you were outside. If she's in town, we'll find her."

"She may call you, Adam," Brenda said. "She doesn't know we have Eric. She might still come to you to play out her act of blaming him."

"Let's hope so," said Stuart. "In the meantime, we've got another big problem. The shooter doesn't know we have Eric either. He's out there looking for Julia, trying to finish what Eric hired him to do. Not that she doesn't deserve it, but we need her testimony."

"How about this?" Brenda said. "We use the media. TV, radio, newspapers. Get them to splash it around that Eric's been arrested. If the shooter hears it, he might call it off." She got a nod from Stuart, then turned to Adam. "What do you think?"

"Maybe." Adam leaned forward. "If…" He waited until he had their full attention. "If Eric hired him."

They both stared at him. Brenda spoke first. "There's that *maybe* word again. What is it, Adam? Back at the hospital, you said something didn't fit, but you never said what it was."

"It struck me as strange," Adam said, "that Eric would send a killer, then come here himself. You'd think he'd stay as far away as possible."

"Don't forget," Brenda said, "he sneaked into town after he told his office he was staying in Philadelphia. He thought he could slip in and grab what Julia had in her box without anyone knowing he was here."

Adam shook his head. "But he went to the hospital to see Chip and told them who he was. Remember the message from Phil?"

She nodded. "I see what you mean. If he wanted to sneak in and out of town, he wouldn't have made a scene and told them who he was."

"There's something else," Adam said.

Brenda sighed. "Okay, Professor, let's have it."

"Do you remember Eric's reaction when he assumed Julia had given us a statement, that she was willing to testify against him?"

"Sure," Stuart said. "He was mad as hell. So?"

"He was mad," Adam continued, "but before that, he was surprised, shocked, that she would turn against him."

Stuart said it again. "So?"

"So if he'd sent someone to kill her, why would it be a shock that she'd turn on him if she found out about it?"

Stuart appeared to mull it over.

Brenda was a step ahead of him. "You're right," she said. "It doesn't fit."

"So you're saying," Stuart said, "that Eric Richards didn't hire the shooter?"

"Eric may be a lot of things," Adam said, "but I don't think he's a killer, not even by proxy. I don't think he has what it takes."

"And what does it take?" Brenda asked, teasing again.

"It's hard to put into words. You might call it, uh, you might say it's..."

"Balls?" Brenda suggested.

Adam bowed his head to her. "Thank you."

Stuart stood. "Okay. *She* did it."

His excitement had returned, and he paced behind his desk, jabbing the air with his finger.

"Listen to this. It all fits. Eric called her and told her Chip was coming to see you. She got worried and decided it was time to eliminate Chip once and for all. She hired the shooter."

He stopped pacing and looked from one of them to the other.

Brenda said, "But what about the shots fired at her at the shopping center?"

"Simple," Stuart said. "It was a set up. Think about it, Adam. No one else knew you were going there to meet her, right?"

"Right."

"Okay." Stuart's enthusiasm appeared to grow as he talked, paced and jabbed. "She hires a man to kill Chip. He almost succeeds, but doesn't. She thinks you know too much, so she agrees to meet you and arranges for her shooter to be there. We think he's shooting at her, but it's really you he's after. When that fails, she comes up with a new plan. She calls you to make you think Eric did it and now he's after her, and she's willing to give him up. That makes Eric look like the one responsible for everything, and she's in the clear."

Brenda asked, "Who trashed her house?"

Stuart frowned, then his face brightened. "She did it herself. To make her story look good." He settled anxious eyes on Adam. "Well, what do you think?"

Adam stood and stretched. "To tell you the truth, I think I'm too tired to think anymore."

He glanced at the clock on the wall behind Stuart. Twenty past midnight. He yawned, then mumbled, "It's been a long day."

Brenda stood beside him.

"I think Adam's right. There's nothing more we can do tonight. Let's pick it up tomorrow morning. We might have more to work with."

They agreed to meet at Stuart's desk the next morning.

CHAPTER
46

"Where's your car?" Adam asked.

He pulled in a deep breath of night air as the door of the station house closed behind them with a soft click.

Brenda looked toward the parking lot. "Right behind yours."

"Where are you staying?"

"The Comfort Inn. Twenty-Ninth Street."

"It's nice," he said. "Not far from my place."

As they walked to their cars, Brenda said, "At least we've got Eric, and Chip is safe."

"Stuart's men are staying at the hospital?"

"Around the clock, for as long as it takes."

"Stuart's a good man."

"Yes, he is," she said. "Even if he does get a little carried away sometimes. But he could be right, you know."

"About what?"

"About Julia White hiring the killer and you being his target. He's missed you twice. She might even be desperate enough to try it herself. Like Stuart said, that could be why she called and said she wanted to meet with you. Don't tell me you haven't thought about it."

"I did, but she hasn't called again. She could be on her way to Canada or South America by now."

"Or she may have given up trying to reach you on the phone. She might be waiting on your doorstep when you get home."

"Thanks for the comforting thought."

"You're welcome."

They reached the LeSabre. Adam went to the driver's side and fished in his pocket for keys. Brenda walked around the front of the car, sliding her fingers across the hood and along the fender. She stopped beside the passenger door.

"By the way," she said, "I meant to tell you before. Nice car."

Adam unlocked his door but didn't open it. "Thanks. It was my wife's."

"Stuart told me how you lost her. I'm sorry."

"It's okay. It was a long time ago."

A soft smile formed on her lips. "You sound like me."

"Like you?"

She broke eye contact and looked away. "I was very close to my dad. He died ten years ago. His heart. People would say things like how hard it must've been to lose him and how much I must've missed him. I'd lie and say it was okay."

"You get to be a pretty good liar," he said, "after awhile."

She turned her head toward him again, and he remembered his first impression of her. Attractive, but cold. He knew now he'd been wrong about the cold part, but not the attractive part. She seemed even more so now. It may have been because he knew her better. Or it may have been because the moonlight added silver highlights to her hazel eyes.

Brenda stacked her hands on the roof of the car and rested her chin on them. "You never remarried," she said. "Ever think about it?"

He shrugged. "Someday. Maybe."

She scrunched her face as though a sudden pain had hit her. "Ooooh, that M word again."

Adam winced. "Sorry." He glanced at her left hand. No ring. Funny. He hadn't noticed or thought about it before. "How about you? Ever married?"

"Divorced. Four years and counting."

"Think you'll jump in again?"

"I don't think much about it," she said, "but you never know. Someday." She gave him a quick playful wink. "Maybe."

They shared a laugh over her throwing his word back at him, and their eyes held for a moment. Adam wondered why he suddenly felt uncomfortable, why he couldn't think of anything to say, why he felt butterflies flapping inside his chest. He was glad when she broke the awkward silence.

"Some people like living alone, I suppose."

Adam's curiosity made him ask, "Do you live alone?" He was immediately sorry he'd asked. It was a stupid question and none of his business.

"No," she said. "I live with three guys."

Adam searched her face for a sign that she was joking. He saw none. She seemed serious and very interested in the small circles she'd begun drawing on the roof of his car with a fingertip.

"Three guys," he said. "That's interesting."

"Chico was my first. We've been together for three years now."

She began making larger circles on the car, watching them intently.

"But then I realized one wasn't enough, so I moved Harpo in. He's the quiet one."

She stopped drawing circles and raised her head. Her expression was dead serious.

"After that," she said, "it was only a matter of time before Groucho came along."

Adam said, "So you live with the Marx Brothers." He was beginning to get a clue. "That must make for a lot of fun."

Finally, her grin broke through.

"It sure does. They're my parakeets. You didn't think..."

Adam shook his head. "No, of course not. I knew all along."

"Sure you did, Professor."

They had another laugh together.

"Okay," Adam confessed, "you had me going for a second. So you like birds. You should talk to Ellie."

"Who's Ellie?"

He waved it off. "Just a friend who thinks she's my mother." He noticed Brenda's complexion. Smooth, soft. He hadn't paid attention to that before either. "What's it like, having birds in the house?"

"Oh, they're a pain sometimes. They can make a lot of racket when they get stirred up, and cleaning bird cages is not my idea of fun. But it sure beats coming home to an empty apartment every night. How about you? Any pets?"

Adam grinned across the roof of the car. "I'm thinking about it."

She grinned back.

Adam felt an awkward silence fill the space between them and couldn't think of anything else to say. The best he could come up with was, "I, uh, guess I'd better get home. In case Julia calls."

Brenda stepped away from the car. "I suppose you're right. It's been a long day, and I'm exhausted."

She raised her arms above her head and stretched. Adam noticed how it pulled her blouse tight across her breasts. In his own chest, the flapping grew louder. Bigger and stronger than butterflies. More like parakeets. "Yeah, I'm kinda beat myself," he managed to say.

"Good night, Adam," she said. "Keep your eyes open for evil blondes on your way home."

He watched her walk to her car and get in. He watched her roll
down her window and turn on the ignition. When she looked at
him with a wide smile and a wave, he smiled and waved back. He
didn't move until her car was out of sight.

It's been a long time, fella. Too damn long.

*   *   *

The flapping in his chest quieted by the time he had driven
a few blocks toward home, but he still thought about Brenda.
Intelligent, resourceful and, contrary to his first impression of her,
a caring and sensitive person. All the qualities he liked in people.
She was the kind of person—the kind of woman—he could...

He caught himself and felt a blush of foolish embarrassment.

*Forget it. You're tired, thinking crazy. A woman like that is bound to have
someone. Engaged or something. Get a grip.*

He reached a hand to the nape of his neck and rubbed hard,
trying to erase the weariness he felt and, with an effort, switched
his thoughts to something more serious. Julia White. Three blows
to the head of a helpless woman and some quick thinking had
bought her a new identity, a comfortable lifestyle, and an obedient
puppet in Eric Richards. Had she seen her masquerade coming to
an end and decided to do whatever was necessary to keep that life?
Eric didn't have the balls to hire a killer, he was sure of that. Did
she? It was possible. But waiting on his doorstep? Not likely. He
reached under the front seat and pulled out the box containing his
Beretta. It needed cleaning. That's why he would carry it inside with
him tonight.

CHAPTER
47

The delivery door on the side of the Endicott House was recessed three feet back from the sidewalk along Thirty-fourth Street, more than enough room for a man of his size to hide in. Every time he heard a car, he'd lean his head out far enough to see if it was a red four-door sedan. Sooner or later, he knew the man he was waiting for would come home, park in the garage down the street, and walk to the side entrance of the Colonial Towers across from where he waited. The opposite of the routine he'd used before the ride up the highway to meet the blonde.

He knew Kingston wasn't home yet. An hour ago, he'd taken the elevator to the top floor of the garage and walked down all four levels looking for the red LeSabre.

He checked his watch. Almost 12:30 a.m.

"C'mon, Adam," he whispered in his dark alcove. "You can't stay out all night. You need your beauty sleep, not that you're going to get any."

He chuckled to himself, but cut it short when he heard a car coming. He leaned out.

No. Not a red sedan. A little gold car, one of those foreign jobs. He pulled back into the darkness and watched it slow and pull to the curb directly across the street. He couldn't see who was driving until the light inside the car came on and the driver turned her head in his direction to pick up something from the passenger seat. He recognized her.

"Well, I'll be damned."

He watched her raise a cell phone, flip it open, and punch in numbers. She sat for a few seconds with the phone at her ear, then closed it with a slap and threw it onto the seat.

"Well now, Adam, old buddy, looks like your bitch is pissed. What'd you do?"

The light inside the car went off, but he'd seen enough to know it was her. He'd gotten a good look at her at that shopping center. She walked right past his car, and he liked what he saw. Tight pants, big tits, full lips, classy but sexy.

He watched her for several minutes more. Twice she slammed her hand against the steering wheel.

"She's really pissed. You're in deep shit, Adam."

Then he got an idea, one he liked very much. It gave him a warm feeling in his crotch and he felt himself swelling. He left his hiding place and walked across the street to her car. By the time he stood beside the driver's door, he had a full erection. Her window was down three inches. He bent over and looked in the narrow opening with a pleasant smile.

"Excuse me, miss."

Her head turned at the sound of his voice.

He broadened his smile. "Hope I didn't scare you."

"What...what do you want?"

"I'm the security guard here at this building." He jerked a thumb at the Colonial Towers behind him. "I saw you sitting here alone and wondered if you needed help."

The security guard bit did it, like always. She relaxed. He liked her eyes. Light blue. He'd never seen eyes like that before.

"No, I'm fine," she said. "I'm waiting for someone. Thank you."

"If you don't mind me asking, miss, I mean it's just my job, security and all, but are you waiting for someone who lives in this building?"

"Yes, as a matter of fact, I'm waiting for Mr. Kingston. He lives here."

He gave her a sad, sympathetic look. "Well, I hate to disappoint you, but I saw Mr. Kingston leave a little while ago. He said he wouldn't be back for a couple of days."

"Oh," she said. He could tell she was disappointed by the way she said it and knew he was playing it right.

"I'm really sorry to be the one to tell you, but he was with another woman, and they looked real lovey-dovey to me, if you know what I mean."

She slumped into her seat.

Soon he'd be balling Kingston's bitch. "But," he said, smiling again, "you don't have to worry about it. I'm twice the man he is."

She looked up at him, like she didn't know what he was talking about. "What did you say?"

"Forget about him. He's nothing. I'm the one you want. I'll give it to you real good."

Now he saw that look on her face, the one they always used when they wanted it real bad, but tried to play hard to get, like they were insulted and mad, like he was a piece of shit.

"I think you'd better get away from here," she said. "Right now."

"Tell you what we'll do, sweetcakes. I've got a room at the Comfort Inn. We'll just hop around there and have ourselves a party."

He watched her face. The look was still there, even better than before. She was real good at playing the innocent bitch role.

"You'd better leave," she said. "I'm calling the police."

She was looking right at him, couldn't take her eyes off him, and patting her hand around on the passenger seat like she really would call the police if she found the phone.

Her hand stopped patting when he stuck the barrel of the gun in the opening of her window.

"Slide over, sweetcakes," he told her. "We're going to have us a real good time."

CHAPTER
48

In Room 128 at the Comfort Inn, Brenda was showered and dressed by 8:15 and on the phone. Timmy Kaminski's wife said he was in the bathroom, but she would get him.

"Dammit, McCort, I was in the shower," she finally heard him say on the other end, somewhat out of breath.

"Overslept again, huh?"

"No, I didn't oversleep. It's only eight o'clock for God's sake, and I'm standing here dripping wet in my birthday suit."

"Actually, it's quarter after eight, but keep still a minute. I want to savor the image of you standing there naked."

"In your dreams, McCort, in your dreams." He laughed. She knew he never stayed mad about anything for long. "By the way," he said, "where the hell you been? You didn't call in yesterday."

"I'm still in Ocean City. Things got a little busy here. Do you have anything for me?"

"Yeah, we located the owner of the Skylark from the garage. Susan Michaels?"

"Good. Where?"

"In intensive care. That's why she never reported her car stolen. She's been there four days, barely hanging on."

"Intensive care? Where? Linglestown?"

"No, Harrisburg. Linglestown is..."

"I know. Right outside Harrisburg. Is she going to make it?"

"Yeah, looks like it."

"Good. What happened to her?"

"She was beaten and strangled, nearly to death. A neighbor heard her screaming and pounded on the door. The attacker ran off, and the neighbor found her in the bedroom."

"So our guy did it, then took her car."

"Looks that way."

"Come on, Kaminski, what do you mean looks that way?"

"Gimme a break. I just got all this late yesterday, and she's not able to talk yet. Let me get my pants on and get to work, and I'll find out."

"Not yet. I'm still enjoying the image."

"And I'm freezing my butt off here."

She laughed. "Okay, but call me as soon as you hear something."

"Right. Oh, by the way. How about that psychic you were going to check out?"

"What about him?"

"Is he for real or what? I know how you feel about those people. Did you check him out or not?"

"Yes, I did."

"So what's he like?"

"He's…all right."

"What does that mean?"

"It means he's all right," she said. "I've got to run. Call me if you get anything."

"Whoa. Wait a minute there, McCort. Your voice cracked."

"It did not."

"Yes, it did. Your voice always cracks when you get that feeling about a guy. What's going on down there? You and that psychic got something going?"

"Put your pants on, Kaminski. Get to work."

"Well," he said slowly, "maybe not."

"What do you mean?"

"I mean Beth's looking at me kinda funny. Maybe I'll go in a little late."

"You're hopeless, you know that? Don't you ever think about anything else?"

"Hey, don't knock it, McCort. There's more to life than chasing bad guys, you know. You should try it."

"Call me when you get something."

After she hung up, Brenda finished packing. Her voice hadn't cracked. Kaminski was crazy. Sure, she'd thought about it for a second or two, but anyone could see Adam Kingston didn't think about any woman but his late wife.

*   *   *

In Room 106 at the Comfort Inn, he put on the same shorts and shirt he'd worn his first day in Ocean City. He'd only packed two changes, and the outfit he'd worn yesterday had been ruined last night. He would've brought more clothes, but he hadn't expected to be here this long. It should've been over by now. Today for sure. He didn't know exactly how yet, but he'd figure it out over breakfast.

He walked to the window and spread the horizontal blinds with his fingers for a look outside. The sun was already bright and hot, and it wasn't eight-thirty yet. Across the swimming pool, he saw a man and woman carrying suitcases out of a room.

"Hope you guys had a good time last night," he said aloud. "I sure did."

He snickered and went back to the bed to finish packing his travel bag. He put the box of trash bags in first, then his new roll of duct tape. He slipped the cell phone he'd taken from the gold Mercedes into his pocket. It might come in handy.

She'd been good, he thought. Real good. A fighter. He liked it when they fought.

He packed his weapons last, wanting them on top. After putting the rifle sections in the bag, securely wrapped in towels, he checked the clip of his handgun to make sure it was full.

First, one in each knee. Yeah. That way he can't run, and there won't be any hurry. Then one in each wrist. Heard that was painful as hell. Maybe the shoulders next. Or the elbows.

He looked around the room one last time. The bed looked fine with just the bedspread over it. He'd stuffed the bloody sheets and his bloody clothes in a trash bag and put it in the dumpster.

Shit. People steal sheets from motels all the time. No big deal.

He'd turned the mattress over so the bloodstains didn't show. It could be weeks before anyone turned it again. He'd be in Acapulco by then, maybe Brazil.

He picked up the travel bag and started toward the door, but stopped, remembering something important.

The magazine. Christ!

He thought for a second before he remembered where he'd left it. On the nightstand by the bed. He went over, picked it up and took another look at the picture of the man he was going to kill.

"Fifteen years," he muttered between clinched teeth. "Fifteen years you owe me. Well, today is payday, old buddy."

He unzipped the bag and shoved the *Newsweek* inside, then pulled the zipper closed with such force the bag nearly slid off the bed. He grabbed it and stomped to the door, thinking he might skip breakfast and go get the son of a bitch right now.

He opened the door a few inches and looked outside. He wouldn't get careless now. No one had seen him bring her into the room last night. He'd made sure of that. And no one would see him leave this morning. The desk clerk wouldn't give a decent description. They never did. They saw so many people every day, and he'd worn the baseball cap and sunglasses.

He checked across the pool first. The man and woman he'd seen a few minutes ago were gone, and he saw no one else on that side. Next, he looked to the left far enough to see the sidewalk going toward the front of the motel. No one in sight. His room was the third from the front. He'd only have to walk that far, sneak past the office, then cross the street quickly to where he'd left the little gold car. He didn't park it on the motel lot. Someone might remember seeing it.

He had to lean out a little farther to check to the right, down past ten or twelve rooms. No one there either.

Wait! Someone coming out of the last door. A woman.

He pulled back inside and closed the door. The woman looked familiar. He stepped to the window and peeked through the blinds for a better view. Light brown hair, nice build, carrying an attaché case and a small suitcase. Dressed nice, like a businesswoman off to a meeting. He watched her come toward him. When she was two doors away, he saw the badge clipped to the waistband of her skirt.

The bitch cop from the garage. Albert. Fuck!

He thought fast, trying not to panic. She had to be here looking for him. How did they track him so fast? He unzipped the bag and grabbed his hand gun, listening as her footsteps grew louder. Her shadow crossed his window. He pointed the gun at his door.

She didn't stop. He hurried to the window and watched her enter the motel office.

Okay. She don't know we're in the same motel. Just stay put until she's gone. Wait. She's got a car. Cops drive big cars. Anything would be better than that little gold piece of shit. And I can use her.

He picked up his bag and put the gun inside, leaving the bag partly unzipped so he could reach in quickly, and went to the door. He opened it carefully and stepped outside as his plan formed in his mind.

Chapter
49

Adam did double time on the treadmill, working up a sweat, thinking about what he had to do. During his years with the Bureau, too many times he had to tell surviving family members a loved one was dead. He'd told parents their child's body had been found and husbands and wives the person they shared their life with was not coming home. Now he had to tell Chip what happened to his sister.

When his aching legs told him they'd had enough, he stopped the treadmill and leaned forward on the handlebar, gasping for breath, letting the stinging wash of perspiration flood over him. It didn't help. What he had to do had never been easy, and it hadn't gotten any easier.

After his shower, he dressed and made his way to the kitchen. The coffee was ready. The phone rang during his first cup.

He grabbed it and answered.

"Mr. Kingston?" a woman's voice said.

Not Julia. Brenda. Calling him Mr. Kingston. An alarm went off in Adam's gut. "Yes."

"My name is Brenda McCort," she continued. "I'm a homicide detective from Baltimore. We've never met, but I have some information for you."

Never met? What the hell is going on? Play along.

"What sort of information, detective?"

"I can't discuss it over the phone. We have to meet."

Adam's mind raced so fast, it was hard to think.

Stall. Keep her talking.

"I'm sorry, detective, but I have other plans. I'm afraid you'll have to tell me over the phone."

"No. We have to meet. It's important."

"How do I know you're who you say you are?"

"You know my captain. Captain Thomas Jackson. He worked with you in Dayton, Ohio."

"Okay. I know him. How is he? Uh, how's his wife?"

"His wife? She's fine. Mary's just fine."

Thomas? Mary? What is she up to?

"Exactly what do you want, detective?"

"Captain Jackson gave me specific instructions. We have to meet in person. It's very important."

Adam listened hard, straining to hear sounds in the background. Faint traffic noises. Nothing else.

"All right," he said. "Where?"

Silence. A change in tone over the line, like a hand over the phone. Faint, muffled voices.

"The police station," she said. "Meet me there. Right away."

* * *

He punched the off button of the cell phone he'd held against her face and tossed it into the back seat. He smiled at the bitch ⌐p in the driver's seat. He'd made her stick her hands through the ⌐nings in the steering wheel, then put her own handcuffs on her ⌐s. With a little effort, she could drive, but that was all.

⌐ou did real good, sweetcakes," he said, pressing the strip of ⌐e back in place over her mouth. "Now, we wait." He jabbed the barrel of his gun playfully into her ribs. "But don't you worry. As soon as I take care of business, we're going to party."

Her hazel eyes were on fire, burning holes in him, and he knew she'd be good, a real fighter. Even better than the blonde. He rubbed his crotch.

"Oh, yeah," he said, "as soon as I'm done, we're going to have us a real good time."

*　　*　　*

Adam punched in the callback code. After five rings, a recorded message said, "We're sorry. The cellular number you have called is not in service at the present time."

"Dammit!" He held the phone tightly between his palms, hoping he could get images, anything to explain her call. It didn't always work with phones, but he had to try. He concentrated, eyes closed, willing himself to relax. Nothing came.

He slammed the phone into its base on the wall and paced, replaying the conversation in his mind. He had to think it through.

She played a game, as though we were strangers. Why? Only one answer. Someone was with her, forcing her to call. Someone who didn't know we knew each other.

She said things that didn't make sense. She said Thomas instead of Leo Jackson and Mary for his wife instead of Lil to make sure I knew it was a game. Then she said Dayton. Okay. That's where I first met Leo, when his wife and son were kidnapped. Was that why she said Dayton? To tell me she'd been kidnapped? That's it. Has to be.

Who? The shooter. He tried for me twice and now he's using Brenda. How did he get her? Doesn't matter. He's got her, using her to draw me out. He wants me. Why? Who the hell is he? Why me?

She said to meet her at the police station. Not likely. Last place he'd want to meet. Somewhere along the way. No. He had that chance yesterday. He wants it face to face. Where? Waiting outside my building? Too public. He's holding her against her will. Couldn't do that outside. People around. Somewhere not public. Where, dammit, where?

Adam continued pacing, thinking, trying to put it together. If only he had something of hers, anything he might use to get images. He took a sip of his coffee.

Coffee!

She'd been there with him the night before. They'd had coffee. He rushed to the dishwasher and pulled out the cup she used.

Holding the cup in both hands, he sat down, closed his eyes, forced himself to relax. After several moments, blurry images began to form, slowly clearing.

Hands, a woman's, within a circle…smaller circles on each wrist, like bracelets…other shapes now, boxy, different colors…green, then black, gray, red, in lines, or rows…taking shape…cars…rows of cars…a parking lot?… maybe…but dark, no sunlight…

The images stopped. Adam concentrated, but nothing more came. He thought about what he'd seen.

The circles on her wrists, like bracelets. Handcuffs. Cars. Rows of cars, but not outside. Inside. A garage. My garage. He followed me yesterday, knows my car, where I park. He's waiting in the garage. A trap. A lousy, stinking trap.

I'm not walking into a trap.

Like hell I'm not. He's got Brenda.

Three minutes later, Adam's finger jammed the elevator button. Ten seconds seemed forever, but it finally arrived. He jumped in and held the Close Door button. He tried to will the door to close faster, the elevator to reach the first floor faster. He had no idea what he was going to do.

He'd thrown on a pair of slacks with a leather belt and a loose-fitting shirt. The shirt covered the Beretta the belt held against the small of his back. It also covered the snub-nosed .38 in the front.

As soon as the elevator door opened, he stepped forward and nearly collided with the Petersons, his elderly neighbors from the eighth floor.

They stopped and smiled, blocking his way out of the elevator. Mr. Peterson, well over six feet, thin and gray, said, "Good morning, Mr. Kingston."

Mrs. Peterson, as thin and gray as her husband but a foot shorter, said, "How nice to see you."

"Good morning," Adam said, hoping he sounded cordial, but wishing they'd move.

Mrs. Peterson said, "We're so sorry about your young friend getting shot the other evening. We hope he's all right."

"He's fine, thanks." Adam tossed a smile and stepped forward, sideways, to slide between them, knowing he was being rude, vowing to apologize to the nice people another time.

He made it through them, and they stepped into the elevator. He took two steps, stopped, turned and grabbed the elevator door six inches before it closed. The Petersons looked astonished when he pushed the door open.

"Do you have a car?" he asked.

The bewildered Mrs. Peterson stared at her husband who answered, "Why, yes, we do."

"Is it parked in the garage?"

"Yes."

"What level?"

"The, uh, second level. Why do you…"

"I'll explain later. I need a huge favor."

CHAPTER
50

Stuart settled at his desk and read the report he'd just received. He had a match. The prints from the suite at the Endicott House and from the Mercury Grand Marquis belonged to a Vernon Lee Dorsey. He checked the clock on the wall behind him. Nine-ten. Adam and Brenda were due at nine-thirty. He couldn't wait to tell them the news.

He read the lengthy report on Dorsey and underlined what he felt were significant points.

...string of seven rape/murders...women viciously beaten and strangled...Dorsey and an accomplice tracked and caught by FBI...testimony from his wife and the accomplice...homicidal, sex-obsessed, psychotic, sociopathic...currently incarcerated...State Psychiatric Detention Center, Newton Falls, PA...

The final paragraph read:

Dorsey swore vengeance on his wife, Susan Michaels Dorsey, for supplying evidence that aided in his conviction; on his accomplice, Albert Joseph Cookson, AKA Albert Cook, for testifying against him; and on the FBI agent responsible for his capture.

The report didn't name the FBI agent. It didn't have to.

"Ho-lee-Ker-rist!" Stuart snatched his telephone and punched in Adam Kingston's number. He let it ring until it clicked over to the answering machine before hanging up. He decided Adam must be on his way to the station.

"Be careful, pal," he whispered.

Next, he fingered through his Rolodex. He had to call the FBI to let them know Vernon Lee Dorsey was no longer in Newton Falls, Pennsylvania; that he was in Ocean City, Maryland; that he had already taken his vengeance on two of the people on his list; and was now stalking the third.

CHAPTER
51

Adam steered the white Lincoln Town Car he had borrowed from the Petersons onto the ramp that would take him from the second level to the third. He had found a floppy fisherman's hat on the back seat and a pair of sunglasses over the visor. Instant disguise.

He turned off the ramp and let the big car drift almost to a complete stop. Three long rows of parking spaces, most of them occupied, stretched out before him, neatly partitioned by white lines on gray concrete. The opening of the stairwell, his usual means of entering the garage, was straight ahead.

The nose of his LeSabre, parked at the far end of the second lane, stuck out two feet farther than the car beside it. Thirty feet of open space separated the LeSabre from the stairwell. Whoever was waiting for him would expect him to come out of the stairwell and walk to his car. They wouldn't expect him to drive up the ramp at the opposite end of the garage in a borrowed car.

He rolled the Town Car slowly forward between the first and second rows, searching the cars, looking for someone sitting in a car, crouched behind one, even under one. Hunched forward and peering through the windshield, he spotted the green Honda Accord Brenda had driven away from the police station the night before, backed into a space in the third row, directly across from the LeSabre.

Brenda was behind the wheel with a wide gray stripe covering the bottom half of her face.

Duct tape. That son of a bitch.

A large man sat beside her in the passenger seat. The stairwell appeared to hold their undivided attention.

The man's head rotated, as though he were looking around the garage. His head stopped moving when it pointed directly at the Town Car, then quickly ducked out of sight. In the same motion, his hand shot up, grabbed Brenda's head, and pulled her down after him.

Adam was certain the man hadn't recognized him. Too many cars between them. He didn't want to be seen by anyone.

Adam reached the end of the first lane and began the U-turn that would take him down the next, between the Honda and the LeSabre. He kept his eyes glued on the front seat of the Honda, watching for any movement. He saw only Brenda's hands stuck through openings in the steering wheel and the handcuffs on her wrists.

Bastard.

His mind raced as he rolled past the Honda.

Go up another level and sneak down the ramp? No. The ramp opens in plain sight. He'll see. Park here? No. He'll hear the car door open. Think, man, think. Something...anything...

Ram him!

His foot moved to the brake and the Lincoln came to a gentle stop. He jerked off the hat and sunglasses, took a deep breath, whispered, "Sorry, Peterson," shifted into reverse, and jammed his foot down hard on the accelerator.

The big Lincoln shot backward on squealing tires, filling the garage with an ear-splitting shriek. Adam spun the wheel hard, throwing its rear end into the front of the Honda with a crash magnified to an explosion in the cavernous garage. Before its echo faded, while the cars shook from the impact and the Town Car's engine sputtered and died, Adam opened the door and slid out from under the deflating airbag. He stepped toward the Honda with his .38 aimed through the windshield, waiting for a head to show.

A bald head came up, and the man's eyes settled on the .38, then rose to Adam's face.

Adam stopped at the rear of the Town Car. "Raise your hands! Get out of the car!" Adam stared through the Honda's windshield, hoping the man would raise empty hands.

The man didn't move at first. Then his face spread in a wide grin, and his left arm rose, bringing Brenda's head with it, his fingers entwined in her hair. His right hand held the Magnum against her temple.

Adam realized his ramming trick hadn't worked. "Put the gun down," he called. "It's over. Get out of the car."

The man held his grin and wagged his head from side to side. "Come on, Adam, you don't want me to shoot this pretty bitch, now do you?"

That face, that voice. Familiar.

"She's nothing to me," Adam said. "You shoot her, I shoot you. What'll that get you?" He stared hard into the man's eyes, but could see Brenda's face, too, her eyes blinking, trying to focus on him through the windshield.

The man's grin widened. "Aww, Adam, come on now," he said, a playful, cocky tone in his voice. "I know you better'n that. You're a boy scout, a goody-two-shoes. You won't let me shoot her. We both know that. No, what you're going to do is put your gun down. Then I'll get out, and we'll talk. We got us a lot of catching up to do."

Adam hesitated, seeing both their faces. Hers, aware now, eyes darting back and forth between the two men. His, familiar, a vague distant memory.

I know him. Where? When?

The man's grin faded. His face twisted into an angry snarl—and suddenly clicked into place.

Dorsey. But...

"Do it, Adam," Vernon Dorsey shouted. "Now. Or we'll see what's inside this pretty head." He jabbed the Magnum hard into Brenda's temple, making her flinch.

"Okay." Adam raised the .38's barrel in the air. "Okay." He bent forward, slowly, expecting to feel the hardness of the Beretta under his belt, pressing against the small of his back. He didn't. It wasn't there.

The impact. It fell out. Dammit!

CHAPTER
52

Adam laid the snub-nosed .38 at his feet and straightened up.

"Good boy," Dorsey said. "Kick it away. We don't want that little peashooter messing up our party, do we?"

Adam did as he was told and watched his weapon slide under the Town Car. "Let her go, Dorsey" he said. "It's me you want."

Dorsey's angry face softened into a grin as he turned the Magnum on Adam through the Honda's windshield. "Ah, you remember me now," he said, playful and cocky again. "That's good, real good."

He released his grip on Brenda's hair, reached his hand across himself, and opened the car door. "I gained a lot of weight while I was away," he said, grunting as he climbed from the car, "and I lost a lot of hair." He pushed the car door closed and stood beside it. "But that's what happens when you get locked up for a long time. I owe you for that, don't I, Adam?"

"We all change," Adam said, staring over the two cars at a man he'd never expected to see again. "We all get older."

"Oh, but not you, old buddy. You haven't changed a bit." He stepped forward to where the two cars met, the Town Car's rear bumper punched into the Honda's grill. His face changed again. His eyes opened into round white circles around dark pupils, his lips stretched into a tight line, his face reddened.

"But then," he said, spitting the words out, "you didn't get stuck away in a lousy hospital for fifteen years, did you? You didn't have to suck up to a bunch of damn shrinks, have to kiss guards' asses to get a decent meal, have to sleep with one eye open because of the nut cases running around, did you?"

"I just did my job, Vernon."

"Your job? Your job?" He was moving again, alongside the Town Car's trunk on the passenger side. Adam moved with him, step by step, along the other side. With no weapon and the car between himself and Dorsey, there was nothing he could do but stall and hope for an opportunity to disarm the man who now had the upper hand.

"You and my dear sweet wife," Dorsey said, "and that little cocksucker, Albert, you did a job on me. Fifteen years, Adam, fifteen fucking years, that's what you sonsabitches did." He raised the Magnum with the contour of the Lincoln's rear window and along the roof as the two of them moved in synchronized steps on opposite sides of the car.

Keep him talking.

"What happened to your old partner? Albert Cook, wasn't it?"

Dorsey stopped. His boiling face formed a sly smile. "Oh, didn't you know? The little bastard copped on me and only got six years. Then he got out and went back to his old name. Like I wouldn't be able to find him. Shit, he was easy to find. What's the matter, don't the Feds tell you anything any more? Didn't they tell you his real name was Cookson?"

Adam shook his head. "I retired. They don't tell me anything. I'm out of it."

"Out of it?"

Newsweek.

"You always were the clever one, Vernon. Tell me something. The shot from the hotel window. That was meant for me, wasn't it?"

"Would've had you, too, a good clean head shot, if it hadn't been for a damn bird messing up my sight. Hit the guy with all the hair instead. He dead?"

"He'll live. I've got to hand it to you, Vernon. You were slick. At the shopping center, I thought you were after the woman I was with."

"Your little blonde bitch? Nah, just you. I'm glad I didn't hit her, though. We had us a real good time last night. By the way, did you know her eyes weren't really blue? Pissed me off when her blue eyes popped out. People have to learn not to piss me off. Did you know about her eyes?"

A chill slid down Adam's back. "I knew about her eyes. Where is she?"

"Hey, I did you a favor. She won't be coming around pestering you any more. You should thank me."

"Where is she, Vernon?"

"Now don't you worry about her. She'll turn up. Say it. Come on. Say thank you." He moved along the front fender of the Town Car, stopping at the front corner. "Say it, Adam, for old time's sake."

Adam didn't move with him this time. The driver's door of the Lincoln, still open from when he had jumped out, blocked his path. He ignored Dorsey's demand and glanced at the Honda. Brenda's face above the duct tape showed both fear and anger. Her hands were white-knuckled fists sticking through the steering wheel. As Adam turned his head back toward Dorsey, he spotted his Beretta under the deflated airbag on the front seat of the Town Car where it fell from his belt.

Dorsey was standing in front of the car now. "I said say it, damn you." He slammed the palm of his left hand on the hood. With his other hand, he leveled the Magnum on Adam's face.

"All right, I'll say it. Thank you, Vernon."

Dorsey glared, then smiled. "That's better. You see? You shouldn't piss me off, old buddy. Like you and that punk cop busting into my room like you did. You didn't even know it was me, did you?"

"No. Like you said, you've changed. It's been a long time. Is that why you followed me to the shopping center yesterday instead of popping me along the way? Because I didn't recognize you in the hotel?"

"Damn right. You pissed me off, Adam. Busting in like that, like Batman and Robin, and didn't even recognize me. You people have to learn you can't piss me off, can't screw with me. But you were so busy grabbing your little blonde bitch, you still didn't know it was me, did you?"

"No, like you said, I was busy."

"I mean, what good would it do if you didn't know who I was? That's why I arranged this little meeting today. So you'd know it was me."

"I'm sorry I didn't recognize you," Adam said. He was thinking about his Beretta only three feet away, and about Brenda's hands.

Can she reach the ignition? The shift lever?

Holding his eyes on the man standing in front of the Town Car, Adam raised his right hand and pointed the thumb back toward the Honda. At the same time, he raised his left hand behind his back. "What about her? What happens to her?"

"The bitch cop? Oh, we've got plans. Big plans. Tell me, old buddy, you ever ball a bitch cop?"

Behind his back, Adam's left hand twisted back and forth, the thumb pressed against the knuckle of his bent index finger, pantomiming the action of holding and turning a key, hoping she saw it and understood.

"I'll be honest with you, Vernon. I tried a couple over the years." He smiled over the car door while continuing the key motion behind his back, hoping she knew what he was trying to tell her, hoping she could do it. "Yeah, I sampled a few, but you know what? To tell you the truth, they're not so hot. Too hung up on themselves, if you know what I mean. You'll be disappointed."

"Well," Dorsey said with a chuckle, "I guess I'll have to find out for myself after I finish our old..."

He was drowned out by the sound of the Honda's engine coming alive, the clunk of a transmission jerking into gear, metal pushing against metal, rubber sliding on concrete.

Both cars lunged forward, the Town Car skidding on locked tires, the Honda's engine racing, straining, pushing with all it had, its spinning tires throwing streams of black smoke against the wall behind it.

Dorsey's face registered shock when the Lincoln's grill struck his midsection. He threw both hands on the hood, one open-palmed, the other gripping the Magnum. He scuffled backward on unsteady feet, trying to keep ahead of the big car pushing him backward toward the red car behind him.

Adam ran beside the Town Car, reached in with both hands, grabbed the Beretta, and brought it out and over the door in one motion.

The cars stopped with only inches between the Town Car and the LeSabre.

"Don't move, Dorsey," Adam shouted.

The seconds that followed seemed like a thousand. Dorsey froze, the color drained from his face, his eyes widened, both hands still pushing against the Town Car's hood, one of them still clutching the Magnum.

Adam hoped Dorsey wouldn't move, hoped he wouldn't have to shoot. But he knew it would happen. He knew Dorsey's eyes would narrow, and his fingers would tighten on the Magnum's grip the instant before he made his move.

"Don't do it, Dorsey. Don't be a fool. You don't have to die."

Dorsey's eyes appeared to reach out of their sockets, down to the big gun in his right hand. His mouth moved with no sound, saliva spilling from the corners. Then his lips tightened in a wavy grin. The voice that only seconds before had bellowed venomous hatred was barely a whisper when he spoke.

"Yeah, well...maybe I do, old buddy."

The barrel of the Magnum jerked up. Adam squeezed the Beretta's trigger. Its blast was followed by one from the Magnum. The garage filled with thunder as the Magnum's bullet tore into a wall a fraction of a second after the Beretta's ripped through the forehead of Vernon Lee Dorsey.

CHAPTER
53

The paramedic who bandaged Brenda's bruised and scratched wrists could not believe she had been able to reach the ignition key and start the car with her hands handcuffed through the steering wheel.

"Impossible," the young man said each time he looked inside the Honda. "No way. Houdini, maybe."

After the paramedics left, Adam sat with Brenda in the front seat of the LeSabre. They faced the quiet half of the garage. Behind them, a dozen men and women in uniforms, plainclothes and lab coats milled around the Honda and the Lincoln. They chatted in groups of two and three, scribbling notes and taking pictures. Their cameras threw soundless flashes of light through the shadowy gray garage like distant lightning in twilight.

Brenda had answered their questions, but had said very little else. She sat, pensive and distant, in the passenger seat, staring through the windshield as though something was out there she should see but couldn't. Adam knew what was bothering her. She needed to talk about it. He would wait until she was ready.

After a while, she said, "So Dorsey wasn't connected with them at all." She didn't look at him.

He turned his head toward her. That wasn't what was bothering her, he knew, but at least she was talking. "Eric and Julia? No, just an old score he wanted to settle with me."

"I wonder what they really were up to."

"Stuart just told me he…"

"Stuart's here?" she asked absently.

"He arrived while you were with the EMTs. He talked with Eric this morning. Eric said Julia wanted him to sneak in the hospital and finish Chip off. All he had to do was hold a pillow over his face, she said. No one would ever know. She told him it was their only chance."

"Was he going to do it?"

"He told her he would, but after she left to meet me at the shopping center, he searched the house for the box. When he couldn't find it, he went to the hospital. He wanted to tell Chip everything and take his chances with the truth. When they wouldn't let him in, he hung around the hospital all day, thinking he could sneak in after dark to see Chip. When he saw us, he panicked and ran."

"Do you believe him?"

"It fits."

"What about Julia?"

"They're still looking."

"Did you tell them what Dorsey said?"

Adam nodded. "I suggested they check the Comfort Inn."

Brenda became silent again. Her eyes were wide and unblinking, her face immobile, her lips slightly parted. He'd seen the look before on the faces of young FBI agents and other police officers he'd worked with.

A man was dead, and she'd been part of it.

Adam had been with police officers before in this situation, some with more years of experience than Brenda. They get used to seeing dead bodies after the fact, but very few participate in a fatal incident. The first one is hard to deal with.

He heard a vehicle moving behind them and glanced in the rear-view mirror. The medical examiner's van was leaving with the body of Vernon Dorsey.

Brenda watched the van roll to the end of the garage and onto the ramp.

Adam wanted her to talk. He searched for the right words to say, but she spoke before he found them.

"How do you justify it, Adam?"

He'd had the question before. He wished there was a perfect answer. "You don't. You can't. There's no way you can rationalize taking another person's life, no matter who it is. You don't even try."

"You've done it before."

He didn't answer. It wasn't a question.

Still without looking at him, she asked, "How do you get past it?"

"Brenda, listen to me." He reached over, took her hand in his, and waited until she turned her head to face him. "You have to concentrate on what would have happened if it had turned out differently. If he had gotten off the first shot, you and I would both be dead."

He gave her a moment to consider the thought. "Sometimes, the best you can do is not think about what happened. You think about what didn't happen."

"You make it sound easy."

"It's not. It's not easy at all, but…"

Adam heard his name being called. He leaned out the side window and saw Stuart beckoning to him.

"I'll be back," he said. "You okay?"

She nodded.

Adam left the LeSabre and walked to where Stuart waited.

When he returned twenty minutes later and climbed in beside her, she looked more relaxed, he thought, but didn't speak for a full minute. Then, "Is it true," she asked, "what you said to Dorsey?"

"What was that?"

A grin played on her lips. "That you sampled a few of us over the years. Too wrapped up in ourselves, huh?"

CHAPTER 54

Brenda followed Stuart to his office. Except for gouges in the front bumper and a punched-in grill, the Honda seemed fine.

Adam stayed in the garage until the Lincoln was towed away. When he visited the Petersons in their apartment and told them about the damage, they were upset at first, even after he promised to take care of all repairs. After they had heard the whole story, their attitudes changed.

As Adam said good-bye to Mr. Peterson at their door, he saw Mrs. Peterson reach for her telephone. He imagined her spending the next several hours telling her friends about the heroic role their car had played.

Adam's next stop was the hospital. He rehearsed what he would say all the way there. When he stepped off the elevator and walked toward Chip's room, he still didn't feel he had it right. It didn't matter. Chip had to know the truth, and there was no easy way.

When he entered the room, Chip lay flat on his bed, staring at the ceiling. He smiled when he saw Adam, but the smile faded as if he sensed bad news.

Adam spent the next thirty minutes telling Chip everything about Lisa, Eric, and Julia. When he had heard it all, Chip sat on the edge of the bed, stiff and rigid, with his back to Adam. After a minute or so, the stiffness went out of him. His head slumped to his chest. He buried his face in his hands.

Adam waited in silence, watching Chip's shoulders rise and fall, hearing his muffled sobs, wishing there was something he could say or do.

It was a full five minutes before Chip straightened. "I'd like to make sure Lisa has a proper burial," he said in a raspy voice. "I know where my parents are buried. There's a place for her, for both of us, with them."

Adam said, "I'm sure that'll be no problem. I'll let the police in Baltimore know."

Chip grew silent again.

Adam waited.

"Adam?"

"Yes, Chip."

"The house in Bethany Beach. Can I live there?"

"No reason why you can't. It's yours."

"I'd like that. I remembered more this morning. My dad and I used to fish together when we stayed there. We had cookouts in the back yard on July Fourth every year, then we'd sit on the beach and watch fireworks over the water. One year, on Lisa's birthday, Dad made homemade ice cream. Strawberry. It was her favorite flavor. We had a lot of good times at that house."

"There'll be good times again, Chip."

Chip turned from the window. His face was pale, his eyes red and puffed. "Adam, I don't know how to thank you for what you've done."

"I didn't do that much," Adam said. "I'm only sorry you're in this place. That bullet was meant for me."

Chip shook his head. "Don't be. It's not so bad." He patted the bandages around his midsection. "The doctors say I'll be good as new in a couple of weeks. Besides, they said the trauma of getting shot is probably what started my memory coming back. It should all return now, a little at a time."

"That's great." Adam stood. "I'd better go. You need to rest so you can get out of here."

"It can't be soon enough for me. I've got a lot of catching up to do."

Adam walked to the door. "I'll come back tomorrow, and we'll talk some more. Is there anything you need, anything I can bring you?"

Chip said, "Nothing I can think of, but when I get settled in the house, maybe you could help me with something."

"Sure. What is it?"

"You know those pictures you have on your wall? I want to gather all the pictures I can get my hands on. My parents, me, Lisa. Maybe you can help me put them up, a whole wall like the one at your place."

Adam hesitated. "I'll be glad to, if that's what you want, but I...well...I'm thinking about taking mine down."

Chip's eyes widened in surprise. "Take them down? Why?"

"It's, uh, about birds. I need to make room for my birds."

"Birds? I don't get it."

"To be honest, I'm still working on it myself. But let's talk about it tomorrow. I think it'll do both of us a lot of good. Are you sure there's nothing I can bring you?"

Chip eyes were moist again. "There's one thing you could bring, if you wouldn't mind."

"Name it."

"If it's not too much trouble, could you bring some ice cream?"

"Strawberry?"

Chip turned toward the window again. He nodded.

*   *   *

Adam's drive to the police station was more cheerful than the one to the hospital. He sensed Chip would get through the loss of Lisa and, in time, would adjust to his new life. Hell, he survived sixteen years on the streets not knowing who he was. He could handle this.

As he pulled into the parking lot behind the station house, he realized he hadn't eaten all day.

Maybe Brenda would like to join me for dinner. To discuss the case, of course.

He parked the LeSabre and scanned the parking lot, but didn't see her car. When he arrived at Stuart's desk, he casually asked if she was there.

"She left about an hour ago," Stuart replied. "I guess she had a lot to do in the big city. Sorry."

"Oh, it was nothing important," Adam said. He waved a hand to dismiss it. "I wanted to make sure she was all right." He shrugged. "About the shooting, I mean." He put his hands in his pockets, took them out again, coughed into one of them, and sat down. "That's all." He shrugged again. "Nothing important."

Stuart grinned. "Sure, big guy. Whatever you say."

Stuart brought Adam up to date. Susan Michaels would recover. The description her neighbor gave of the man who drove away in her Buick Skylark fit Vernon Dorsey, the man she divorced after testifying against him.

The hospital in Newton Falls, Pennsylvania, Stuart said, knew Dorsey had escaped, but didn't report it. They thought they could find him and bring him back before anyone found out he was gone. They didn't want publicity about their lax security system. Stuart said he wouldn't want to be in their shoes when the Feds and the State of Pennsylvania got through with them.

And they'd found Lisa's gold Mercedes parked near the Comfort Inn.

"We're still checking the rooms," Stuart said. "If she's there, we'll find her. I told them to make sure they checked under the beds."

Adam nodded, remembering the package Dorsey left under a bed at the Endicott House.

"She was a real piece of work," Stuart said. "I still think she was planning to take you out. Don't you?"

"Anything's possible, I suppose, but we'll never know now."

"Well, it makes sense to me. She thought Eric was going to finish Chip off at the hospital. All she had to do was take care of you, and she could go on being Lisa. Everything would be hers. Yes sir, a real piece of work. She just didn't figure on Eric copping out."

"And," Adam said as he stood to leave, "she didn't figure on running into Dorsey."

As they shook hands and promised to get together for a beer soon, Stuart's telephone rang.

Adam walked away as Stuart answered. He'd only gone ten steps when he heard Stuart's voice.

"Adam, wait."

Adam returned to the desk and heard Stuart say "Uh-huh" and "Right" several times, then finally, "I'm on my way."

Stuart replaced his phone. "They found Julia White."

"Bagged?"

Stuart was on his feet, pulling on his sport coat. "And taped. Under a bed. You want to go along?"

Adam shook his head. "No, she's all yours."

"There's something else, Adam."

"What?"

"They found her purse under the front seat of the Mercedes. She was carrying a .32 semi-automatic, fully loaded. Looks like I was right. Your old pal, Dorsey, might've saved your life. You should've thanked him before you blew his head off."

"As a matter of fact, I did," Adam said, walking away. "He insisted on it."

*   *   *

Adam drove up the ramp of the Colonial Towers parking garage wondering what he would have for dinner. He'd thought about stopping at a drive-through on the way home, but decided against it. He didn't feel like talking to anyone, especially through a squawk box.

I'm glad she didn't stay around. Who cares?

He felt tired and grumpy from all the excitement, and he was hungry. Starved. He tried to remember if there was anything in the fridge he could throw in the microwave.

She could've stayed long enough to say good-bye, dammit. Professional courtesy.

When he came off the ramp on the third level, he saw Brenda's green Honda parked in his reserved space. She was kneeling in front of it, examining the damage to the grill. His window was down when he brought the LeSabre to a stop beside her.

"It doesn't look too bad," he said.

"Nah," she said as she pulled herself to her feet. "It's fixable."

Adam said, "I saw Stuart. He said you'd left for Baltimore."

Brenda smoothed her skirt. "I started to, but it's a long ride on an empty stomach. You want to go get something to eat?"

"I think I could eat a little something," he said. "Uh...do you like omelets?"

She grinned.

He looked for a place to park.

ACKNOWLEDGMENTS

Writing is a lonely endeavor with only you, a keyboard, and a blank screen hungry for words. But there are times when you must reach out to others for camaraderie, encouragement, and help. You call them friends, writing partners, critique group or, if you're as lucky as I've been, all three. Here are some who are special to me.

The Raven Mavens: Dee Stuart, Carolyn Smith, Tricia Allen, Mark Troy, Kevin Tipple, and always in our hearts, Liz Scott.

At the Four Star Coffee House: Bunnie Bessell, Terry Calvin, Jan Christensen, Jan Clark, Chuck Gatlin, and Jonathan Shipley.

Back in the Gainesville days: the wonderful InkPlotters.

Transcending time, space and geography via the Internet: Rachel Downs, Joyce Holland, Cynthia McClendon, Donna Nigon, and the rowdy redhead from Lubbock, Marcia Kiser.

With special nods and tons of hugs, and I don't have to say why: Babs Lakey, Patti Nunn, and Ant Jan.

Ocean City, Maryland: Finally, this story and the people in it are entirely fictional, but Ocean City, a family resort town on Maryland's Eastern Shore, is real. My family and I have wonderful memories of weekends and vacations there. I hope the town and its people forgive me for taking certain liberties. For one, I extended the Boardwalk to Thirty-fourth Street and placed the Colonial Towers there. I also gave them a full-size hospital, which they did not have on our last visit.

There's one thing, though, that is fact, not fiction. Ocean City is a charming, clean, and cozy family getaway destination and, for my money, the jewel of the Atlantic Coast beach resort towns.

Derringer Award-winning author Earl Staggs served as editor of *Futures Mystery Anthology Magazine* and as president of the *Short Mystery Fiction Society*. His short stories have appeared in numerous magazines and anthologies. He welcomes comments on his work at earlstaggs@sbcglobal.net.